Murder Vision

BOOKS BY RAEGAN TELLER

Murder in Madden

The Last Sale

Secrets Never Told

The Fifth Stone

Time to Prey

Murder Clause

Murder Vision

MURDER VISION

Raegan Teller

Pondhawk Press LLC
Columbia, South Carolina

Copyright © 2024 by **Raegan Teller**

All rights reserved. No part of this publication may be reproduced, distributed, or transmitted in any form or by any means, without prior written permission.

Pondhawk Press LLC
PO Box 290033
Columbia, SC 29229

Publisher's Note: This is a work of fiction. Names, characters, places, and incidents are a product of the author's imagination. Locales and public names are sometimes used for atmospheric purposes. Any resemblance to actual people, living or dead, or to businesses, companies, events, institutions, or locales is completely coincidental.

ISBN 979-8-9880730-2-4

Dedicated to local newspaper reporters everywhere—
the unsung heroes who tirelessly serve our communities.

"Sometimes, our journey leads us back to where we started, but with new eyes and a wiser heart."

Unknown

CHAPTER 1

Death is not something most people think about every day. That is, not unless you're an oncologist, trauma doctor, or funeral home director. Or a fortune teller.

Cassandra thought about death every day, because she was afraid. Not of dying but of seeing other people dead or dying. As a third-generation seer, she had the "gift," as her grandmother explained to her. Cassandra's mother, also a seer, called it a curse.

Today, Cassandra was working with a new client, Mara Sterling, the wife of a prominent financial advisor. As she always did, Cassandra had her client read a disclaimer and sign it. The disclaimer stated that no one, including Cassandra, was totally accurate, and the readings were for reflection, consideration, and primarily for entertainment. Cassandra, the document stated, was not responsible for actions taken by the client as a result of her readings. Despite this disclaimer, no one who worked with Cassandra had any doubt of her ability or her accuracy. And they understood her visions could not be turned off and on. Some days, Cassandra saw nothing and rescheduled the client's session. Rarely did she go more than a day or two without having visions, even though she asked God every night to make them go away. Before committing suicide, her mother, too, had prayed to be relieved of the curse that eventually drove her mad.

Mara Sterling was a later-in-life new mother. At thirty-one, she had finally conceived the child she had always wanted. Her husband, Grant Sterling, advised upper income families on how to maximize their returns and minimize their taxes. All for a hefty fee, of course.

Cassandra could learn a lot about her clients by how they were dressed, how they sat, how they spoke. "Do you have any questions about the disclosure form?" Cassandra asked.

In response, Mara signed the form and put the clipboard back on the table. "No. I understand the need to protect yourself." She smiled. "My husband trained me well." She laid the pen on top of the clipboard. "But you came highly recommended."

"Can you tell me who referred you?"

Mara shifted in her seat. "I'd rather not, if you don't mind. But you've seen her for several years, let's just say that." Mara glanced around the room, as though she was looking for something.

Cassandra had many clients she had worked with long-term, and many of them were about Mara's age. "That's fine. I was just curious."

"Is Cassandra your real name, or a stage name, so to speak?"

"Yes, it's my real name."

"I remember reading about Cassandra in Greek mythology. It was a terribly difficult course, and the professor was *boring*," Mara said, drawing out "boring" and rolling her eyes. "As I recall, the god Apollo was smitten with her and gave her the gift of prophecy in order to win her affections. But when she didn't reciprocate his feelings, he put a curse on her, so that no one would believe her prophesies, even though they were true. So when Cassandra warned about the fall of Troy, no one believed her. I even had to read *Homer's Iliad,* but I just read the CliffsNotes.

Of course, Cassandra had heard all of this many times from her grandmother, who had insisted on the name. "I'm surprised you remembered all that. I can barely remember my studies."

"I have a good memory. Or at least I did when I was using my brain routinely." Mara shifted again. "I understand this process, I mean your process, works best when you have specific questions to be answered. Is that correct?"

Cassandra smiled. If it was only that simple. "Sometimes that helps. But I'm not a psychic. I am a seer, which means I only see the future. Sometimes it's specific, sometimes symbolic."

"And sometimes you see a picture or an image, according to my friend."

Cassandra shifted in her seat. It was true that sometimes the future of a client played like a movie in her head. Those were the most accurate predictions, but often hard to interpret until after the fact. "Sometimes, yes." Cassandra held out her hand. "May I take your hands?"

Mara quickly put her hands in Cassandra's. "Yes, of course, I mean if that's how it's done."

"Sometimes I use cards and sometimes the vision comes from touch. At times, I see things after the client, and if that happens with you, I'll contact you to come back in so we can discuss it."

"Of course." Mara's hands were soft and her nails perfectly manicured. She wore a pale pink polish that matched her skin and provided a subtle canvas for a large diamond ring.

"What questions do you have about your future?"

Mara shifted in her seat. "Lately, I've had this sense of dread. Like something was about to happen to me. Or my baby. I want to know what my future will be like." She hesitated. "And I want . . . I want to know how to be happy again. What kind of wife does Grant need?"

Cassandra had learned not to judge the questions people had. She wanted to dig deeper into the last question but knew it was really none of her business or necessary for her vision. "I'll keep those questions in mind but I can't guarantee the vision will be related. Or, as I said, it might be symbolically related."

Mara nodded. "I understand."

"Now, please don't speak again until I tell you to. The silence helps my vision."

After all these years, Cassandra still wondered why people came to her. Especially people like Mara. Her clients were typically women, and a few were wealthy, as Mara appeared to be. But there was something different and unsettling about Mara. Something Cassandra couldn't put her finger on.

Pushing all these extraneous thoughts aside, Cassandra invited the vision in. When she was doing readings, she had no concept of time. Her clients often said it was "quick" or "I thought you had gone to sleep," but to Cassandra, all readings felt like the same length. In the past, this phenomenon had caused scheduling problems, so she had learned to allow ample time for each session.

At some point, the familiar, yet dreaded, feeling took over and the movie began playing. Sometimes there was no sound, like a silent movie. Rarely, Cassandra heard running water, cars crashing, or something else.

Cassandra's vision was unusually clear today. She saw Mara in her house, in her kitchen, looking out the large window over the sink, as though she was looking for someone in the backyard. Suddenly, Mara turned around and the vision went blank. Cassandra forced herself to stay focused on the feel of Mara's soft hands and the energy of the woman across from her who wanted to know what her future held.

When the vision returned, Mara was lying on the floor in a pool of blood. She was on her side, her body slightly twisted, with her face staring up, toward the ceiling. The eyes caught Cassandra's attention. Unlike the eyes of the vibrant woman who had come to see her today, Mara's eyes in the vision were lifeless. Blood rushed from the slash in Mara's neck. In the distance, Cassandra heard one of those rare sounds. A baby crying. And then another vision. A man was leaning over the body and then looked right at Cassandra, as though she was standing right there with him.

Cassandra's hands were shaking when she opened her eyes.

"What did you see?" Mara asked.

CHAPTER 2

Cassandra released Mara's hands immediately and clasped her own shaking hands. "Give me a moment, please. I need to reflect and to collect my thoughts."

Cassandra recalled her grandmother's teachings, that a vision of death is often symbolic. The brutality of what she saw could mean that changes in Mara's future would mean giving up something, or making drastic changes that went against her nature. The change would not be easy.

Cassandra rarely saw actual death, unless someone was suffering from a known illness, like cancer. In which case, the client often wanted to know how long they had left. Of course, there were no calendars in Cassandra's visions, so it was impossible to be specific. Typically, her visions were about change, like someone who was stuck in a job that was killing their soul, depleting their joy.

But this vision was so *real* that it unnerved Cassandra.

She cleared her throat and forced herself to relax her taut facial muscles. "I saw a difficult time ahead for you. You're going to give up something precious and you won't like it."

Mara's eyes reflected her concern. "I'm not sure what that means exactly. Should I be worried?"

Cassandra took another deep breath. "It could also be a danger ahead. I saw some conflict in your home. Your kitchen specifically."

Mara made a pouty face, much as a child might when told to clean up her room or finish her veggies. "I love that kitchen. We spent a fortune remodeling it last year, but Grant doesn't like it."

"Why is that?"

"As I said, he's a financial advisor, so he always watches our money closely. He thinks I spent too much on the renovations. He really flipped out when I ordered reclaimed wood floors from a barn up in the North Carolina mountains."

Cassandra recoiled slightly at the mention of her home state. Visions of her own life, pattering around barefoot on the wide wooden floors that were worn smooth by several generations of her family. "In my vision, at least, it was beautiful." Cassandra paused. "Is this something that causes ongoing tension between you and Grant?"

Mara looked off into space momentarily and then nodded.

"I can't be sure of the timeline, but just be careful around your house and when you're in the kitchen." She paused. "I saw you looking out the window. Does your child play in the backyard?"

"Oh, goodness no. She's barely a year old. But I often look out the window. We have a nice backyard, although it's not as large as I'd like."

"Well, then just be careful, keep your doors locked, and don't let strangers into your home." Seeing the question on Mara's face, Cassandra added, "Just standard advice when I see, well, danger or symbolic danger ahead for someone." Cassandra couldn't bring herself to say "death." She looked at the calendar on her phone. "Can you come back sometime later this week? You can think about what we've discussed, and if it has any meaning for you. Just think about big decisions ahead or anything you may have to give up, especially related to your home or family."

Mara gave her a smile that Cassandra was sure Mara used often at dinner parties—that superficial smile that sometimes covered up so much hidden truth.

CHAPTER 3

Approximately a week after Cassandra's vision session with Mara Sterling, this article appeared in newspapers across the South.

Tragic Mystery in Columbia: Mother Found Dead

Columbia, SC - Tragedy struck a serene and affluent neighborhood in Columbia this past weekend, as local residents awoke to the shocking news of a mother's untimely death. Mara Sterling, 31, was found dead in her family home late Sunday evening by her husband, Grant Sterling, a well-known financial advisor.

According to the Richland County investigator, officers were called to the scene around 8 pm following a 911 call from Mr. Sterling. Upon arrival, they discovered Mrs. Sterling deceased under circumstances that have led investigators to pursue the case as a homicide. The nature of her injuries has not been disclosed, as authorities are withholding details during this early stage of their investigation.

The couple are known for their philanthropic efforts and active involvement in local charities. Their infant daughter, who was home at the time of the incident, was unharmed.

As the investigation unfolds, the Richland County Sheriff's office has appealed to the public for any information related to the case. "We are doing everything in our power to bring the perpetrator to justice," stated Lieutenant Albright. "We urge anyone with information, no matter how insignificant it may seem, to come forward."

The loss of Mara Sterling has left a void in the hearts of those who knew her, with friends and neighbors describing her as a loving mother and wife. The Sterling family has requested privacy during this difficult time as they grapple with this unimaginable loss.

This is a developing story, and more details will be released as they become available. The community stands united in mourning and in hope for justice for Mara Sterling.

CHAPTER 4

Enid was alone in the small house she and Josh rented near downtown Columbia. Josh was traveling and wouldn't be home until the next day. Since they were new to the area, they had decided to rent the modest brick bungalow in an older neighborhood near uptown Columbia instead of buying.

Their one-car garage was still full of boxes and things they would most likely discard or donate later when they had a chance to fully unpack. The yard was full of leaves, as Fall was approaching. Since they had both jumped into new jobs immediately upon arriving in town, these kinds of household chores had taken a back seat to more pressing matters.

The second bedroom was an office space she shared with Josh. He had his own uptown office in the consulting firm in the Vista district, but he often worked from home. Most of his work required travel anyway: visiting clients and gathering information on the target's background. Most days, Enid had the small bedroom to herself and could work uninterrupted.

Tiffany, owner of the consulting firm where Josh worked, had asked him to attend a large event this evening in Greenville, South Carolina, to observe a target, a woman who was up for a big corporate promotion.

Enid had smiled when she saw Josh packing a suit and tie earlier that morning. Having spent most of his life in law enforcement, first in New Mexico, where he often worked undercover, and then as police chief in Madden, and later as the Bowman County sheriff, terms like "business casual" or "formal attire" were foreign to him.

Their client was Bob Larkin, former governor of the state. Josh had worked a couple under-the-radar assignments for Larkin, who had then recommended Josh to Tiffany, the consulting firm's owner. He and Enid moved to Columbia when Josh took the job.

With the quiet house to herself, Enid focused on her assignment for the paper, an article featuring several food vendors at the weekly Soda City market in uptown Columbia. When her cellphone rang, she instinctively looked at the screen with the intent to let it go to voice mail. But it was Enid's editor at the newspaper, so she answered. "Hi, Grace, what's up?"

"I'm sorry to bother you, but there's a woman here asking to see you. I told her you didn't work from this office, but she insists that she *has* to see you. Do you want me to get her phone number and you can call her?"

"Do you have any idea what she wants?" Enid asked.

Before Grace could answer, Enid heard her say, "Wait, she's . . .Ma'am, I asked you to wait in the lobby."

"Grace, just let me talk to her if you don't mind," Enid said. "I'll make it quick." She heard some kind of movement and then a woman's voice.

"I apologize for being so pushy, but I must talk to you," the woman said. "I need your help. We can meet anywhere you want. And I'll try to be brief. Please, Ms. Blackwell. It's, well, it's life and death."

Enid took a deep breath and wondered how she could get rid of this woman who was clearly disturbed about something. "I'm working on an assignment this afternoon, but I can meet you at Indah Coffee on Sumter Street around 2:00 pm. Do you know where that is?

"Yes, I know it well. I've seen your picture, so I'll be able to recognize you. And thank you. I'll explain everything when we meet."

CHAPTER 5

Indah Coffee Company is a small coffee shop located in the Cottontown neighborhood of Columbia. It's known locally for its excellent coffee and typical coffee house vibes. Parking is always an issue in the uptown area and today was no exception. Enid parked a block away on a side street, where a man walking in tattered clothes and mismatched tennis shoes eyed her suspiciously. Enid knew from several articles she had read that street people were a growing problem in Columbia.

Inside the coffee shop, she inhaled the intoxicating aroma of roasted coffee, a smell she had learned to love after marrying Josh, even though she liked the smell of coffee more than the actual taste of it. Today she would forgo her typical cup of hot tea and make an exception for a cup of what Food and Wine Magazine claimed to be the best coffee in South Carolina.

After receiving her order, Enid looked around and saw a slender woman sitting at one of the tables. Her exotic looks—dark hair and olive skin—made her attractive enough to be a fashion model. When the woman saw Enid, she stood and walked toward her.

"Ms. Blackwell, I'm Cassandra." The woman motioned for Enid to join her at the small table against the wall. "I apologize again for being so aggressive at the newspaper office, but I had to see you."

After settling in her chair, Enid asked, "How did you get my name? I don't typically get bylines in the *State*."

"Karla, a friend of mine, recommended I get in touch with you."

Enid's memory was instantly flooded with flashbacks of working with Karla when they were trying to locate the town of Madden's missing historian. As an empath, Karla had an extraordinary ability to sense and absorb the emotions and energies of others, which she said was both a gift and a challenge. "I haven't seen or heard from Karla in a couple years. How is she?"

"She's doing well and living in a small village in upstate New York, but we stay in touch."

"I remember her visiting Lily Dale often, but I didn't realize she had moved there." Karla had explained to Enid that Lily Dale, a quaint hamlet in southwestern New York, is renowned as the world's largest spiritualist community. More than fifty professional mediums live there permanently. "So why did Karla suggest you contact me?"

Cassandra looked around the coffee shop at the half dozen or so customers who were scattered around at different tables. "I need your help." She paused, glancing around again. "I saw a murder."

Enid gasped. "Oh, my. That must have been upsetting. I'm so sorry." She studied Cassandra's face, hoping to see beyond the mysterious facade. "But I'm sure you've talked with the police. And the paper's editor would have to approve my doing any kind of story. I don't get to pick the stories I'm assigned."

"The story has been reported in all the papers. A mother was killed in her home about a week ago."

Enid studied Cassandra's face, trying to determine where all this was going. "I remember reading about it. Such a tragic death. But the police are investigating it, right?"

"Yes, so they say."

"And as a witness, you talked to them, right?" Enid asked.

Cassandra waited momentarily before answering. "I witnessed it, but I wasn't physically there."

Becoming annoyed now with the mysterious woman, Enid took another sip of coffee to collect her thoughts. "I'm not sure what you're asking of me, but if you've talked to the police, and you don't want an article, there's nothing I can do." Enid leaned over to pick up her tote bag sitting on the floor, signaling her exit.

Cassandra leaned forward and spoke softly. "I'm sorry, it's just that this is . . . I'm not sure where to start."

Trying to hide her frustration, Enid said, "The beginning is always a good option. If you want me to stay and hear what you have to say, then just say it."

Cassandra took a deep breath and pulled a business card out of her jacket pocket. She put it on the table and pushed it toward Enid. Enid picked up the card and read it. "Fortune teller? Are you serious?" Enid said. And then realizing she had offended Cassandra, Enid added. "Look, I'm sorry but this conversation is very confusing. Are you saying you're a psychic?"

"No, I can only see the future. Psychics have a much broader view that includes the past."

"So what do you do with these visions?" Enid asked.

"I help people make decisions about their lives, their work, their relationships. I realize this is all confusing and you're skeptical, as you should be. There are plenty of fakes out there." Cassandra then told Enid about her session with Mara Sterling.

"Wait, are you saying you saw this woman being killed?"

"Yes, and no. I saw her dead, murdered, a week before it actually happened. And, yes, it was during a session. But I didn't see the actual murder take place."

"And did you tell her what you saw?"

Cassandra glanced around the coffee shop again. "Not exactly." She pulled out her phone. "I realize this is awkward for you. You don't know if I'm crazy or just a liar, so I'm going to text Karla and ask her to vouch for my character at least, even if you don't believe in my visions. Does Karla know your mobile number?"

"She had it at one time." In less than a minute, Enid's phone rang."

"Enid, it's Karla. I'm sorry to bother you, and I'll be brief. Cassandra says you two are in a meeting. I can fill in more details later, but if you trust me, then I can vouch for her. She's a true seer. Her gift is uncanny, although she considers it a curse. We can talk later if you'd like. Just call me back on this number. And I apologize for not giving you a heads-up that I suggested Cassandra contact you. I've been doing sessions at a retreat for the last few days. In fact, I need to go now."

"Thanks for calling me," Enid said. "Let's catch up later." Before she could say anything further, the call ended.

CHAPTER 6

Enid rubbed her temples. "I admit that working with Karla, I was impressed with her empathic skills, even if I didn't totally understand how it worked. But this is a lot to take in. What can I do to help?"

"I read in one of your articles that you became a reporter because you want to find the truth."

"That's always been my goal."

"The truth doesn't always set you free. I would never lie to a client, but I'm careful about how I tell them what I've seen."

"I'm afraid I don't understand."

"If I saw you being killed on the way home today, would you want to know that?"

"Of course. I could take a different route or do something to prevent it."

"Exactly. So I tell my clients to be careful and that I see a possible accident in their future and suggest they take a different route. But nothing more. Remember that any legitimate seer is not one hundred percent accurate. If I told you that you were going to die today, you might make decisions or alter your life in ways that are irreversible. And my vision could be wrong. Or merely symbolic, like the messages you get in dreams." Cassandra bowed her head slightly and then looked back at Enid. "Let me tell you a little more about my background."

"I'm happy to listen, but I've got to tell you that despite Karla's endorsement, I'm skeptical. And I'm not sure I want to be involved in any of this."

"I understand. You see, my grandmother was the first seer in our family. When she was very young, she began to see people's futures. I grew up in North Carolina, in the Appalachian mountains, which has no shortage of people with special gifts. Granny studied with several of them, and she was grateful for her gift. To show her gratitude, Granny tried to help as many people as she could. And she never withheld the truth from anyone, as unpleasant as it might be."

"But you don't follow that practice."

"No, I don't, and here's why. My grandmother passed her gift of seeing the future onto my mother. My grandmother lived until she was ninety-eight, but my mother couldn't handle it and killed herself at thirty-three." She smiled slightly. "I'm the same age now as my mother was when she . . . when she died."

"I'm so sorry. How old were you when your mother passed?"

"Sixteen." Cassandra took a deep breath and continued. "I try to remember her for being a wonderful mom, a great storyteller, and talented cook. Sometimes I admit, I curse her for passing this ability to see visions on to me. But I know she couldn't have prevented it."

"I can see how your feelings and memory of her would be conflicted."

"After my mother died, my grandmother took me under her wing and encouraged me to develop her own budding gift, to use it to help others, as she had done. Each day I saw my grandmother work with clients who paid with stewing chickens and root vegetables, and sometimes a jug of moonshine or scuppernong wine. My grandmother told her clients exactly what she saw and put the responsibility on them to deal with it. And she encouraged me to do the same."

"But you just said you withheld some information from your clients."

"One day, less than a week before my mother took her own life, I held her hands in mine. That's when I saw my mother's lifeless body sprawled on the floor."

"That's so sad. What did you do?"

"I threw up, sick with fear. Then I went to my grandmother and asked for her advice. She told me I was likely just worried about my mother and reminded me that no seer was totally accurate, not even her. And that my mother's death could be a message, not a literal death. She encouraged me to tell my mother what I saw."

Cassandra wiped away the tears spilling down her cheeks. "After I told my mother about my vision, I begged her not to die. She held me close and we cried together. The next day, she announced she was taking a trip up into the highlands to see an old friend." Cassandra paused. "That's the last time I saw her alive. She took a potion, a poison, likely one her friend concocted for her. When she went missing, we didn't know where to look for her, so it was several weeks later before we found her decaying body in an abandoned cabin one of her relatives had owned."

Enid put her hand on Cassandra's. "I'm so sorry."

"For years, I felt responsible for my mother's death. Maybe if I hadn't told her ... Anyway, that's the last time I told anyone when I foresaw their death."

"I can understand your confusion when you were younger, but you know now that you didn't cause it, don't you?"

Cassandra shrugged, "Somehow in my immature mind, I thought I had given my mother the idea, that she wouldn't have done it if I hadn't told her about my vision. Like maybe somehow she felt it was a prophecy she had to fulfill. Anyway, I know it's not rational, but that guilt is embedded in my psyche. Some days are better than others. Look, I'm not asking you to believe in fortune tellers or seers. And I'm not asking for your sympathy. I just wanted you to know a little more about me and why I withheld the actual vision. What I'm asking is that you help me."

"But your client is dead, so there's nothing you can do to prevent it. And what can I do?"

"In my vision, my client was killed in her home, so I warned her to lock her doors and to not let strangers in. She assured me she would. I told her I saw danger but stopped short of telling her the entire vision."

"What was her reaction?"

"She was confused. I explained that there are more kinds of death than physical death." Cassandra looked down at her hands in her lap. "She seemed relieved and said she would be careful."

"I see now how your conflicted feelings about telling your mother the truth affects your work with clients. But given all you've told me, why not just go into another line of work?"

"I can't turn the visions off. Believe me, I would if I could. And my visions are not always tragic. In fact, I rarely see someone's death. Instead, I help people get clarity in their lives."

"Well, at least I'm glad you've come to some kind of peace with your gift. Did you share any of this with the police?"

"One thing I haven't told you about my vision is that I saw the killer."

Enid sat up in her chair. "You saw his face?"

Cassandra shook her head. "No, not exactly. But I saw his bare back and a distinctive tattoo, so I told them to look for a white man, no older than forty, with an insect tattoo."

"An insect? What kind?"

"I'm not sure. It appeared to be a wasp or something with wings."

"Could you draw a sketch of it?" Enid asked.

"I tried, but art is not one of my skills. I asked the police detective to let me work with a sketch artist, but he just smiled and sent me home, saying they'd be in touch. I haven't heard anything from them."

"I may know someone who can help us."

"Us? Does that mean you'll help me?"

Enid stood. "I'm not sure at this point, but I'll be in touch soon."

CHAPTER 7

Enid sat in her home office, alone in the quiet house, while contemplating her disturbing conversation with Cassandra. Was she legit? A nut case? Enid couldn't decide, but since Karla had vouched for her, Enid at least owed her the courtesy of checking out her story.

When she glanced out the window, she saw Kibo, the gray cat next door, chasing a squirrel. He was named after Mount Kibo, the highest point in Africa, and supposedly belonged to the recently deceased ninety-year-old neighbor. The woman's great granddaughter, Sophie, was now living in the house and had apparently adopted Kibo, who always seemed to be hungry. Despite all the warnings Enid had ever heard about not feeding a cat unless you wanted to own it, she often put a few leftovers out on a paper plate at the back door. So far, Kibo had readily taken the food but hadn't tried to move in.

Enid had talked with Sophie the week before when she came over to apologize for Kibo's wandering ways. Enid didn't mention that Kibo especially loved the Boar's Head sliced turkey that Enid often bought for Josh. During their brief conversation, Enid found out Sophie was an artist, who had done police sketches, among other things, when she lived in Atlanta. Her layoff had coincided with her great grandmother's death, so Sophie decided Columbia seemed as good a place as any to explore new options. She was currently teaching art classes at a community college until she figured out her next move. Soon, she told Enid, AI programs like DeepFaceDrawing and others could put all the police sketch artists out of work.

Enid slipped a slice of turkey into a small plastic bag and headed next door. Kibo was stalking something in a pile of leaves but immediately abandoned his search when he saw Enid. As she tore the turkey into small bites, Kibo was devouring them faster than she could deliver. When the last bite was gone, Kibo went back to scouting his prey in the leaves. "You're welcome," Enid said as her feline friend abandoned her.

Enid walked to the front of the house and rang the doorbell, which produced an awful sound, loud enough to wake the prior resident from her grave. When Sophie opened the door, she had on an artist's smock with various paint stains on it. "Hey, neighbor. Come on in."

"It looks like you're painting, and I don't want to disturb you. I can come back later."

Sophie laughed. "Don't be silly. I'm baking cookies. Come back to the kitchen with me."

Enid followed Sophie down the narrow, dark hallway to the small kitchen at the back of the house. The cabinets were painted white enamel, now cracking and yellowing with age. The entire room looked like a throwback to the early 1950's when the house was likely built. "That old O'Keefe & Merrit stove is a beauty. People love to restore them."

Sophie smiled. "Look at you. At expert in antiques, no less."

"When I lived in Madden, a small town about an hour from here, the old inn originally had an O'Keefe & Merritt stove in it." Enid left out the part about the human remains in the wall behind the stove that Theo, the inn's owner, had discovered.

"Someone offered me $500 for it recently," Sophie said. "When we finish cleaning up the house and settling the estate, I told him I'd give him a call." She opened the oven door to check on the cookies. "This old thing still works good though." She took the cookies out and offered Enid a seat at the small round, maple-stained table. "Please have a seat. As soon as these cool a bit, we can sample them."

"They smell delicious," Enid said.

Sophie pulled out a chair across the table from Enid and sat. "This is a nice neighborly visit. To what do I owe this pleasure?"

"When we talked last week, I didn't notice your slight British accent."

Sophie laughed. "I was born in Yorkshire but came here with Mum when I was five. So technically, I have dual citizenship. When I spend time with my mum or grandma, my accent slips out. Mum was here last week to help me go through all the stuff in this house. You know, for the estate."

Enid had a flashing memory of Cade, her ex-husband, now working for the Associated Press in London. Why were all these memories popping up recently? "Well, I love your accent. I apologize for dropping in unannounced, but I was wondering if you might help me with something. I'd be more than happy to pay you." Enid smiled. "A small fee, hopefully. Right now, until we get settled in Columbia, I haven't pursued assignments with other news outlets. And I don't make much as a freelancer."

"I'm sure we can reach an agreement on payment. Like maybe some chocolate chips for cookies, that is, if I can help you. Whatcha need?"

"I remember you telling me you had been a sketch artist."

"Yeah, before the damn . . . oops, sorry for my loose mouth. Before I was let go."

"I'd like for you to draw a sketch from a witness description."

"Won't the police do that?"

"She asked them to, but she said they brushed her aside."

Sophie made a face. "What? Why would they not listen to a witness?" She jumped up and began taking cookies off the tray on the counter. "I can tell now we need a cookie and a cup of tea for this conversation." She busied herself making tea and putting four cookies on a small white plate with roses around the rim. "Here you go, now tell me more about your witness." She bit into one of the cookies, "Hmmm. These are good."

Enid tasted a cookie and agreed. "I'm not much of a cook but better than I used to be. Josh, my husband, is the chef in our family."

"I've seen your man in the driveway. Yummy." She and Enid both laughed. "Sorry, but he is hot. That dark hair and nice bum ... well, anyway, the fact that he cooks makes him even more awesome. But I promise not to go after him." The two women laughed again, reminding Enid how much she missed having female friends.

"I'm not sure where to start." Then Enid remembered chiding Cassandra to just start at the beginning. "But here goes. This woman, Cassandra, contacted me through the newspaper. She had been referred to me by a friend, an empath I had worked with on a story a few years ago."

Sophie grinned and clapped silently. "I'm loving this already. Go on."

"Cassandra is a professional fortune teller."

Sophie leaned back in her chair. "No way! Are you serious? Is she legit?"

"To be honest, I'm not sure I buy into this whole seeing-the-future thing, but I know my friend wouldn't vouch for her if there was any question about her character."

"Well, go on, let's assume she's legit."

"A little more than a week ago, Cassandra was working with a client and saw her murdered in a vision."

Sophie's hand flew to her mouth. "What? You're serious? Did she tell her client?"

"Well, not exactly. Cassandra saw her in the kitchen of her house, looking out the back window into the yard. So she told her client not to let strangers in the house and to keep the doors locked. You know, all the usual precautions."

"It that ethical, to withhold information?"

"It's a long story for another time. Anyway, the woman was murdered about a week later. Just like in Cassandra's vision."

"Geez. I'd hate to have that kind of power, to be able to see things. I'm sure Cassandra was devastated." Sophie sighed. "Now I see why the police didn't take her seriously. How sad."

"Here's where I need your help. Cassandra saw the murderer, a man, but not his face. She saw his back and a tattoo of an insect on it."

"A tattoo? Of an insect? This is getting weirder by the moment. So you want me to draw the tattoo, is that right?"

Enid nodded. "I don't know how much detail Cassandra can give you."

"And what will you do with this sketch once you get it?"

Enid took a sip of the now lukewarm tea. "That's a good question."

CHAPTER 8

The next morning, Enid was finishing an article to upload to Grace. After tossing last night, she decided to connect Sophie and Cassandra, and then let Cassandra do what she wanted to with the sketch. After all, what could she do to help? And what Enid needed desperately now was more normalcy in her life, not this kind of thing.

Enid stayed busy the rest of the day, and the hours passed quickly. Several times, she realized she was fighting boredom, a feeling that was somewhat foreign to her. After years of working with Jack Johnson at the *Tri-County Gazette* in Madden and being drawn into several investigations, her career was now floundering again. Her and Josh's brief stay in Blakeley had left her confused and adrift. The *State* and her editor were treating her well, but she wasn't essential. She missed being essential.

Glancing at the new Apple watch Josh had given her for her birthday, she realized he would be home soon. She looked forward to his smile, his holding her in his arms. She also wanted to share her news about Cassandra with him.

About thirty minutes later, she heard his voice. "I'm home."

As she ran down the stairs, she remembered she had not put dinner on to cook and would now have to improvise, which wasn't her strong suit in the kitchen. Thankfully, Josh wasn't a picky eater, but after two days on the road and eating hotel food, she felt sure he would relish something simple. "Hi, Babe," she said as she threw her arms around him. "I'm so glad you're home."

He pulled her close. "Me too."

Enid stepped back and looked at him. "You look tired. Are you okay?"

He laughed in a way that she knew wasn't a happy laugh. "Rough trip. And on top of that, Roo quit."

Ruby-Grace Murray, nicknamed Roo after the Winnie the Pooh character, was a former freelance insurance investigator and the niece of Madden's town historian. She and Enid had teamed up to find the missing woman and had remained friends. Roo had also helped solve the murder of the spouse of a descendant of the town of Blakeley's founding family. After ruffling too many feathers during her investigation of the murder for a life insurance company, Roo had agreed to accept Josh's offer to be his assistant in Tiffany's research firm. While Roo was spontaneous and often unpredictable, she and Enid had become friends immediately. "What? Why? I thought she was happy working with you?" Enid asked.

"Roo said I wasn't the problem. She and Tiffany were like two alley cats swatting at each other." He pulled his tie off and thew it on the sofa. "I hate ties."

"I'm sorry I don't have a delicious home-cooked meal ready. How about a glass of wine, some cheese, crackers, and some of that chicken salad you like from Publix?"

"The wine sounds good, but I'm not too hungry. Just want to crash."

"Want to sit out on the patio or stay inside?"

"Definitely outside. I've been cooped up for two days in cars and hotels."

Enid busied herself setting the small table outside, complete with linen cloth and napkins, and their best wine glasses. A small candle flickered in the late afternoon dusk. As they sat down, a few leaves fluttered onto the table. Enid grabbed one and threw it over the rail into the yard. "I guess I'll need to rake soon."

Josh put his hand on hers. "I'm sorry I'm gone so much. I miss doing things like raking the yard."

"Do you want me to call Roo and convince her to stay?"

Josh smiled. "Don't bother. I think Tiffany's comment was something like, 'I hope the door doesn't hit her in the ass when she leaves.'"

"Ouch. That bad, huh?"

Josh nodded. "They're both good people and hard workers but the chemistry was bad, for both of them. Tiffany has to be conservative and low-key to gain people's trust and to do what she does."

"You mean spying on people?"

Josh smiled. "I guess that says a lot about how you feel about what I do."

"Not necessarily."

"And you know Roo. More like a bull in a china shop, although a sweet and hard-working bull."

Enid laughed. "Yep, that's her."

"So how were your couple of days?" Josh asked.

Enid wanted to tell him about her meetings with Cassandra and Sophie, but she was pretty sure he wasn't in the mood right now. "I'll tell you later. Just relax and enjoy being home."

After a few minutes of silence, Enid asked, "Will you replace Roo?"

Josh shrugged. "Tiffany has left that up to me. Roo was really good at online research, something I'm not good at and definitely don't enjoy."

"I know where you can get some good, cheap help with that."

"Who?" Josh asked.

Enid grinned. "I'm happy to help you."

Josh leaned in and kissed her. "Thanks, Babe, but I know you've got your own work to do."

"Yes, but . . ." Another conversation they'd have later. "The offer remains open if you need me."

Josh leaned back and appeared to be studying Enid.

"What?" she asked.

"I just missed, you, that's all." He sipped his wine. "And you don't look very happy yourself. Are you? Happy, I mean?"

"I'm okay. It's just that I have no input into my assignments, and I feel non-essential."

"Then go to work full-time, as a reporter for the paper."

Enid shook her head. "I'm not sure that's what I want."

Josh leaned back in his chair again. "You tired of being a reporter?"

Enid rubbed her temples. "Right now, I'm just tired."

"Do you like living here, in Columbia?" he asked.

"It's a nice, small city. It's fine."

"Do you miss Madden? And Jack?" he added.

Unexpectedly, tears filled Enid's eyes. "I miss having friends. We didn't make any in Blakeley."

Josh laughed. "Now *that* was a different experience." He took her hands in his. "I want you to be happy. I want *us* to be happy."

Enid squeezed his hands. "Me too."

Josh held up a finger. "Ah, I forgot to tell you. I got a phone message today from Big D."

"Am I supposed to know who that is?"

"Drake Harrow. You may have met him when we were in Madden. He's a detective for Bowman County and he's on temporary loan here, to Richland County, for some additional training. He wants to meet with me, just to reminisce, I guess."

"That's nice. You can invite him here if you like."

"I'll just meet him somewhere in a couple days. That way, you can take the night off."

And do what?

CHAPTER 9

When the alarm went off the next morning, Enid was surprised Josh's side of the bed was empty. Then he appeared coming out of the bathroom, with a towel around his waist. "Hey, sleepyhead. I thought we might go out for breakfast."
Enid sat up in bed. "You going in late?"
"Well, I can if you're interested in breakfast."
Enid swung her legs out of bed. "Give me about ten minutes. Are we going anywhere I can't wear jeans?"
"I thought we might go to Lizard's Thicket, down on Elmwood. You know, get a real breakfast for a change." He dropped the towel and rummaged in the tall wooden chest for underwear. "Besides, I got the impression you needed to talk about something last night. I'm sorry I wasn't more receptive. It was just one of those days."
Enid went over to him and put her arms around him. "You're so sweet."

. . .

In less than an hour, Josh and Enid were sitting in a booth at "the Lizard," as it was often called. "I've eaten here once or twice," Josh said. "Tiffany won't come. She's more of a bagel and smoked salmon kind of gal."
"I've heard of this place. The locals seem to like it."

After they ordered grits, eggs, and toast, Josh leaned back against the padded booth. "So what's on your mind, my beautiful wife?"

Enid sighed. "I need your advice on this woman who contacted me."

"About a story?"

"Well, that's what I thought at first. But no. She ... how can I explain this? She's a fortune teller, a seer, as she calls herself."

Josh leaned forward. "A what? Are you saying she reads palms?"

"I know you're skeptical, and so was I. I guess I still am somewhat. But Karla, you remember her, she called me and vouched for Cassandra."

Josh took a sip of coffee. "I know Karla helped you on an investigation, but I never was sure about her either, to be perfectly honest."

Enid paused while the waitress placed two steaming plates in front of them. "I'll bring some more coffee, but can I get you anything else?" she asked.

"No, thanks. We're good for now," Josh said.

"For the purposes of this conversation, can we just agree on our joint skepticism but consider Cassandra may actually be legit?"

Josh opened a small container of butter. "I love these," he said pointing his fork at the grits.

Enid laughed. "You'd think you grew up in the South, instead of New Mexico. I assume you didn't have grits there."

"We had a lot of things made with cornmeal but no grits." Another sip of coffee. "What was it Cassandra told you that's on your mind?"

"She saw someone get killed."

Josh's fork stopped midair. "She what? Where?"

Enid told Josh about Cassandra's vision and the woman's murder, which then occurred just like Cassandra had seen it. She also told him about Cassandra's withholding some specifics of the vision from her client.

"That's an incredible story, even if only half of it is true. But why didn't she tell her client?" Before Enid could answer, Josh held up his hand. "No wait. I'm not sure I'd want to hear that kind of prediction, considering that it might not be true."

"That's exactly what Cassandra said. She warned her client to be careful and especially not to let strangers in the house." Enid paused when the waitress came over to fill their cups and then continued. "But then it happened, exactly as she saw it."

"I would have loved to be in the room when Cassandra told all this to the police. I guess it would be asking too much to hope that she saw who did it."

"Well, she kinda did. But she didn't see his face, only his back."

"Well, that won't be much help. We don't have a way of identifying backs like we do faces."

Enid smiled. "You do realize, don't you, that you said 'we'? You still think like a cop."

Josh shrugged. "Just habit, I guess."

Enid studied Josh's face, trying to read his thoughts. "Anyway, she did see a tattoo. It was a winged insect."

"The police sketch artist can help with that."

Enid shook her head. "They dismissed Cassandra and her vision."

The waitress brought their check and smiled. "See you next time."

Josh smiled and nodded. Then he said to Enid, "So I'm almost afraid to ask, but how are you involved?"

"I've arranged for Sophie, our neighbor who used to be a police sketch artist, to draw Cassandra's vision of the insect tattoo."

"Well, that could be helpful. Once you get it, I'll be glad to ask Big D to make sure it gets some attention. He's a bit more open than some to these kinds of things." He paused. "And that's it, right? That's all you're going to do?"

"I'm not sure at this point, but why does that sound like a command instead of a question?"

Josh's cell phone pinged to notify him of an incoming text. "It's Tiffany. I told her I'd be in shortly." He put the phone back in his pocket. "I'm sorry if my tone sounded like a command. But …" He paused. "Ever since I've known you, you've put yourself in danger several times to—"

Enid held up her hand and cut him off. "To find the truth. That's what you did in law enforcement too. So why is it crazier when I do it as a reporter?"

"Fair enough. But we need to talk more about this later. I've got to drop you off and get to the office."

"I've learned to use Uber. It's kind of fun living in a place big enough for taxis and ride sharing. I can get home."

"You sure? I'm not crazy about you getting in the car with—"

She cut him off again. "Stop worrying and go snoop on some people."

Josh put his hand over his heart. "Ouch. That hurt."

CHAPTER 10

On the drive home, Enid found out the Uber driver was a University of South Carolina graduate who was now working toward a degree in music therapy online through Colorado State University. "I played a few gigs around town, you know, acoustic guitar stuff," he said. "But my grandma got Alzheimer's and she worked with a music therapist. I got to talking with the guy and he encouraged me to check it out." He grinned at Enid through the rear-view mirror. "Besides, I'm tired of eating instant ramen. That's about all most musicians can afford."

"That's fascinating," Enid said. "I know music therapy is used for autism and other conditions also. But are you willing to give up being a musician?"

"Music therapy is *all* about the music, the vibe. So I'm just using my skills in different ways. Besides, I can still do a few gigs here and there if I want to." He pulled into her driveway.

"It was nice talking with you," Enid said. "Good luck with your studies."

"Stay true to yourself," he said as she got out of the car.

"Thanks, and good luck with your new career path."

Sophie came running across the yard toward Enid. "I'm ready to help with the sketch. Want me to set it up with Cassandra?"

"Well, sure. That would be good. Let's go inside and I'll ask her to contact you. I'd like to be there too when you do it, if that's okay."

Sophie put her hands on her hips and grinned. "Well, of course, I was counting on it."

They went inside and Enid called the number on Cassandra's business card. It went to voice mail, so Enid assumed she was with a client. She left a message to call Sophie to set up the sketch.

Sophie was halfway out the door when she called over her shoulder. "I'll let you know when I hear from her."

Enid made herself a cup of tea and sat at her small desk to work on an assignment. Less than an hour later, Sophie called and said Cassandra was on the way to Sophie's house to work on the sketch. "I'll be there in a few minutes," Enid said. She finished the paragraph, gave it a quick review and uploaded it. Most of the paper's readers were boomers, so she had to write accordingly. And younger people typically relied on online sources, social media, and podcasts for their news. Enid sighed and closed her laptop. She couldn't stop the way journalism was heading. Instead, she tried to be open-minded and to consider that maybe newspapers really were outdated. Finding things online might make it easier to get information, but that didn't always mean the truth was easy to find.

. . .

Enid and Sophie had just finished a cup of herbal tea when they heard a knock. Sophie jumped up and ran to the door. "Hi, you must be Cassandra." Sophie held out her hand and then quickly withdrew it. "Sorry, no offense, but if I'm going to get killed by a meteorite crashing to earth this afternoon, I'd rather not know about it."

Cassandra smiled slightly. "I'm pretty sure that's not how you'll die." She leaned in and whispered loud enough for Enid to hear her. "But don't take a train today."

Sophie's hands flew to her mouth. "Seriously?"

Cassandra smiled. "No, I'm fooling with you." She looked toward Enid. "Hello again. Thanks for setting this up."

"You're welcome. I hope it will be helpful."

Sophie, who still appeared to be a bit shaken by Cassandra's comment, pointed to the sofa. "You can sit here beside me so you can see what I'm doing."

After everyone had settled in their seats, Sophie began. "Tell me what you saw in as much detail as you can."

Cassandra nodded. "May I lean back just a moment and close my eyes? I need to get the image in my mind again."

"Of course," Sophie said.

Once Cassandra closed her eyes, Enid began studying her. She was dressed in all black, so she had probably been working that morning. That mysterious persona was part of Cassandra's brand, Enid discovered. What was Cassandra like when he wasn't "on stage"? Or was she dark and mysterious all the time? She had the figure of a slim athlete and had moved gracefully, almost floating from the door to the sofa. Enid recalled making the same observation about Karla once.

The room was eerily quiet as Enid and Sophie watched Cassandra and waited. When Cassandra spoke, her soft voice was barely audible. "He had broad shoulders. Very muscular. He turned slightly and he had a slim nose with the tip turning down slightly at the end. Not a lot, but his nose was regal looking, like a hawk's. He's attractive though."

Enid watched Sophie sketch quickly, capturing Cassandra's description on the large pad of paper. When Sophie's pencil stopped moving, Cassandra, whose eyes were still closed, continued. "His hair was dark. Not black, but dark. No gray. He's bare from the waist up." She rubbed her forehead with her fingers, as if trying to stimulate the image. Sophie glanced at Enid but both remained silent.

"There's a drawing, a tattoo, on his upper back. It's wide, no color, just an outline in black. It's an insect. Perhaps a wasp. It has wings, but its body is not as slender as a wasp's."

"Describe the body," Sophie said.

"The insect's body is robust, and the frame, the texture of its body, is etched with fine lines. Very detailed."

"That's good," Sophie said. "Now describe the wings."

Cassandra was silent momentarily, as though she had not heard the request, so Sophie waited. Enid tried to imagine how different this must be from the times Sophie did sketches witnesses provided, asking dozens of questions and trying to pull the details from their memories. Witnesses' memories were notoriously flawed, but Cassandra was no ordinary witness. The image she had seen was seared into her mind. It was amazing to watch how, with little or no prompting from Sophie, Cassandra could pull that image into consciousness.

"The wings are splayed, spread out. Delicate and intricately etched with lines or veins. Very detailed."

"Good," Sophie said as she sketched furiously. "Now tell me about the head, legs, or anything else you can remember, or see, I mean."

"The insect has short, bristle-like antennae protruding from its head, which is compact, with prominent eyes that seem to bulge a bit at the sides. The legs are thick and sturdy."

"Anything else distinctive about it?"

Cassandra sat up straight and opened her eyes. "That's it."

Sophie put the final touches on the sketch and held it up for Cassandra to inspect. "Is that close to what you saw?" Sophie had drawn the back of a man, turned slightly sideways, whose angular nose gave him an aristocratic appearance. The black lines of the tattoo Cassandra described covered most of his upper and middle back.

Cassandra's hand clutched the fabric of the sofa, holding it tightly. "Yes, that's what I saw."

Sophie threw the sketch pad on the coffee table and jumped up. "I'll be right back."

She disappeared down the hallway but quickly returned with what looked like a textbook in her hand. She flipped pages furiously and then turned the book around for Cassandra to see. "Is this the insect you saw in the tattoo?"

Cassandra nodded. "Yes."

Sophie walked over to the chair where Enid was sitting and showed her the drawing in the book. "What is it?" Enid asked.

"A cicada," Sophie said.

CHAPTER 11

For a moment, neither Sophie, Enid nor Cassandra uttered a word. Finally, Enid said. "Why would someone get a tattoo of a cicada?"

Cassandra remained quiet, her brow furrowed.

"Well," Sophie said, people get weird tats all the time. I knew someone who had a ... Well, never mind. I'm just saying people do weird stuff."

Finally, Cassandra commented. "It's more than that. It really means something to this man, but I don't know what."

Enid took a photo with her cell phone. "I'll send you a copy," she said to Cassandra, who was staring at the drawing. "Josh, my husband, has connections with the police. He used to be in law enforcement. And one of his friends is here on loan from another county. They'll make sure this drawing is entered into the case file."

Without a word, Cassandra stood and walked to the door. As she was walking out, she turned to Sophie. "Thank you." And then she left.

"She's a bit strange, don't you think?" Sophie asked.

"You've got to remember what she's been through. First she sees the murder, and then no one believes her. But now she's got an image that may help us find the killer."

"Us?"

"I mean Josh and his friend."

Sophie leaned back against the sofa. "This is like totally none of my business, but you seem worried. Or maybe just distracted. Like I said, I don't know you very well, but if you need to talk, my friends all say I'm a good listener."

Enid smiled slightly. "Thanks, I may take you up on that offer." She stood. "But for now, I've got an assignment to work on."

"Oh, what's that?"

Enid started to explain but then stopped. "It's nothing, just a local story no one will likely read."

...

Back in her small home office, Enid stared at the blank screen. *What is wrong with me? I can't focus.* The assignment was about a restaurant that had been in business for more than forty years and was now closing. There seemed to be a lot of that happening these days. She looked at her interview notes from a few days ago and forced herself to write. She knew all too well that perseverance was perhaps more critical than talent when it came to writing.

By the time she finished the article, she had a headache and her stomach was growling. When was Josh coming home today? She couldn't remember his schedule. Finally, she decided to make a sandwich instead of waiting for him.

In the kitchen, she found an end piece of whole grain bread and a little bit of black bean hummus. After scraping all she could from the container, she spread it on the bread. Josh was the cook in the family, but he'd been traveling so much lately and often came home too tired to care about cooking. They were eating more takeout food and frequenting more restaurants than they ever had.

Sophie had offered Enid a walnut brownie after their meeting with Cassandra. Now Enid was glad she had taken it. She took it and the rest of her tea back to her desk and began an online search for information about cicadas.

Most of the information she found explained there were two types of the insect. The annual type emerged every year; the other type, the periodicals, emerged every thirteen to seventeen years, and South Carolina was expecting an emergence this year. Could there possibly be a connection to this event and the mysterious tattoo? She decided to leave it to Cassandra to make meaning of the cicada vision.

Enid laughed and said aloud to herself, "Next you'll be joining conspiracy groups. Get a grip, Enid." Just as she was ready to close her laptop, an article caught her eye.

The Enigmatic World of Cicada 3301: More Than a Decade of Mysteries and Conjectures

In the shadowy corners of the internet, a cryptic entity known as Cicada 3301 emerged over a decade ago, sparking intrigue and debate among cyber-sleuths and cryptography enthusiasts worldwide. This anonymous group, recognized for orchestrating a series of complex puzzles and alternate reality games (ARGs), has become a modern enigma, blurring the lines between virtual challenges and real-world mystery.

The origin of Cicada 3301 can be traced back to January 2, 2012, when the first of three sets of puzzles appeared online. Each puzzle set, released annually between 2012 and 2014, embarked on a quest to recruit "intelligent individuals" by presenting an array of challenges that tested participants' proficiency in cryptography, data security, and steganography—the art of hiding messages within plain sight.

The initial puzzle set the tone for what was to follow: a complex and layered journey through a digital labyrinth. The image of a cicada and the enigmatic number 3301 featured prominently, becoming synonymous with the group's identity. The subsequent rounds of puzzles, launched in January 2013 and 2014, continued this trend, deepening the mystery and drawing more curious minds into its web.

Cicada 3301's puzzles were not merely a test of skill; they were a showcase of the importance of internet anonymity and the depths to which data can be encrypted and concealed. The last known communication from the group appeared in April 2017.

The true identity of Cicada 3301's members remains a topic of intense speculation. Theories range from the group being a recruitment platform for international intelligence agencies like the NSA or MI6, to suggestions of a "Masonic conspiracy" or a cyber mercenary group. Some believe Cicada 3301 to be an elaborate alternate reality game, yet no individual or company has claimed responsibility or attempted to monetize the phenomenon.

As we mark more than a decade since Cicada 3301's first puzzle, its legacy persists in the collective imagination of the online community. The group's activities and motives remain shrouded in mystery, serving as a digital-age reminder of the endless possibilities and mysteries that lurk within the vast expanse of the internet.

Enid copied the article and pasted it into a digital file she had started on Cassandra. Could there be any connection between the tattoo and this secret group?

CHAPTER 12

When Enid's cell phone rang, she glanced at the screen. An unknown caller. When she answered, the caller introduced himself as Silas Marlowe.

"How can I help you, Mr. Marlowe?"

"Just Silas, please. I'm calling because your name came up in a conversation with a friend, and I wanted to reach out to you."

"I see. And who might that friend be?" Enid asked.

"He says you're the best thing that ever happened to Madden."

Enid paused, irritated with what felt like a game they were playing. "And how is Jack doing? I haven't talked to him a while."

Silas laughed. "He said you need to call him and catch up. But I'll get to the point of this call. I'd like to offer you a job."

"A job? Who are you with?"

"I'm the founder of the *Palmetto Post*, an online newspaper—"

Enid cut him off. "I'm familiar with your … your paper."

"Hmmm," Silas said, laughing. "Do I detect a bit of snobbery?"

"I appreciate your offer, but I'm a newspaper reporter. You know, the traditional kind."

"Ah, the kind that's laying people off left and right? That kind?"

Enid was ready to end the call. "As I said, I appreciate—"

"Don't hang up. Please. I know I threw that curve ball at you without warning. My apologies. Can we meet for coffee? Anywhere you'd like. I'll give you more details then."

Reluctantly, Enid agreed to meet Silas at Indah Coffee, where she had met with Cassandra. It was safe enough and the coffee was good.

. . .

When she walked in, the coffee shop was nearly empty, so she spotted Silas right away. He had described himself as slender, sandy blond hair, and "old enough to know better, but still young enough to get into trouble." He also mentioned he was a "halfway Millennial," referring to those born between 1981 and 1996. Midway would have made him around mid-thirties.

As Enid approached his table, Silas stood and offered his hand. "Enid, it's a pleasure to meet you." A Millennial with good manners was unexpected.

Enid shook his hand.

"Buy you a cup?" Silas asked.

"No, but thanks." Enid was beginning to regret agreeing to this meeting. She was behind on her assignment and wanted to do some research on Mara Sterling's murder.

As if reading her mind, Silas said, "I know you're busy, and I'll keep this brief. I'm hoping that meeting in person will help relieve some of your doubts about our paper. And I want to answer any questions you have."

When Enid didn't respond, Silas continued. "We are based in South Carolina and have reporters throughout the state and even into Charlotte, since it blends into the Rock Hill and York areas. Our readership is about 500,000 unique visitors per month."

"That's impressive."

"Thanks. I realize it's not as impressive as the *State's* footprint, but we do okay."

"Are you a journalism grad, or did you just decide to start a paper?" Enid asked.

Silas threw back his head, laughed, and grabbed his chest. "That was definitely a dagger! But a fair question. Yes, I graduated from the University of South Carolina with a degree in journalism. I was a few years behind you because I took off some time to walk the Appalachian Trail." He leaned forward and lowered his voice. "Sorry, I did a little research on you. That's how I know when you graduated."

"And did you work for a traditional newspaper?"

"Yes, I worked for the *News and Observer* in Raleigh after I graduated." He sighed loudly. "Sadly, I became disillusioned with the whole traditional journalism route. It's gotten worse now for print reporters, but even then, there was little room for a rookie like me who wanted to do investigative reporting. I realized soon after graduation that online reporting was the future."

"So you just started your own paper?" Enid asked.

Silas nodded. "The *Palmetto Post* originally operated with a small team of dedicated, like-minded journalists, and very limited resources."

"I remember now. Your paper did a series of articles exposing a major political scandal in South Carolina. Jack and I followed those stories."

"That series was our lucky break. We got some national attention and our readership grew significantly." Silas paused. "If you have more questions about the *Palmetto Post*, or me for that matter, I'm happy to answer them. But then I have some questions for you."

"What would you like to know?" Enid asked.

"Jack told me a little about you. That you went to Madden several years ago to investigate the murder of a young woman. A cold case, as I recall."

"Yes, it was my ex-husband's cousin."

Silas continued. "And you went to work for Jack, which at the time was the *Madden Gazette*. You pretty much solved the case on your own, at least according to Jack. I read your reporting on it. Well done."

"Thanks. Sounds like you already know a lot about me. Jack helped me get back into journalism." She paused. "I'll always be grateful to him for his support. And his friendship." She felt a lump growing in her throat.

"So why are you wasting your time doing crap assignments at the *State*?"

Enid found it difficult not to react. "I'm not ready to go to work full-time. Not yet."

"And why is that?"

Good question. "As you likely know, we just moved to Columbia and we're trying to get settled in."

Silas tilted his head and appeared to be studying her for a moment. "Okay. I won't pry. But I'm betting that you're ready to commit to something you believe in." His phone beeped and he glanced at a text message. "Sorry for the interruption." He turned his phone face down on the table. "Jack and I met at an oncologist's office."

"I've wondered about his cancer but I didn't want to pry too much. He claimed to be in remission when I left."

"I'm sure you understand I can't talk about that with you. But you need to contact Jack and catch up. In fact, he told me I needed to tell you that." Silas grinned. "And I'm okay. Thanks for asking."

Enid found herself liking this guy, despite the fact that he was a bit of a smart aleck at times. But something about him made her feel she could trust him.

"Anyway, Jack and I stayed in touch and I recently contacted him when I was looking for a new editor. He told me about you, and I did some research."

Enid held up her hand, her palm toward Silas. "I can stop you right now. I have no interest in being an editor. Surely Jack told you I filled in for him while he was out and that it wasn't my cup of tea."

Silas grinned. "Yeah, he might have mentioned that. But relax. I'm not here to offer you that job, that is unless you really want it. I want you to come to work for the *Palmetto Post* as a salaried employee. Full benefits. And I can pay you a decent salary."

Enid leaned back in her chair. "Well. I wasn't expecting that."

"As you know, we focus on crime reporting, especially unsolved crimes. I'm sure you've read about Mara Sterling's murder."

Enid froze momentarily while she collected her thoughts. "Yes, I have."

"I want you to investigate and report on that story for the *Palmetto Post*. Whaddaya say?"

CHAPTER 13

After Enid put away the last dishes from the dinner table that night, she said to Josh, "I've got a couple things to run past you. Can we talk?"

Josh put down his iPad and looked up at her. "Sure. Everything okay?"

"I just need your input on something. Two somethings, actually."

They settled down on the sofa with cups of coffee, and then Josh turned so he was facing Enid. "What two things?"

Enid took a deep breath, trying to decide which topic would be easier, and then decided both would likely concern Josh. "First of all, I want to show you something." She showed Josh the photo of the cicada drawing Sophie had done for Cassandra.

Josh studied it. "I don't understand. What is it?"

"It's a cicada."

"You mean one of those flying things that makes so much noise late summer?"

Enid nodded. "Yes, exactly. Sophie, our neighbor, drew it for Cassandra. This is the tattoo Cassandra saw in her vision. It was on the man's back."

"You mean the one where she saw the murder?"

"She didn't see it happen, only the aftermath."

Josh studied the photo again. "Was he naked?"

Enid slapped him lightly. "No silly, just from the waist up."

"I would think that's an unusual request, you know, to get a cicada tattoo," Josh said. "Should be easy to trace through the tattoo artists. They usually keep up with who's doing what in their community."

"You're assuming he had it done locally," Enid said.

"Good point. It's a good, detailed sketch. The detective handling the case should be happy to have it."

Enid made a face. "They should, but they don't believe her."

Josh leaned back on the sofa and took a sip of coffee. "I remember reading about this case in the newspaper, so your editor is unlikely to let you do another story on it."

"You're right. There's a reporter assigned to do follow-ups on this story." Enid sighed and ran her hand through her hair. "You know, I took this gig to freelance with the *State* because I wanted us to get settled in before I committed to full-time work."

"I think there's more to it than that."

"Like what?" Enid asked.

"Like you want to make sure I can actually work in something other than law enforcement, and you want to make sure we'll stay in Columbia before you commit."

Enid reflected a moment before answering. "I admit, there's some of that. But if you like it here, then we'll make it work."

"You don't like Columbia?"

"It's fine. Actually, yes, I like it."

"Are you having second thoughts about being a reporter?"

Enid was silent for a moment. "Today, I met with the owner of an online investigative newspaper. Jack recommended me to him."

Josh laughed. "Good ol' Jack. Always in your life somehow."

Enid sat up straight. "What does that mean?" Before he could answer, she added, "Are you jealous of Jack? Still?"

Josh reached out and took her hands in his. "I'm sorry. That was a cheap shot I made. Guess I'm just tired. You know I like and respect Jack. So tell me about your conversation with this guy."

Enid eased her hands away from Josh's grip. "Silas is his name. Silas Marlowe. He offered me a full reporter position with benefits."

Josh drained the last of his coffee. "Okay, so help me understand. You're not interested in working full-time for one of the most respected newspapers in the state, but you'd go to work for an online paper?"

Enid exhaled and shifted in her seat. "Actually, yes. Print papers are dying. You know that yourself. They're always laying people off. And I like the idea of doing investigative reporting, but I'll be in a long line of reporters waiting for those assignments at the *State*."

Josh looked directly into Enid's eyes. "Now I get it. You want to investigate this murder, the one your fortune teller saw."

Enid was surprised at herself when she felt tears filling her eyes. "I know you'd rather I write other kinds of stories, but this is what I want to do. It's what I'm good at."

Josh took her hands in his. "Yes, you are a good investigative reporter. And it's almost gotten you killed. Several times."

"And when you were in law enforcement, I worried about you constantly. But I didn't ask you to give it up, because it's who you are and what you love."

Josh wiped away a few errant tears that ran down Enid's cheeks. "No, you didn't. You've always been there for me." He pulled her close and held her. "And I'll support your decision, whatever it is." He kissed her hair. "But I won't stop worrying about you."

CHAPTER 14

The next morning after Josh left for work, Enid tapped on Jack's name in her phone contacts. After several rings she was ready to leave a voicemail, and when Jack answered, her mind had wandered back to her conversation with Silas. Was this really what she wanted to do?

"Enid, what a nice surprise."

"It's so good to hear your voice. How are you?" she asked.

"Better now that you've called."

"Do you have a few minutes? I just wanted to thank you for referring me to Silas. And to catch up a bit."

"Sure. How did the meeting with him go?"

"How did you know I met with him? Did he report back to you?"

Jack laughed. "Always the reporter asking questions. No, I didn't ask him to report back to me, but he said you two had a good meeting."

"Silas said he met you in the doctor's office. What do you think of him? Is he legit? Trustworthy and all that?"

"You mean is this someone you should work for? I wouldn't have recommended you if I had any doubts. I just regret I never got the *Tri-County Gazette* online so that I could offer you a remote job."

"Are you still looking for a buyer for the paper?"

"I'm sure you and Silas talked about the current state of print newspapers, so I won't bore you by reiterating the industry's woes."

"What about you? How are you?" she asked.

"We can talk about me later, but I can tell you Silas is top-notch. He's young, dedicated to finding the truth, just as you are, and he hires only trained journalists. None of these do-it-yourself reporters who are popping up on podcasts and online junk papers. I think you'd be a good fit for the *Palmetto Post*, but that's your decision. All I can do is tell you that as far as I know, Silas is a solid guy." Jack cleared his throat. "Sorry, this last medication I'm on dries me out like crazy. So how's that solid guy of yours?"

"Oh, I forgot to tell you Josh says 'hello.' He's working hard and learning how to be a snoop."

Jack laughed. "Uh oh. Do I detect a bit of sarcasm?"

"That's kind of an inside joke with us."

"But does he enjoy the work?"

"Honestly, I don't know. He's trying to make the best of it. For both of us. We want to settle down in Columbia. The last few years have been hard on both of us."

"Josh is a top-notch lawman. I'm sure Richland County or the South Carolina Law Enforcement Division would be happy to have him."

"I agree. But that's another conversation for another day. As soon as I can, I'll call you to set up a time to ride to Madden and have coffee."

"Don't wait too long."

After the call ended, Enid wondered if there was more to Jack's last comment.

CHAPTER 15

Josh surveyed the large crowd in the ballroom of the Marriott hotel on Main Street in Columbia. Dozens of round tables with white cloths and linen napkins filled up much of the area. A speaker's podium was set up at one end of the ballroom.

Josh was there to observe a target, the person their firm had been hired to investigate. Their client was ex-governor of South Carolina Bob Larkin, who now managed a Political Action Committee that was considering funding the target's political campaign for the state legislature. The PAC wanted to know if there was anything about the target that might jeopardize its investment in him.

Tiffany had sent him an email with some basic information, and Josh pulled the printout from his pocket. Ordinarily, Tiffany would have kept this kind of assignment for herself since she enjoyed fancy luncheons and dinners, as well as mingling with the who's-who-in-Columbia folks. But Tiffany had a past relationship with the target of their background check and felt her report to their client might be more objective coming from someone else.

But Josh's thoughts kept drifting back to his conversation with Enid, which had troubled him and was still on his mind. He didn't want to be one of *those* husbands who interfered with his wife's career. He wanted Enid to be happy with her work because he knew how important it was to her. But still, he worried. Once she went after a story, there was no stopping her. And if he was honest with himself, he was annoyed with Jack's recommending her for the job, given that he knew Enid's history of getting in too deep with her investigations. But Josh also knew Jack, like Enid, was a reporter at the core. Josh understood that kind of devotion to one's work. He had it once.

A buzz of conversation in the room interrupted his thoughts. The man who had walked in was Bob Larkin.

For the next few minutes, Larkin droned on about how wonderful the man standing beside him was, and what a great asset he was to the state of South Carolina. Josh tuned out until he heard the guest begin speaking.

"Thank you for that wonderful introduction, Bob. And thank you all for being here today."

As Caleb Thornhill continued to charm the crowd, Josh studied him and observed his movie star qualities: tall, dark, and handsome. He didn't just project charm; he oozed it. His voice reminded Josh of the narrator for a recent novel he had listened to in the car on the way to an assignment. Thornhill never hesitated or fumbled a word and had no notes. A born politician.

Josh's mind wandered to other things until he heard Thornhill say, "And now let's enjoy this wonderful meal and then mingle a bit."

From two tables away, Josh watched Thornhill laugh, chat, nibble on a few bites of food, and mesmerize his entire table, including several men who seemed as equally fascinated with their celebrity table mate as the women were.

As Josh took a bite of the chicken covered in some kind of sauce, he reminded himself not to judge Thornhill as a politician, but as a man. What kind of character did he have? What secrets was he hiding, if any?

After the meal, there was a social period for mingling that seemed to be winding down. Josh made his way over to Thornhill, who had been working the room like a pro. Josh introduced himself as a citizen concerned about crime.

Thornhill proceeded to check all the boxes he assumed Josh wanted to hear: more funding for police, more law enforcement hires, higher salaries to attract quality law enforcement, and so on. It was a well-rehearsed and expected response. Josh asked a few more questions but decided he would learn little about Thornhill this way.

After their conversation ended, Josh felt a tug on his elbow. "Well, if it isn't Joshua Hart." Larkin held out his hand. "Good to see you again."

Josh shook his hand but started mentally formulating an exit strategy. Josh didn't dislike Larkin. But he didn't trust him.

"Did Tiffany assign Caleb's background check to you?" Larkin asked.

"I'm just a concerned citizen interested in where Thornhill stands on law enforcement."

Larkin threw back his head and laughed. "Right, I know."

"So you're now running a PAC, right?" Josh asked.

Larkin flashed a well-rehearsed smile. "Yes, I'm doing what I can to help our party identify quality candidates and get them elected."

Josh tried to imagine Larkin doing anything other than being a smiling politician. "Well, I need to run. Good to see you again."

"Tell that lovely wife of yours, Edith, I said hello."
"It's Enid, sir. Her name is Enid."

CHAPTER 16

Enid sat across from Silas at the small office of the *Palmetto Post*. Silas explained that since their reporters worked remotely most of the time, there was no need for renting a large office to drain their operating budget.

"Silas, I want to thank you for the offer to come to work for you. Josh and I talked about it and—"

Silas interrupted, "Please don't say no."

Enid laughed. "I was going to say I'll take it."

Silas threw his hands in the air. "Terrific." Holding out his hand to her, he said, "Welcome aboard."

"Thanks. I admit I'm a little nervous about working for an online paper but Jack gave you high scores."

"What about your current assignments with the *State*? Do you need to give them notice?"

"I have a couple small assignments, but I can finish those pretty quickly." Enid paused. "There is one thing I need to tell you, though."

Silas leaned back in his chair. "I hate it when someone says that. It's usually not good." He waved his hands in the air. "Go on, lay it on me."

"The story you want me to work on, Mara Sterling's murder, I already have some connection with it."

"What does that mean exactly, a connection?" Silas asked.

Enid told Silas about Cassandra contacting him and asking for her help, and about her vision. For now, she withheld the information about the sketch. That would be another conversation.

Silas threw his hands up again. "Wow. I mean, like, wow. Are you friggin' serious? What a story! I mean, that's not a problem at all, not from my end at least. It's a bonus."

Ever since Silas had told Enid he wanted her to work on Mara's murder, Enid had felt uneasy. Cassandra had come to her for help. Was she betraying Cassandra by accepting this story as an assignment? And what about the sketch? That was done for Cassandra, so Enid shouldn't use it without her permission. And the investigator assigned to the case would surely not want the press to publish a potential clue like that. That is, if they even took the sketch seriously. But if she withheld the sketch from Silas, her new employer, what did that say about her trust in him?

And then there was Josh's reaction, which she had expected. He worried about her, in the same way she worried about him when he had been in law enforcement. Love and worry seemed to go together, so she couldn't fault Josh for his feelings. But there were deeper undertones to their conversation she needed to think about.

"Enid?" Silas asked.

She refocused her attention. "Sorry. I was just thinking about the story."

"That's good. As you know, all the major newspapers around here have reported on the murder and a few follow-ups were done. But we need to dig deeper than that. That's what we do here—dig deep. So get yourself up to speed and don't hesitate to ask if you need research or other assistance. We've got a small but quite competent staff. I'll answer any further questions you have, then I'll connect you with the service that handles our HR stuff. They'll email you all the paperwork to fill out. Just leave the references section blank, and I'll take care of that on my end. And I'll make sure you get access to our online databases, query services, other newspapers and wire services, and your company email address." He stood up. "On your way out, I'll introduce you to some folks and show you our two conference rooms you can schedule online to use if you want to meet with anyone here. Again, Enid, welcome aboard the *Palmetto Post*."

. . .

As Enid drove back home from her meeting with Silas, her mind drifted from one topic to another. The radio was on a local news station, but since she wasn't paying much attention, it just became background noise.

When she heard the newscaster say, "Grant Sterling, a prominent financial advisor, has been arrested for the murder of his wife, Mara Sterling," Enid snapped to attention and turned up the volume. Was the story ending this simply? The husband did it?

Enid's cell phone rang and Cassandra's name appeared on the screen. "Did you hear the news?" Cassandra asked.

"I just heard it. I'm in the car. Let me call you when I get home."

"He didn't do it," Cassandra said. "They're wrong."

CHAPTER 17

Enid had barely got inside her house when the phone rang. This time it was Silas. "I'm sorry to bother you, but we need to get right on this. Can you work on the article this afternoon?" he asked.

"Well, yes. I can. But I haven't had time to—"

"Yes, yes, I know." Silas sighed. "Sorry, I just want us to be on top of this one. I can assign it to someone else to fill in until you're ready."

"No, I'll take it. I'll talk to you later and let you know what I've found out."

So this was how it was going to be? With virtually no contacts in Columbia, it was going to be a challenge to build trusted resources as quickly as she needed them.

Then she remembered she needed to call Cassandra back. "It's me, Enid. I'm home now."

Without any preamble, Cassandra said, "You've got to convince them that he didn't do it."

"How can you be so sure?" And then Enid realized that was the wrong thing to say.

A brief period of silence, and then, "I thought you believed me."

"I'm sorry, it's been a crazy day." Enid sat down at her desk. "Cassandra, I have to be honest. I *want* to believe you, and I respect your insights and skills, but as a reporter, I need solid information."

"But you're not doing a story on this. I didn't come to you for that."

"Cassandra, I'm not an investigator, at least not in the way you want me to be." Enid took a deep breath. "Are you familiar with the *Palmetto Post*?"

"I've heard of them. Why?"

"I accepted a job with them. Today."

There was silence on the line.

"Cassandra, are you there? Talk to me."

"So what does this mean? For helping me, I mean?"

"Nothing, except I've been assigned to report on the Sterling murder. That means I can officially ask a lot of questions. I withheld the sketch because it's yours, not mine. And the police need to know about it before the public does."

Enid heard a soft sob.

"I'm sorry. It's just that I don't know how to handle all this myself," Cassandra said.

"You don't have to. In fact, I can help you more now. But first, let's get the sketch to the authorities and go from there."

. . .

Enid and Cassandra waited in the lobby for the lead investigator to meet with them. After twenty minutes, a large man with dreadlocks and light caramel skin approached them. "I'm Detective Drake Harrow. How can I help you?"

Cassandra stood, while Enid remained seated. "You're not the detective I talked to," Cassandra said. "Is he in?"

"Lieutenant Albright is not in right now, but I'm assisting him on the case and can help you. Would you like to come to the conference room and talk?"

Cassandra looked at Enid. "She needs to come too."

Detective Harrow smiled, revealing brilliant white teeth. "Of course, just follow me." He looked at Enid. "Both of you."

When Enid and Cassandra were seated at the small conference table, Harrow shut the door and sat down across from Cassandra. "How can I help you?"

Cassandra laid the sketch on the table in front of him. "That's what I saw."

Enid raised her hand slightly. "Excuse me for interrupting, but are you familiar with the case at all?"

He shrugged. "Somewhat. I'm here on loan from another county to assist, so I know a little about it."

"Which county?" Enid asked.

"Bowman."

Enid suddenly felt a little lightheaded. "Do you know Joshua Hart, the former sheriff there?"

Harrow smiled broadly. "Yes, I know Josh. He's straight up. You related?"

Enid considered her options for answering and decided on the truth. "He's my husband."

Harrow's face lit up. "No. For real?"

Enid nodded. "He mentioned a detective he knew was on loan here."

Harrow shook his head. "Small world. Indeed." He turned his attention back to Cassandra. "Are you the woman who saw the vision?" He smiled. "I heard about you."

Cassandra nodded and pointed to the sketch on the table. "This is a sketch of the tattoo I saw on the killer."

Harrow studied the drawing. "Very nice. Are you the artist as well?"

"No, it was done by a former police sketch artist," Enid said. "My neighbor."

"Ah, you are a resourceful pair, I see," Harrow said with a slight island accent—either Bahamian or Jamaican.

"The other detective, Lieutenant Albright, didn't believe me," Cassandra said. "So we had to be resourceful."

Harrow studied the sketch again. "It's a cicada, is it not?"

Enid nodded. "It is."

Harrow pulled a notepad from his pocket and wrote a few words. "And where on his body was this tattoo?"

"Just like in the sketch, on his back, across the shoulders and down the center," Cassandra said.

"Why don't you tell me about your vision," Harrow said. "I'm not sure your full statement is in our file."

Enid spoke up. "I doubt any of Cassandra's vision is in your file. She said no one took her seriously."

Harrow put his pen down and leaned back slightly. "I'm sorry if that's the case, but surely you understand how unusual this kind of thing is."

Cassandra started to protest, but Harrow held up his hand to silence her. "Please let me finish." He leaned back slightly in his chair. "My mother was Jamaican and her family practiced Obeah. Are you familiar with it?"

Cassandra nodded. "It's a form of voodoo that can be used for good or evil. My grandmother knew an Obeah practitioner, a woman who lived in the mountains near us. She was a healer."

Harrow dropped his head slightly and shook his head. "Obeah is so misunderstood. But that's another conversation for another day. So you come from a line of seers, is this true?" Harrow asked.

Enid found herself growing impatient with his casual approach to interviewing but reminded herself she was here to support Cassandra, not to interfere. And then she remembered Silas' pressure for an article. What, if any of this, could she use ethically?

Cassandra told Harrow about her grandmother and her mother, including her mother's failure to make peace with her gift and her ultimate suicide. Cassandra seemed to be warming up to Harrow. At least he was listening to her.

When Cassandra finished talking, Harrow leaned forward. "Thank you for trusting me with this information." He looked at the drawing. "So the man in your vision had no shirt on. It must have been some kind of ritual for him."

"He was bare from the waist up. A broad, muscular back with this large tattoo."

Harrow scribbled more notes. "Was the tattoo a color?" He looked up and smiled. "I guess the right question is do you see in color, or just in black and white?"

"Both. Some visions are detailed and very colorful. Others are vague, almost like shadows. This vision was mostly black and white, but I got the impression it was a black ink tattoo, no color. Very detailed, just like the sketch."

Harrow ran his finger across the paper, as if he were able to feel the delicate wings Sophie had drawn. "Are you aware of an organization called Cicada 3301?"

Enid responded, "It came up in my research. It seemed to have been a group of intelligent people trying to solve puzzles."

Harrow nodded, his brow furrowed. "Yes. That's what they were back then. Around 2012 to 2014, as I recall." He smiled, "I did a little research myself during that time, for a case." He turned to Cassandra. "May I make a copy of this?"

"You can keep that. We'll make another copy," Enid said.

Harrow stood, looking directly at Cassandra. "I need to go to a briefing but I assure you that I heard you. By the way, I assume you know Mr. Sterling, the husband, has been arrested."

"That's why we're here," Cassandra said. "The man I saw was not her husband."

Harrow handed a business card to both Cassandra and Enid. "I need to hear more. But we'll have to have another meeting. Call me and set something up."

"Who is the investigator on the case, you or Albright?" Enid asked.

"Technically, Lieutenant Albright is."

Cassandra stiffened, "What does that mean exactly?"

Harrow opened the conference room door. "It means we'll talk later. Call me." He motioned for them to leave and then followed them out the door.

Walking through the lobby to leave, Cassandra turned to Enid. "Maybe I should just try to move on, forget what I saw."

"Could you do that?"

. . .

As they walked out of the police station, Cassandra fingered one of the bracelets on her arm. "Your husband, he used to be in law enforcement."

"He did. Now he works for a consulting firm that does background checks, mostly on politicians or executives." Enid studied Cassandra's face. "Does that concern you?"

Cassandra looked up from the bracelet. "I'm more concerned about you being a reporter."

Enid braced herself for the inevitable conversation. "I was a reporter when you came to me. You knew that."

"Yes, but you weren't doing crime reporting."

"But that's why you came to me originally, because of my experience. Right?"

Cassandra's eyes filled with tears. "I don't know anything anymore. I'm so upset, I've had to reschedule my appointments for the next few days because I can't focus." She wiped the tears with a tissue she pulled from her pocket. "Sorry. I'm usually not emotional. I just keep thinking about my mother. For so long, I've been angry with her for giving up, for killing herself. Why wasn't she stronger?" Cassandra let out a loud sigh. "But now I get it."

Enid put her hand on Cassandra's. "All this is a lot to handle, for anyone. Don't let it get to you. I'll do what I can to help." Enid pulled her hand away gently. "But we need to talk about my new job and what all of this means. I promise not to betray you, not intentionally. If you ever feel that I have, let me know. Promise?"

Cassandra nodded.

"I won't report on anything you tell me off the record. I'm going to make notes about some things I need to ask you right now, but that doesn't mean I'll print it. Understand?"

Another nod.

"How can you be so sure it wasn't the husband you saw?" Enid asked.

"I can't explain it. I just know. And I saw his photo in the news. He's not the same shape as the man I saw."

"Then do you have any idea who it was in your vision?"

Cassandra shook her head, side to side, slowly. "Someone who is evil. I know that seems obvious from what he did, but I could feel the hate and violence in him."

"Perhaps someone Mara Sterling knew?" Enid asked.

"I don't think so. I felt no connection between the killer and the victim. But I can't be sure."

As if talking to herself, Enid asked, "Why would a stranger kill someone? And in her own home? That kind of up-close killing is usually personal."

Cassandra stood. "I'll give all of this some more thought when I can focus. "Thanks for helping me find the strength to deal with it."

And now I've got to find my own strength, Enid thought.

CHAPTER 18

The section of Forest Acres where the Sterlings lived was typical of upper middle-class suburbia. About five miles from downtown Columbia, it was mostly older homes, many of them large, two-story traditional houses. Mercedes, Lexus, and other luxury cars were parked in many of the driveways.

A couple of weeks earlier, right after Mara Sterling was found murdered, the neighborhood was likely overrun with press vehicles. Now, it was quiet.

Yellow crime scene tape still covered the front door of the Sterling house. In the yard next door, the one to the right, an older woman walked around, tending the plants at the front of her house.

Enid parked her car in the street and walked toward the woman. "Excuse me." The woman fixed her gaze on Enid but said nothing. "May I talk with you for a minute?" Enid asked. When the woman remained silent, Enid continued walking toward her.

When Enid was within earshot, the woman said, "I'm a bit hard of hearing. Who are you?"

Enid produced her press pass. "I work for ..." She hesitated, almost saying the *State*. "For the *Palmetto Post*. May I ask you a few questions?"

The woman pointed to two chairs under a large front portico with a red brick floor. "We can sit there, if you like."

Enid followed the woman, being careful not to get too close or to alarm her in any way, although the woman didn't look like someone who was easily spooked. The woman sat down in the chair closest to the front door and motioned for Enid to sit in the other one. "Thought all you press people were done with us," the woman said.

"I bet you had a lot of them here right after it happened."

The woman threw back her head and laughed. "Couldn't spit without hitting a reporter."

Enid liked her. "I appreciate your talking to me. I won't keep you long."

The woman shrugged. "Not much else going on. Since Dan, that was my husband, since he passed on, it's been pretty quiet around here." She nodded toward the Sterling house. "Until all that horrible stuff happened."

"May I take notes?" Enid asked. "If you need to tell me anything you don't want me to use, just let me know."

The woman laughed again. "Off the record, huh? I watch a lot of TV these days. Lots of cop shows, but occasionally there's a reporter involved." She seemed to be studying Enid. "Why'd you become a reporter, if you don't mind me asking?"

Enid was amused that the woman had taken over the questioning now. "To find the truth. I know that sounds lofty, but it's what drives me."

"Not lofty at all. I respect that. Now what kind of truth do you need from me?"

"How well did you know the Sterlings?" Enid asked.

"I said hello when I saw them in the yard or drive, you know, that kind of thing. They're much younger, obviously. Young people don't like to hang out with us seniors too much. But they were nice enough. At least she was friendly."

"What about Mr. Sterling?"

The woman's shoulders stiffened. "He was alright, I guess. Just a bit stuffy. One of those financial guys. Seemed to be smart as a whip, but not much personality, if you know the type. I had a nephew like that. Money smart but people dumb." She laughed at her own joke.

"Do you know how they got along?" Enid asked.

The woman shook her head. "Not really. I wasn't invited to their parties. They entertained a lot." She waved her hand toward the street. "Had cars parked way down there. Upset some of the older residents, them taking up so much of the road."

"Were you surprised when Mr. Sterling was arrested?"

The woman shook her head. "Not really."

"Why is that?"

The woman leaned forward slightly and lowered her voice. "That smart ass policeman seemed hell-bent on blaming the husband from the git go."

"Why do you say that?" Enid asked.

"Kept asking me questions but didn't seem to care what I said. Had his mind made up, it seemed. Now mind you, maybe the husband did kill her. That's not for me to say. But ... well anyway, I'm not sure that detective was looking for the truth, like you say you are. I think he was looking for an easy out."

"Can you think of anyone who might want to harm Mrs. Sterling?"

The woman shook her head "Don't know enough about them to say." She paused. "There is one thing though. They had a guy doing some renovations. Kitchen work, I think.

Mara told me that one day when we were in the yard talking. I knew the contractor. Talked to him myself once but another neighbor warned me he was a crook and couldn't be trusted."

"What's the contractor's name?"

"Dunno, but no need to worry about it. Smart Ass said he'd check it out, and when I asked him about it when he came back, he brushed me off."

Enid handed the woman her business card, one from the *State*. "I'm actually leaving here to work for the *Palmetto Post,* but this is my personal cell number on the card. Please call me if you think of anything else. You've been very helpful, and I enjoyed talking with you."

The woman stared intently at Enid, her eyes squinting slightly. "Good luck with your story, sweetie. Come back anytime you want to ask me more questions." She smiled. "I like you. Don't know why, but I do."

CHAPTER 19

Josh sat across from Tiffany in her tastefully decorated office. Each time Josh was in her office, he eyed the unusual painting hanging on the exposed-brick wall. She had mentioned how much it cost—much more than Josh would ever consider for a painting, especially an abstract he didn't understand.

"So, how did the luncheon go?" she asked.

Josh knew she expected him to give Caleb Thornhill a glowing report. "I know you two were close at one time," he said.

Tiffany tossed her long blond hair over one shoulder. "Look, I know he's not your kind of guy, but can you put that aside?"

Josh wanted to agree with her, that Caleb wasn't someone he wanted to spend time with but refrained. "He was smooth and handled himself well. He barely touched a glass of wine and never seemed to get too friendly with the female guests." Josh smiled. "And he's full of BS."

"You don't like politicians very much, do you?"

"I guess I can't shake my experiences with them from my law enforcement days. Not to mention my work with our client, ex-Governor Larkin, who was, by the way, in attendance today."

"I'm not surprised. Larkin is heavily invested in making sure the *right* people get elected."

Josh wanted to say something about Larkin's "right kind" of people but refrained. "From what I could tell, Caleb would be that right kind of person. But I'll do some more in-depth checking and give you a formal report."

Tiffany nodded. "Good. In a few days, I hope?"

"I'll do my best."

"This should be a slam dunk. Let's give Larkin a report and collect our fee. Move on to the next one."

"I'll be working from home and snooping around on Caleb, so I can wrap this up." Josh smiled to himself when he used Enid's term *snooping*. "Just call if you need anything." He walked out of Tiffany's office feeling uneasy, but he couldn't pinpoint exactly why. He agreed this guy Caleb was the right kind of guy for politics: handsome, well built and smart. What else could a PAC ask of someone they were about to invest heavily in?

...

After ditching his office clothes and changing into jeans at home, Josh walked to the kitchen to make coffee. Enid was sitting at the small table making notes and looked up when she heard him. "Hey, I didn't know you'd be home today. You still working?" she asked.

"I've got to do some more snooping on a guy." He leaned over and kissed her. "What about you?"

"I took the job, the one with *Palmetto Post*."

Josh sat down beside her. "I assumed you would."

Enid rubbed his arm gently. "Can we talk about this story I've been assigned? I need your input."

Josh laughed. "You got an assignment already? That was quick. And you want my input on a story you're working on? Seriously?"

"Silas wants me to do an in-depth follow-up on the Mara Sterling murder."

"You mean, the one your fortune teller saw?"

"Cassandra. That's her name. And yes, that murder. We went to talk to the detective today to give him a copy of the sketch Sophie did."

Josh stood up to pour a cup of coffee, not waiting until the brewing was complete. "I would have loved to have seen his face. What was his reaction to Cassandra's vision?"

"Detective Harrow was open minded."

Josh's coffee cup stopped midway to his mouth. "Drake Harrow? Big D from Bowman County?"

"Yep, that's the one. Your friend. He is pretty imposing, I admit. But a nice guy. Told us about his mother practicing Obeah."

"You must have hit it off pretty good."

"I think he was just letting Cassandra know he didn't think she was crazy. Is he one of the good guys?"

"Far as I know. I never worked a case with him, but the talk around was that he's honest, fair, and gets results." Josh laughed. "Imagine that. Big D working the case you're writing about. Small world."

"He said he was helping another detective, Lieutenant Albright."

"I know him too." Josh paused to take a sip. "Or at least I know about him. Sadly. I heard he's near retirement and his drinking has gotten worse since his wife died. Hate to hear that Albright is the one assigned to work with Big D."

Josh took a deep breath. "So what do you need my input on? A law enforcement question?"

"Well, not exactly. As you know, Cassandra came to me through Karla and asked for my help. It was before I accepted the new position, which came with the assignment to work on the Sterling murder."

Josh's brow furrowed. "I'm not sure I understand the dilemma."

"The problem is Cassandra said explicitly she wasn't looking for me to write a story about her vision."

"And now you are?"

Enid threw her hands up in the air. "That's the dilemma. Exactly. When I told Silas what I knew about the case, about Cassandra's coming to me, I didn't tell him all the information."

"Such as?" Josh asked.

Enid reached into a folder and pulled out a sketch of the cicada. "Such as this."

"What is it?"

"That drawing I showed you, the tattoo on the killer's back that Cassandra saw in her vision."

"But you gave this to Drake, right?"

Enid nodded. "Yes, but I haven't told Silas, and I'm worried that I might be starting off a new job withholding information. For a reporter, that's pretty serious."

Josh leaned back in his chair and looked up at the ceiling momentarily. Then leaning forward and refocusing on Enid, he asked "Have you talked to Cassandra about this?"

"Yes, of course. She was understanding, as far as I could tell. I told her our conversations would be off the record unless she gave me permission to use something."

"So your dilemma is with Silas, not Cassandra."

"Now that we're talking, I'm not sure I have a problem. Maybe I just needed to talk it out."

Josh took her hands in his. "You seem to have a knack for getting into these kinds of situations. It used to be a conflict of interest between us, when I was in law enforcement."

Enid squeezed his hands. "I know. I guess it's the nature of my work."

Josh leaned over and kissed her. "Want me to talk to Big D? Off the record?"

"Do you think he'll talk to you?"

"I don't know, but I can ask. Besides, it will be good to catch up with him."

"I appreciate that. Oh, and I'm sorry. I didn't ask how your day went."

Josh sighed. "Oh, just another day of snooping, rubbing elbows with pompous politicians, and eating rubber chicken. You know, one of those days."

Enid studied Josh's face, trying to read his thoughts. "Is the job not what you expected?"

"I don't know. Not sure what I expected."

CHAPTER 20

The next day, Josh pulled into the parking lot of the Waffle House. There were others closer to town, but Drake insisted they meet at this one just outside of Columbia. When Drake saw Josh, he stood and grinned. "Josh, my friend, how have you been?"

They shook hands and then embraced in a man hug. "Good man, how about you?" Josh asked.

"Never better." He motioned toward a booth where they could sit. "As I recall you liked one egg, I forgot how though. And grits with raisin toast."

Josh laughed. "You have a great memory. I haven't eaten at a Waffle House in a long time."

Drake threw back his head and filled the space with his booming laugh. "Nuttin ever change here, mon. Nuttin."

"I see you still haven't lost the accent."

Drake leaned forward and whispered. "It comes in handy sometimes." He leaned back and smiled. "Besides, the women love it."

Josh glanced at Drake's hand. "But none of them enough to marry you?"

"No, mon. I keep muh freedom."

After they ordered their food, Drake said, "I met your woman yesterday. She's a looker. Why she pick you?"

"Because I'm charming? Or maybe she just loves my chili."

"Could be. But you didn't come here to BS with me. What's up?" Drake's face was serious now, and Josh was reminded how imposing the investigator could be.

"I won't put you in the position of sharing anything you're uncomfortable with—"

Josh was interrupted by their wait person putting their food on the table and refilling the coffee cups. "There you go, hun. Let me know if you need anything else."

After they thanked her, Drake said, "I trust you, my friend. So I'll tell you what I know and trust that you'll handle the information as a lawman."

"A former lawman."

Drake stirred his scrambled eggs into his grits. "Yeah, I heard you were snooping these days."

"Something like that. And I appreciate your trust."

"That means I trust you to tell your missus only what she needs to know."

Josh slathered a piece of raisin toast with apple butter. "We've learned how to keep confidences. If you trust me, I hope that you'll learn to trust her as well. She'll do what's right, and if she has a question when it comes to the law, she'll come to me."

"Must be nice to trust someone that much."

Josh wiped his mouth with a napkin. "It gets tested at times, but we work it out."

"So what do you want to know?"

"Enid says you met Cassandra as well."

Drake shook his head. "I must say, this is a first. Having a fortune teller see a murder before it happens."

"Do you believe her?"

"As I told the ladies, my grandmother practiced Obeah on the island. She was a seer too." He shook his head again. "Thankfully, she didn't pass that gift on to me. Don't think I want to see the future."

"So you do believe Cassandra?" Josh asked.

"Let's just say, I'm taking it at face value. For now, at least."

"But the husband has been arrested, and Cassandra is adamant he wasn't the killer."

Drake reached into his pocket and pulled out his phone. Flipping through the photos, he showed the sketch of the cicada to Josh. "You seen this?"

Josh nodded. "Enid showed it to me. What do you make of it?"

Drake shrugged. "Maybe nothing. Maybe something. Your woman knows about the old Cicada 3301 society. May have no connection." He raised an eyebrow. "But may be worth checking into. Ask her to let me know if she finds something."

Josh nodded. "Have you talked to Albright about the sketch?"

"What do you think?" Drake said, laughing. "I will, but he's not going to listen. Too busy counting the days to retirement."

"Is that why you're here? To take his place?"

The waitress came to clear the plates. "One check or two?"

Josh held up a finger. "I'll take it."

Big D said to the waitress with a beguiling smile, "He make a lot of money, not like me and you. We work hard for ours, don't we?"

The waitress smiled. "You got that right, sweetie." She scribbled on the order pad, ripped it off the pad, and plopped it in front of Josh. "Y'all come back now." She glanced at Drake again and smiled before walking away.

"I think she likes you," Josh said.

"All da women, dem all love mi." Big D glanced over his shoulder to make sure she wasn't within earshot. "I just came here to learn from another county. Richland has got a much bigger operation than Bowman. More technology, more training, all that. But I'll be ready to go home when I can." He paused. "By the way, your old stomping ground, Madden, is looking for a police chief."

"Really? What happened to Pete?"

"He's going to SLED. You know, bigger fish to catch. Why don't you come home, take the job?"

Josh pushed back on the edge of the table. "Thanks for your vote, but we're here to settle in."

Drake raised an eyebrow. "Whatever. Just wanted to let you know. Anyway, Albright is fixated on the husband."

"Why's that?"

"Says the husband has a lot of debt, some rumors about him having a mistress and a big insurance policy on his wife."

"That certainly gives the husband motive. What about opportunity and means?"

Drake laughed. "I love it when you talk lawman." His smile now gone, he continued. "The husband was in Charlotte, but Albright says he had time to drive back and kill her within the timeframe of her death and then get back to his meeting."

"Really? In I-77 traffic in the middle of the afternoon?"

"I know. Seriously. And no one can confirm he was still in Charlotte at the time of the murder."

"But would a husband kill his wife and leave their baby on the floor beside her?" Josh asked. "What kind of cruel bastard would do that?"

"The world is full of them, my mon. Full of 'em." Drake's phone pinged an incoming message. "Albright. Got to go." Drake stood to leave. "Thanks for the breakfast. I'll get the next one, even on my meager salary." He leaned to whisper in Josh's ear. "I don't think the husband did it either."

CHAPTER 21

On the short drive back to Columbia, Josh called Pete on a whim. Today must be his day for reconnecting with old acquaintances. He still had Pete's private number in his contacts, as well as the number for the Madden police station. Josh tapped on the private number.

"Josh, is that you? Pete asked. "How are you?"

"I'm good. Just had breakfast with Big D, remember him?"

"Yeah, he's pretty unforgettable, especially around these parts. Stands out like a sore thumb. I mean, you know, a good sore thumb, of course. But I guess a sore thumb isn't a good thing. Anyway, I've always liked him."

"He seems to be pretty solid. But what about you? I hear you're going into state law enforcement."

"I'll be leaving in a few weeks."

"SLED is lucky to get you. I wish you all the best." Josh paused. "So who's taking your place? Just curious."

"We were all hoping you'd come back. We got a new mayor and Jack and I have been working on her."

"I appreciate it, really. But I'm setting into a new job in Columbia."

"So I heard. You like it?"

"It's something new. Nobody is shooting at me. Not yet, anyway." Josh cleared his throat. "How's Jack doing? His health, I mean."

"I don't know but he looks like he's losing weight. And he's really pale."

"I hate to hear that. I know he was trying to sell the paper. He find a buyer?"

"Not that I know of, and I'm afraid it will get sucked up by one of the bigger papers and we'll lose our three-county identity. Or maybe Jack will just shut it down." Pete laughed. "You know Jack. It has to be the right person. And he hasn't found that person yet." Josh heard some people talking in the background. "Look, I'm sorry but I've got to run. Let's talk again," Pete said. "Think about taking the job. You were the best police chief Madden ever had. We all miss you both."

. . .

Josh decided to go to the consulting office since Enid would be working at home and he didn't want to disturb her. Working from home had its benefits, but it also had drawbacks. Besides, he needed to make an appearance at the office. His last meeting with Tiffany didn't feel right, but he couldn't pinpoint why. He wasn't ready to admit it was because he wasn't used to working for a woman. Could it be that simple? But then Tiffany was no ordinary woman, at least not like the female officers he had worked with.

When Josh walked into the office, his mind was on Jack. If Enid knew, why hadn't she mentioned it? And if she didn't know, he hated to be the one to tell her, considering that she worshiped the man.

"Josh. Did you hear me?"

He turned around to see Tiffany is a sleek black dress, looking more like a fashion model than a background search consultant. Her hand was on her hip. "I need to see you."

Josh followed her into her office. "What's up?"

"I've been calling you all morning. Where have you been?" She then held up her palm to Josh. "Don't answer that. That was a bitchy question. Sorry."

"It's okay. I was meeting with a police investigator."

"As part of your background check on someone?"

Josh tried to get comfortable in the stylish, but torturous, chair across from Tiffany's desk. "No, a personal matter. I should have let you know where I was."

"Don't be silly, I'm not that kind of boss. You need to either ignore me or push back." She tossed her hair. "Anyway, our client wants a report on Caleb as soon as possible. They're ready to invest in him. Are you making any progress?"

"Working on it. I'll try to speed it up." The uneasiness Josh felt during their last meeting was back. "How quickly do you usually report to a client?"

Tiffany frowned. In spite of Josh's many years of reading people, he admitted he was stumped when it came to Tiffany. Perhaps it was because she was just as she said she was. No hidden layers. But Josh was wary and couldn't figure out why.

"There's no set time frame, but this one should be straightforward. Anything else we need to discuss?"

Josh stood. "No, I'll get on it."

CHAPTER 22

Josh changed his mind and decided to work on Caleb Thornhill's background from home. Why was he uncomfortable doing it at the office? Josh chided himself for his uneasiness.

Enid had gone out so he had the house to himself. Before settling down to work, he looked around the small bedroom he and Enid had divided into two separate areas. They had even put a set of bookcases between the two areas to act as a room divider. For the most part, it worked well, mostly because it was rare for them to both work from home at the same time.

Starting where most searches began, Josh checked Caleb's online presence: social media and even a Google search. After more than an hour, he looked at the notes he had copied and pasted into his digital file. Most of the information supported Josh's first impression of Caleb. He supported a variety of charities, none of which would raise an eyebrow. He even listed St. Jude's Hospital as one of the organizations he recommended to others. Nowhere was there a mention of a Mrs. Thornhill, other than Caleb's brief reference to his late mother who taught him "how to be successful."

Josh felt a familiar uneasiness growing. He recognized the tightness in his shoulders, a dead giveaway. Sometimes he felt it in his chest, as if his body was preparing to fight. But during his years as an undercover detective, Josh had developed these survival responses and they weren't easily discarded. In fact, the other day he felt it when looking for a parking space. Maybe it was just plain tension. After all, he and Enid were both acclimating to new jobs, a new city, and life in suburbia. That was a lot to absorb.

Momentarily, he managed to file his uneasiness away, but there was still something about Caleb that bugged him. What?

For one thing, Caleb's life was too sanitized. No photos of birthday parties or other social events, other than what appeared to be business gatherings. Caleb had apparently blocked his birth date from his profile, as there were no "Happy Birthday" posts anywhere to be seen.

One thing that caught Josh's attention was Caleb's participation in Intellecta. Josh was only vaguely familiar with the group. One article he found explained it this way:

> Intellecta is an international high IQ society founded in 1951. The organization was created as a society for individuals with high IQs, with the goal of fostering human intelligence for the benefit of humanity. Intellecta is a non-political and non-sectarian organization, open to anyone who scores at or above the ninety-eighth percentile on certain standardized IQ or other approved intelligence tests, which equates to an IQ of roughly 130 or higher.
>
> The society's activities include local, regional, national, and international gatherings, discussions, and seminars. Members often engage in a wide range of intellectual pursuits and are encouraged to share their knowledge and interests with others in the society.

Josh filed the connection to Intellecta away as "interesting but probably not relevant." But who was this intelligent, impersonal man?

Frustrated that his search had yielded only superficial information, Josh decided to do something he was now doing with more frequency: check the dark web. Individuals subject to background checks often hid their private lives in its murky depths.

Using his Tor browser, Josh signed on with his fake ID. He knew how to do rudimentary searches on the dark web but he was far from an expert. First, he checked some known hate groups he had become familiar with during his police investigations. He also checked extreme political groups and conspiracy groups. But Caleb was too smart not to conceal his identity. If his IQ was high enough to get him into Intellecta, then he was certainly smart enough to avoid detection.

Frustrated, Josh signed off and resumed his traditional search. He needed a name or two of individuals he might interview. Their client had listed Caleb's occupation as investor, and when Josh had asked Tiffany what Caleb invested in, she shrugged and said, "real estate, tech stocks, whatever's hot." She went on to gush about how "lucky" Caleb seemed to be in his investments.

Another thirty minutes of search yielded little, so Josh decided to try something else, Asking local law enforcement what, if anything, they knew about Caleb. Drake was new to this area, but he might be able to point Josh to someone.

On the third ring, Drake answered his phone. "Hey, mon. What's up?"

Josh explained his need for information on Caleb Thornhill and that he had failed to find much about the elusive guy.

"You need to be careful playing in the dark web. Nothing good there, and you could expose yourself."

"I didn't just wander in from the desert. But I appreciate your concern."

Drake released a loud infectious laugh. "That some kind of New Mexico say'n?"

"Yeah, probably."

"I'll check on your man, see what I can find out. Might be a couple days. I'm knee-deep in filing some reports that are overdue."

"You're the best," Josh said. "Whatever you can find out will be appreciated."

After ending the call, Josh stared at the smiling man in the photo in his file. "Who are you, Caleb Thornhill?"

CHAPTER 23

When Enid arrived home, she was surprised to see Josh's pickup in the yard. "Josh, it's me," she called out as she went inside.

Josh emerged in torn jeans and paint-stained tee shirt. "Hey, hon." He kissed her cheek.

Enid studied Josh. "Pretty clear you aren't going back to the office today."

Josh looked down at his attire and smiled. "I guess so. What about you? You home or have to go back out?"

"I've got to interview Lieutenant Albright, if he'll talk to me. But I doubt it will yield anything worthwhile. I'm curious as to why you're home though, even though it's nice."

"I'm doing some online research of one of our targets."

"How's it going?"

Josh sighed and ran his hand through his dark mane. "It's not. The guy's like a plastic facade. I have no idea who the real man is behind the mask. All I know is he's wealthy and brilliant."

Enid put her arms around Josh. "Is he available? I might be interested."

Josh smiled. "He seems to be."

"I'll remember that." Enid headed to their joint office. "Will I bother you in here? I can use one of the rooms at the news office."

"No, I'm done working online. Got time for a cup of coffee first?"

"Sure, you make the coffee and I'll drop these files off on my desk."

...

After a few minutes of catching up on the capers of Sophie's cat Kibo, who earlier had dropped a dead rodent at their front door, Enid asked Josh, "Can I ask you a work question?"

"Sure."

"Remember the cicada sketch Sophie drew?"

Josh nodded. "Sure."

"I know this may sound silly but I've got something bouncing around in my head I need your take on."

"Sure," Josh said. "Go on."

"I found a reference to the cicada emergence in South Carolina while I was doing research."

Looking puzzled, Josh motioned for her to continue.

"This year, we're going to have a double emergence of cicada broods eight and nine."

Josh threw back his head and chuckled. "What? Sorry, go on."

"I know you think I'm crazy, and maybe I am. Anyway, South Carolina is one of a handful of states that will have this double emergence this year. The last time that happened here was 221 years ago.

Josh leaned back in his chair. "I'm not sure where you're going with all this, but it's interesting."

"So, don't you think that's it's quite a coincidence this rare occurrence happens the same year a person with the cicada tattoo kills a young mother?"

Josh sat up straight. "Whoa, now. First of all, you're buying this whole vision thing?" He held up his hand to stop her from interrupting. "Just hear me out. Maybe, just maybe, Cassandra read the same article, and it got stuck in her memory and fed this image she saw."

"Maybe. Or maybe the killing was something ritualistic."

Josh stood up to get another cup of coffee. "Geez, Enid. I mean, I know you want to connect all the dots, but sometimes they just don't connect."

"Or . . ." She paused. "Or maybe you just can't accept Cassandra's abilities."

Josh pulled his chair closer to Enid. "Have you forgotten I grew up the land of medicine men and women? We had hatałii in New Mexico who healed and often had visions. You, of all people, should know I'm open-minded about things that can't be fully explained." He took her hands in his. "And I know you're just trying to find out what happened. But please don't confuse my concern with skepticism. Cassandra may have very well seen what she claims. Just keep an open mind yourself. Okay?"

"Sorry. It's just that this all seems like too much of a coincidence."

"I know you'll keep digging until you find out if there is a connection. Wish I felt as optimistic about my investigation."

"Want to talk about it? Or is it off-limits?"

"I'm not worried about talking to you. Our cases are hardly connected in any way. Besides, I don't have any dots to connect. My target is clean. Too clean."

"Is this the man Tiffany knows?"

"I think they used to have an intimate relationship, but she hasn't confirmed it. That's why I'm doing the investigation, so there can't be any hint of impropriety in our report."

"I'm surprised she took the job. Maybe she hoped to control how much you'd learn?"

Josh sat up straight. "Whoa. I didn't see that coming. Are you serious? Do you think she could manipulate me?"

"I didn't mean to insult you. Sorry." She patted Josh's hand. "I absolutely know you can't be manipulated. But she doesn't know you as well as I do, so maybe she thinks she can."

Josh felt the tension in his shoulders and chest tighten. "I didn't mean to overreact, it's just that ... Anyway, this guy, Caleb, has nothing personal online. No family photos, nothing that provides a look beneath the polished exterior."

"Maybe he changed his name."

"That thought crossed my mind, but why would he?" Josh paused then answered his own question. "Unless he's hiding something awful from his past."

CHAPTER 24

Albright was not happy to see Enid in his office, or any reporter for that matter. His disdain for the press was well known. It was only after Enid dropped Drake Harrow's name that he agreed to *briefly* talk to her.

"Thank you for seeing me, Lieutenant Albright."

He made a snorting sound that reminded Enid of a horse. "Get on with it."

"Can you tell me what evidence you have against the husband, Grant Sterling?"

"We have enough to convict him, but I can't go into the specifics." He glared at Enid. "You married to Joshua Hart?"

Enid wanted to ask him what that had to do with this interview but didn't want to risk antagonizing him further. "Yes, I am."

"He was a hulluva lawman when I knew him. Why'd he give it up?"

"I'm sorry but I don't feel comfortable discussing my husband with you. Perhaps you should ask him."

Unexpectedly, Albright laughed. "Touche, Mrs. Hart, touche."

"I kept my last name, Blackwell, for professional reasons."

Albright scratched his stomach. "Yeah, that seems to be the trend these days."

"Is there anything you can tell me about the investigation of Mara Sterling's murder?"

"It's ongoing."

"But it appears you've made up your mind that Grant Sterling killed his wife in front of their infant child and left the child to crawl in the mother's blood. Does that about cover it?" Enid felt her frustration growing and pulled the sketch from her file. "Have you seen this?"

Albright glanced at the cicada sketch. "Yeah, Harrow showed it to me. So what?"

"Are you dismissing Cassandra's vision completely?"

Albright glanced at the large clock on his wall. "You got one minute. Make good use of it."

"Cassandra asked that I not report on this information because she didn't want to compromise your investigation. Can you show her the same respect?"

"What exactly is it that you want me to do, Mrs. Hart?"

Enid's jaw clenched. "Your job, Lieutenant Albright. Check out this tattoo."

Albright glanced at the clock again. "I'll get Harrow to check it out. Looks like it might be some kind of gang symbol. But I still don't see any connection with the Sterling case."

Enid stood. "As my time is up, I'll leave." She leaned forward slightly toward Albright who was seated at his desk. "From what Josh has told me, you had a reputation for being fair and thorough." She stood up straight, pulling her shoulders back. "I can't even imagine how losing your spouse can alter your perspective on life, and I'm very sorry for your loss. But think of Grant Sterling, how he must feel losing his wife, and if he is innocent, how awful his life must be right now."

...

Enid was nearly to the front door of the police station when she heard her name. "Enid, wait up." She turned around to see Drake jogging toward her. "You got a minute?" he asked.

"Hi, Investigator Harrow."

"Just Drake, ma'am. Josh calls me Big D, and that's OK too."

Enid smiled. "I'll just go with Drake."

He nodded toward the door. "Let's go to your car and talk. Too many nosy bodies in here."

Enid led him to her car, which was parked near the front entrance. When they were inside, he glanced around his surroundings as if looking for someone.

"Sorry," he said. "Habit, I guess. As you know, we undercover cops are a jumpy lot."

"Even in front of a police station?"

Drake laughed. "Sick, ain't it." His smile disappeared. "I'm going to tell you something in confidence, but you can't print it. Not yet anyway." When Enid remained silent, he continued. "I could lose my job, talking to a reporter."

Enid leaned her head back against the headrest. "I'm married to a former undercover detective, police chief, and county sheriff. And I've had to sit on far more information than I've reported on over the past few years." She turned her head toward him. "Give me some credit, okay?"

Drake threw up his hands in surrender. "Sorry. Point taken. Anyway, what I wanted to tell you is that I found another case involving a cicada."

Enid turned to face him. "What? Where? And did you find the tattoo artist?"

Drake threw up his hands again. "Whoa. One thing at a time. No, I haven't found the tattoo artist and probably won't. If the tattoo is as detailed as the sketch you gave me, it isn't likely a local job. Maybe Atlanta or Charlotte. Or anywhere in the world for that matter. But I did find a reference to an insect tattoo in a case file. It wasn't identified as a cicada, but when I laid the sketch beside the photo of the suspect's tattoo on his arm, it was a near perfect match."

To prove his point, Drake showed her a photo on his phone. "Take a look."

Enid gasped. "Oh, my. It *is* a perfect match. What are the odds?"

"Pretty astronomical, I'd say."

"So this man could also be Mara Sterling's killer."

Drake put the phone back in his shirt pocket. "Not likely. He died in prison last year. Somebody knifed him with a toothbrush shiv."

"A toothbrush?"

"Inmates often create shivs from toothbrushes by sharpening one end against a concrete wall, then melting and shaping the handle into a point." Drake shook his head. "Unfortunately, they're very resourceful."

"Did this guy belong to a gang of some sort? I just met with Albright and he said he'd get you to check on gang symbols."

"I'm way ahead of him. Eddie, the tattooed guy killed in prison, was heavily involved in just about anything illegal. He went to prison for killing another gang member."

"The research I did on Cicada 3301 indicated its members were highly intelligent problem solvers. That doesn't seem to fit with what you've told me about Eddie."

"Agreed. I'll do some more digging."

"Albright is convinced the husband did it. What do you think?"

Drake looked out the window, his jaw tightening. "That guy. I know he's grieving and in pain, but ... Never mind. I'm only peripherally involved in this case, so I haven't studied it like he has. But, based on what I do know, I can't see it being the husband. If he did it, and he left his baby like that by her dead mama, then he's one sick bastard is all I can say." He put his hand on the car door to open it. "You need to be careful. Don't get in over your head."

CHAPTER 25

When Josh walked into the consulting office, Tiffany immediately approached him. "I've been trying to find you. Do you have the Thornhill report finished yet?"

Josh frowned. "Mind if I get in the door first?"

Tiffany tossed her hair. "Sorry. It's just that I'd like to wrap this up as quickly as possible."

"Can we talk about it?" Josh walked toward one of the conference rooms to divert her from heading to her office. He wanted this conversation to be on more neutral grounds. Seated at the table across from Tiffany, Josh said, "I need some clarification on Caleb Thornhill."

"I don't understand. It's pretty straightforward, and I've known Caleb a long time."

"Isn't that an issue, with this assignment I mean?"

Tiffany leaned forward and put her hands on the table. "You obviously have something on your mind. Just say it. I'm busy." She tossed her hair again, something Josh noticed she did when annoyed.

"I haven't been working with you very long, but I haven't seen you rush another assignment like you have this one. Are you afraid I'll find something?"

Tiffany opened her mouth to talk but then stopped and leaned back in her chair. "Go on. Get whatever is bugging you out on the table." Another hair toss.

"How involved were you with Thornhill? Was it a close relationship?"

"Are you asking because you're a nosy son of a bitch, or is this fodder for your report?" She held up her hand. "Sorry. My bad." She exhaled deeply. "We were ... an item once. We were both single, but it just didn't work out. Caleb is a brilliant man but ... how can I say this, he's deep, complicated."

"But you obviously still care for him."

Tiffany shrugged. "I care for you, too. As a friend. Caleb is a friend, that's all."

"Then let me do my background investigation. If he's being considered for a high-level position then we don't want any surprises down the road."

Tiffany momentarily stared intently at her perfectly manicured nails before refocusing on Josh. "How much longer do you need?"

"Another week at least. Maybe more."

Tiffany leaned forward again. "Let me ask you something, Josh. Do you think your years in law enforcement have made you paranoid?"

Josh considered his answer. "I'm sure it's had some effect on me. But why do you ask?"

"When you've spent years looking through a magnifying glass, every shadow starts to look like a secret, and every smile hides a lie." Tiffany walked out of the conference room leaving Josh sitting alone at the table.

CHAPTER 26

Enid tapped away at her laptop, searching for information on Grant Sterling. Unable to find anything useful beyond numerous references to his expertise as a financial consultant, she checked social media. He wasn't on Facebook or Instagram, but when she searched for him on LinkedIn, she found him.

Most of what he shared was more professional information, a few references to articles he had written, and a few accolades from others. But one comment about an article caught Enid's eye. "Your big sis is proud of you." The post was from Audrey Sterling. Enid checked Audrey's account and discovered she is a college professor of economics for an online university, living in Charlotte.

Enid searched Audrey Sterling further until she found a possible phone number. When she called, she got a message prompt, so she requested a return call. Enid then added to her message. "If you are Grant Sterling's sister, please know that I'm trying to help him. Call me."

Enid searched again and found a reference to Grant Sterling speaking at a conference last year. One of the comments referenced his Intellecta affiliation. Enid stared at the keyboard trying to piece bits of information together in her mind. Cassandra had seen a cicada tattoo. While no connection had been confirmed, there had been a Cicada 3301 group of intellectuals who solved online puzzles.

Intellectuals, like those in Intellecta. Grant Sterling was involved with the group, or maybe even a member.

Enid's phone rang. "Hello," she said, but no one responded, She started to hang up, but then glanced at the number and recognized it as the 704-area code she had called a few minutes ago. "Audrey Sterling?" Enid asked.

"You called my number. Are you a reporter?"

Enid hesitated. "I am, but please don't hang up. We can talk off the record. As I said in my message, I'm trying to help."

A brief silence, and then, "I've refused to talk to other reporters. Why should I talk to you?"

"Just because your brother has been arrested doesn't mean I'm going to stop looking for the truth. I'd like to sit down with you to give you some additional information I have and ask you a few questions. Depending on how it goes, maybe I can publish a story about Grant and show another side of him."

Another period of silence, then, "I'm in south Charlotte. But I can meet you in Rock Hill."

"Great. Send me the address, date and time, and I'll be there. And thank you for agreeing to meet with me."

"I'll do anything to help Grant," Audrey said. "He's innocent, I'm sure of it."

...

Before leaving for Charlotte the next morning, Enid texted Josh to remind him where she was headed. He had left early for an out-of-town appointment. Since she was overdue reporting to Silas about the story, she decided to call him while she was driving up I-77.

But before she had a chance to call Silas, he called her just as she was leaving Columbia. "I was just going to call you," Enid said. "I'm on my way to see Grant Sterling's sister."

"That's good. When can I get a story to run?" Silas asked, his tone unusually sharp. Before she could answer, he added, "Why do I get the feeling you're holding onto something you don't want to share?"

Caught off-guard, Enid stammered, "I'm not, I mean, I'm checking on a few things before I can submit a story."

Silas exhaled deeply. "Sorry. I'm coming across as one of *those* kinds of bosses. It's just that I was hoping we'd have something by now."

Before responding, Enid had to remind herself of her commitment to Cassandra. "Silas, look, I told you before I took the job that I was already somewhat involved in this story due to Cassandra's confiding in me. I'm wrestling a bit with how to balance the confidentiality I promised her and the need to report to you. I think it'll all work out but you'll have to be patient. I can't use information she gave me confidentially, not without her permission." She hesitated. "Maybe hiring me to do this story wasn't such a good idea."

"Don't be silly. I'm the problem here, not you." Silas laughed. "But I do need something from you on this story soon. Got it?"

"Got it." Enid ended the call with the familiar uneasiness she had felt when she and Josh had conflicting interests. Was nothing ever simple? She vowed to herself to have a conversation with Cassandra and put it all on the table.

CHAPTER 27

Enid walked into the small mom-and-pop restaurant just off I-77. Audrey said she'd be wearing a green jacket, and Enid immediately saw a woman, alone in a booth. The woman stood and offered her hand. "Hi, you must be Enid."

"I am." Enid extended her hand. "Nice to meet you, Ms. Sterling."

"Audrey, please." She motioned to the booth. "Is this okay with you? I mean this place. It's not fancy but the food is pretty good."

"It's fine. I'm not hungry but please feel free to order for yourself."

"I have, thanks," Audrey said, motioning to the waitress approaching their table. "Would you like some coffee or tea?" Audrey asked Enid.

"I'll have a cup of tea please," Enid said. "I want to thank you again for seeing me. I know this must be a traumatic time for your family."

Audrey nodded. "Grant and I are the only ones left of our immediate family. And, of course, there's Mara and Grant's daughter, Zoe."

"That's a beautiful name. How old is she now?"

"Zoe is a little over a year old." Audrey blinked back tears. "Ironically, her name means 'life' in Greek." She pulled a tissue from her pocket and dabbed at her eyes.

"I'm sorry for your family's loss. Where is Zoe now?"

"She's with me, for now. I've hired a woman I've known for years, a former schoolteacher, to stay with me and care for Zoe. I've never had kids and know nothing about caring for an infant." Audrey smiled slightly. "She's an adorable kid. But I worry about both of our futures. I wasn't planning on becoming a mom at my age, but I can't forsake Grant, you know, in case he's ..." Her voice trailed off. "They can't convict him, because he's innocent. I'm sure of it."

"He's your brother, and of course, you know him better than anyone, but people often hide parts of themselves others aren't aware of."

Audrey squared her shoulders slightly. "I'm aware of that. Believe me, I've tried to remember any signs of conflict between them. But I never saw anything, other than the occasional marital spats. Besides, he would never have left Zoe sitting there beside Mara's body. Never."

"I'm sure the police have asked you these same questions, but bear with me. Did Grant have any enemies you're aware of?"

"Grant is a genius. I mean that literally. He belongs to Intellecta, and he often seems to show more concern for facts and figures than people. That's not true, but it's the impression he sometimes gives."

"He appears to be very successful, so his clients must like him."

"Grant is more than just a financial advisor. He's a wealth manager, meaning that all of his clients are millionaires at minimum. And many of them are like Grant, more interested in their money than in forming a close relationship with him—or anyone else."

"Are there any disgruntled clients that you know of?"

Audrey waited until the waitress filled her coffee cup and left the table before continuing. "He grumbles often about how difficult his clients can be, but he understands they are successful because of their determination and drive, so he accepts them for who they are."

Enid scribbled some notes and then asked, "I know this will be uncomfortable for you to respond to, but what can you tell me about Grant's affair?"

Audrey slapped her palms on the table, causing the couple at the table across from them to stare at her. "That's preposterous. I don't know where they got that information. But it's simply not true."

"But why would the police fabricate something like that, especially since it provides a motive of sorts."

Leaning forward, Audrey said in a soft voice, "I don't know, but it's a vicious lie. Someone is trying to frame him."

Enid knew all too well that people having affairs were adept at hiding it from their spouses, as well as others in the family. But the truth eventually comes out. "Did Grant and Mara have a lot of social acquaintances?"

"They were always entertaining, you know, dinner parties, cocktail parties. Mara was a great cook, which is why they spent a fortune remodeling their kitchen not long before …"

She paused. "But I got the impression they were more work-related acquaintances, you know, Grant's clients."

"I want to ask you more about Grant's involvement with Intellecta. Do you know how long he's been associated with them?"

Audrey shook her head. "Not really. He told me once that one of his clients recruited him."

"Do you know who that client was?"

Audrey shook her head again. "I don't know the names of any of his clients. He's very cautious not to reveal anything like that to me. He says he has a strict confidentiality agreement with them."

"Has he seemed upset about anything recently or acting differently in any way?"

Audrey stared at her hands resting on the table and appeared to be deep in thought. "Not exactly." She paused and looked up at Enid. "But I was visiting them in Columbia, and I overheard him on the phone, not long before Mara's murder. He had raised his voice, so I couldn't help but hear it. He was trying to explain why an investment had lost money. Or at least that's what I got from the brief snippet I heard."

"And you have no idea who it was?"

Audrey shook her head and stared at her hands again.

Enid hesitated before asking the next question. "How was your relationship with Mara?"

Audrey sat up straight. "My relationship? Surely you don't think I—"

"No, not at all. I just want to you ask you about something she may have told you, something personal."

Relaxing her posture a bit, Audrey leaned back against the back of the booth. "We got along fine. Of course, with them being in Columbia and me being in Charlotte, we only saw each other every couple of months."

"Did she ever mention to you that she was seeing a fortune teller?"

"A what?"

"Fortune teller. Does that seem typical of something she would do?"

Audrey exhaled deeply. "I sure didn't see that question coming. The only thing I can say is that Mara was a talented woman. She had written several books of poetry and illustrated them herself. Of course, all this was before Zoe came along." She paused. "I got the sense that Mara missed having her own identity."

"What do you mean?"

"After Zoe was born, Mara became a mother and Grant's personal assistant. Not paid or formally, of course, but after she gave up her writing and art, she ran errands for Grant and did all the things he didn't feel comfortable asking his secretary to do."

Enid scribbled in her notebook. "Do you have his secretary's name?"

"No, I don't." And then as if talking to herself, she added, "Isn't that odd." Audrey seemed to be refocusing her thoughts. "But why did you ask about a fortune teller, of all things?"

"It's just that I know she consulted one. Perhaps to discuss or take more control of her future, as you suggested." Enid glanced at the time on her phone. "Just a couple more questions and I'll let you go. Do you know of anyone, a man, who has a large tattoo on his back? Perhaps Grant has a tattoo?"

Audrey leaned back and appeared to study Enid. "You're asking very strange questions." She shrugged. "But to answer you, no, I have no knowledge of anyone like that. And as far as I know, Grant doesn't have any tattoos. In fact, I would be shocked if he does. He often talks against them. Is that person, someone with a tattoo, a possible suspect?"

More than you know, Enid thought. "It's just one of those bits of information that came up. Nothing to worry about." Enid handed Audrey her business card. "I'd like to write a story about Grant, as your brother and as a good family man. If you're right about him being innocent, maybe it will help in some way."

"He is innocent, and I will not stop fighting to clear his name," Audrey said. "He's a victim too."

CHAPTER 28

Cassandra held the woman's hands in hers. Nothing. No vision, no impressions. Nothing. It was almost like a blessing to feel like a normal, unseeing person. "I see a bright future ahead of you," she told the woman, feeling more like a fraud today than a true seer.

"Should I marry him?" the woman asked.

Cassandra held up her hand, signaling for the woman to stop talking. *Please be quiet.* Slowly a vision formed, like a small television screen. The colors were vivid, her client was laughing. The man turned to look at Cassandra, at least that's what it felt like. As if he knew she was watching. His thick blond hair gave him the carefree image of a surfer.

The image broadened as if someone were filming him and switched to a wide-angle lens. Her client was sitting on a picnic blanket, along with a sandy haired girl, who was intent on eating ice cream from a cup.

"What color hair does your boyfriend have?" Cassandra asked.

The woman looked confused but answered, "He has dark brown hair, almost black. But why do you ask?"

"Do you know, or have a relationship with, someone who has a thick mane of blond hair?"

The woman's hand flew to her mouth. "Well, yes, I ..." She sat back and stared at Cassandra. "I've been seeing ... Oh, this is embarrassing."

"I'm not here to judge you. Is he important to you?"

The client began wringing her hands. "I'm a good person, but, you see, I'm so conflicted about George's proposal, and I've been putting him off. So I became involved with a friend at work. His wife died in childbirth three years ago, and we became friends through all of that. It was so sad."

"So you're romantically involved with him?"

"Keith, yes, he keeps telling me George isn't right for me." More hand wringing. "I'm embarrassed to admit that I was unfaithful to George."

"Do you love Keith?" Cassandra asked.

A slight smile spread across the client's face. "Yes, I think I do."

"I'm going to tell you what I see in your future, but remember, I'm not infallible. You'll have to weigh the vision against your own judgment to assess its merit. Understand?"

The woman nodded, appearing anxious for Cassandra to continue.

"I saw you with this blond man and a small child. She was sitting on a picnic blanket eating ice cream."

Before she could continue, the client gasped. "Oh, my God. Penelope, she's Keith's daughter, loves ice cream and picnics. One reason I've held back on letting my relationship with Keith develop is that I never wanted children." Then she added, "But Penelope is adorable."

"It seems you, Keith, and Penelope, if that's who I saw, were happily enjoying each other." Cassandra felt as if she was cheating the woman by not telling her more. But that was all she had seen.

As if reading Cassandra's mind, the woman said, "This is a wonderful gift. I have so much clarity now." She squeezed Cassandra's hand. "Thank you. You're amazing."

Cassandra waived the woman's payment, lying by saying that she often did so and asked the client to donate it to her favorite charity. The client happily agreed to do so, promising to make a generous contribution.

After the woman left and Cassandra was alone, she put her face in her hands and wept. How many times had she prayed the vision would go away? And yet, she now worried that it might. Who was she without it, the thing that had defined and shaped her entire life?

CHAPTER 29

As Josh walked into the plush office that housed Larkin's consulting firm, he questioned the wisdom of making an appointment to talk with the ex-governor. But even though Josh had reservations about Larkin, he trusted Larkin's judgment. Most of the time, at least.

When Larkin saw Josh walk in, he stood and walked toward him, hand extended. "Josh, what a pleasure to see you. Come on in and have a seat." Larkin directed Josh to a corner office with dark paneling, thick carpet, and expensive-looking furniture. Josh couldn't help but think Larkin had recreated his former office in the state's capitol building.

"I appreciate you taking the time to see me. I won't keep you long." Josh waved his hand around the office. "Nice digs."

Larkin smiled. "Thanks. Have to keep up the appearance of a successful political consultant, if you know what I mean."

Josh smiled and nodded. "Mind if I ask you a few questions about Caleb Thornhill?"

Larkin tapped his fingertips together and appeared to be contemplating his response. "Yes, of course, but I don't want to influence your background check in any way."

"Why? Is there something to hide?"

Larkin's brow creased. "Do *you* have doubts about Caleb?"

Josh tried to relax the tension that had crept into his shoulders. "This job is a lot like law enforcement. It doesn't matter what I feel if I can't back it up with facts."

"But you don't like him."

Josh stopped himself from saying he didn't particularly like *any* politicians. "That's irrelevant. I'll do a fair report and move on to the next target, but only once I feel I can write an honest report."

Larkin leaned forward. "That's fair. You know, Josh, that's why I hired you for those assignments you completed for me. You're honest, even if a bit stubborn at times." He paused. "I'll tell you what I can, but don't quote me as a source in your report." He held up his hand to keep Josh from interrupting. "I know that may feel dishonest to you, but I've got to live in this town and work with these people."

"I can live with that. You'll be like a CI, a confidential informant."

Larkin chuckled. "Always the lawman. Anyway, what do you want to know?"

"Let's start with the big question. Is Caleb one of the good guys?"

Larkin rested his head against the back of the tall leather desk chair. "You don't make it easy, do you?" Josh waited for Larkin to consider his reply. Larkin tapped his fingertips together again. "I honestly don't know. As you've seen, he's charming and smart as a whip."

"But?" Josh asked.

"But let's just say, I'm not quite sold yet. It's my firm's job to help get him elected if we decide to back him, and that's what I'll do. That is unless something changes my mind."

"What makes you have reservations?"

Larkin smiled. "Maybe I'm just jealous. My wife idolizes him. What's not to hate? The guy is handsome, smart, and rich." He glanced out the window, appearing to gather his thoughts. "But my impression is that he would do whatever it takes to get ahead. That kind of ambition scares me."

Josh laughed. "I've heard people say that about you. Everyone assumed you'd run for the Senate."

"This may surprise you, but I hate politics. It's necessary but dreadful. I'd like to be a horse rancher if I could. When you talked about growing up in New Mexico, I envied your childhood. My dad was a district judge and expressed his expectations early on that I would go into law and then politics."

"But it's not too late to get out."

"I will. When the timing is right, I'll move on." Larkin laughed. "Hopefully before I'm too old to enjoy a new life." He sighed. "But I digress. You're here to get the dirt on Caleb."

"So you think he's got something to hide?"

"We all do, Josh." Larkin glanced at the gold desk clock. "I've got to leave for a meeting, but I'll tell you this. The age-old adage is to follow the money. That's where I'd start."

"But I thought he was from a wealthy family."

Larkin's left eyebrow raised. "That's his story. He made his money himself, mostly with smart investments."

"Before I leave, I need to ask. It seems you're actually wanting a deep investigation of Caleb. And if that's the case, why did you hire Tiffany's firm, knowing she had a prior relationship with him?"

"Because I knew she'd recuse herself and turn the investigation over to you. And I knew if there was any dirt on Caleb Thornhill, you'd find it."

CHAPTER 30

Enid stared at the big gleaming plaque in the hallway outside Grant's office: "Sterling Wealth Management." Enid smiled to herself at the irony of his last name, considering his profession. Enid opened the door and stepped inside. Finding Grant Sterling's secretary was easy enough, because when Enid stepped inside, there she was, dutifully holding down the fort while her boss sat in jail awaiting a bail hearing for the alleged murder of his wife.

The woman sitting at the enormous mahogany desk flashed a well-rehearsed smile. "Hello, how can I help you?"

"Are you Grant Sterling's secretary?"

The woman stiffened. "Executive assistant. How can I help you?"

Enid judged the woman to be in her late forties, which would make her slightly older than her boss. Enid produced a business card and her press credentials.

The woman glanced at them. "I'm sorry, but I have been instructed not to talk to the press."

"By whom? The police? Or Grant Sterling?"

The woman's shoulders slumped. "I'm sorry if I sound short with you, but as you might imagine, it's been a bit stressful around here. On top of Mara's murder and now Grant's arrest, someone broke into the office and stole files."

"I'm sorry for all you're going through. I won't keep you long. May I sit?"

The woman looked hesitant but nodded, letting out a long sigh. "I know you're just doing your job, but I really can't talk to you." And then added for emphasis, "I have nothing to say."

"I want to tell you upfront that I think Mr. Sterling is innocent," Enid said. "I've met with his sister Audrey Sterling, and my paper is running an article in tomorrow's paper about how he's a great brother, husband, and father. I'm trying to report the truth, that's all."

"You might be the only person, other than me and his sister Audrey, who believes he didn't do it."

"If you talk to me, I assure you I'll do what I can to help clear him."

The woman looked intently at Enid. "But why? I mean why are you so sure he's innocent?"

"I can't tell you the details, but I'm working with a confidential source."

"If there's someone out there who knows Grant is innocent, he or she needs to go to the police." The secretary tapped her finger to make her point.

"My source *has* talked to the police." Seeing the confusion on the woman's face, Enid continued. "It's complicated. But trust me when I say we're trying to find out what really happened." She paused. "May I please ask you a few questions? Off the record?"

The secretary relaxed her shoulders and nodded. "I'm Olivia. Nice to meet you."

"Nice to meet you, Olivia. May I begin by asking you about the allegation that Grant was having an affair?"

"The police quizzed me about that also. I guess people think I know more than I do." Olivia played with the ballpoint pen in her hand, clicking it repeatedly. "Grant works away from the office much of the time. So even if he was, having an affair, I mean, I wouldn't have known."

"How well did you know his wife Mara?"

Olivia shrugged. "You know, just superficially. I went to their house several times for dinner, and Mara and Sterling were both gracious hosts."

"Did you get the impression they had a good relationship?"

"As far as I could tell. You never know what goes on behind the scenes. But, yes, I'd say they at least gave the appearance of a happy couple."

"And was he happy about the baby, Zoe?"

Olivia clapped her hands together silently. "Oh my, yes. He loves Zoe more than anything in the world. And he was always buying her presents, talking about her, showing everyone the latest pictures."

Enid tried to reconcile this information with the horrific image of Zoe beside her mother's body. "I read online where Grant is an Intellecta member, so I assume he's pretty smart."

"He's brilliant, absolutely brilliant. He's made millions for his clients." Olivia frowned slightly. "That's why the recent losses were so confounding."

"Recent losses? You mean investments?"

Olivia nodded. "Grant does extensive research before he makes any recommendations to his clients. He learned about a technology that was going to revolutionize something, though I'm not actually sure what. I believe it was AI related."

"And what happened?"

"Like I said, he always does extensive research and then, if warranted, makes recommendations to his top tier clients to invest. He usually tells them the investments are long-term, but his clients have plenty of money and are accustomed to waiting for returns." Olivia blinked back tears. "But then he got these new clients that were impatient for big paybacks quickly, so he directed them to some high-risk stocks." She stopped to compose herself. "He warned them right from the beginning. And it all fell apart. They lost millions and millions."

"I'm sure they were upset, but if they are experienced investors, they've surely had some bad investments before. Nothing is guaranteed in the stock market."

Olivia shook her head. "He has a reputation of never losing big. It was unlike him to take that kind of risk with a client."

"Did you tell the police all this?"

"Most of it. I didn't want to make Grant look like a fool."

CHAPTER 31

Drake Harrow took a deep breath to bolster his courage. He was a big man and stood nearly a foot taller and at least fifty pounds heavier than Lieutenant Albright. And at least twenty years younger. But Albright was the one with the power, and he held Harrow's future in his hands. Even though Albright was now seen by many as a broken man, saddled with grief and trying to drown himself in rye whiskey, he was still held in high esteem in the department. Like all dedicated lawmen, he had sacrificed a lot for his career. Late nights, too much overtime, and persistent stress had taken its toll. When Albright's wife died, he had little in reserve to fight off the persistent loneliness and pervasive guilt of not spending more time with her over the years.

"Sir, may I have a word?" Harrow asked.

Albright was sitting behind his desk, staring at a file, its contents spread out in front of him. "What's up?"

"I know you're the lead investigator on the Mara Sterling case, and I'm not trying to step on your toes. But I'd like to do some work on it. On my own time, if necessary."

Albright squinted at Drake over his half-frame reading glasses. "Why's that? You think I'm not doing enough?"

"No sir, I mean, yes, I think you're doing what's necessary." The conversation was not going the way Harrow had hoped. "No offense intended, sir, it's just that I'd like to work on the vision that woman Cassandra claims to have seen. Maybe I can put it to rest, you know, tie up that loose end."

"Surely you don't believe in that craziness." Albright cleared his throat, making a snorting sound. "Go on, sit down."

Harrow was beginning to doubt his decision to talk to Albright. He sat down gingerly in the wooden chair that looked like it had come over on the Mayflower.

Albright threw his reading glasses on the table and leaned back, his chair squeaking each time he moved. "You know, with Fort Jackson nearby, there's no shortage of fortune tellers, ink artists, whores, and other nut cases trying to cash in on young, unsuspecting men. What makes you think this woman is any different?"

"I don't know one way or the other, but I'd like to find out."

"I've a mind to say no. Plenty of other cases you need to work on. Chasing this vision thing is a waste of time, if you ask me." He paused. "But I know that reporter snooping around here is married to one of the best lawmen I know."

Drake relaxed a bit. "Yes, sir. Josh Hart is definitely one of the best."

Albright closed his eyes and remained quiet for a moment. Harrow wasn't sure if his commanding officer was dozing off or just thinking. Without opening his eyes, Albright said, "I may retire soon, you know. Just can't get my head and heart into it anymore, not since …" His voice trailed off as he opened his eyes. "So, if you want to go chase that crazy fortune teller's vision, have at it. Besides, if we don't, I'm sure we'll see a newspaper article about how the police ignored her." Albright waved his hand as a sign of dismissal. "But keep me informed. No surprises. Hear me?"

"Yes, sir. I hear you."

...

Drake knew exactly where to start: his tattoo artist connections. It wasn't something he could do by phone though, so he got in his car and drove a little more than an hour back to Bowman County. That's where he had worked undercover, where he had met Josh and where he had met the man he was going to see.

Drake pulled up to the motorcycle shop where they knew him from both sides—as an investigator in the Bowman County Sheriff's Department and as Whistler, an undercover drug dealer.

"Hey, if it ain't the Whistler," said a man whose arms were covered in grease. "Or are you the cop today?"

"Hey, mon." Drake gave him a man-hug, oblivious to the grease now on his own arms. "Some would say it's all 'da same."

The man laughed. "I'd be one of 'um." His smile faded. "What you need?" Drake pulled out the print of the cicada tattoo. "Whew, that'd set you back a penny or two. Nice work." He looked at it again. "But it's not you, man."

"Not for me, not my style, you know, noisy bugs don't turn me on. Who could do work like this, you know, this kind of detail?" Drake asked.

The man held the printout and studied it, squinting at it and holding it close. "Damn, I hate getting old. My eyesight ain't worth shit these days." He handed the paper back to Drake. "Only one I know is Kirk the Kite."

"You mean that crazy SOB that tried to shoot me? The one you warned me was always high as a kite on something?"

"That'd be him."

Drake folded the paper and put it back in his pocket. "He still up there off Hwy 21, way back in the woods?"

"Far as I know. He's not someone I visit on a regular basis, know what I mean?"

"I hear 'ya, mon. You take care now, and stay out of trouble. I'll be back in a few months, coming back here to keep your sorry ass in line." The two men hugged again, laughing. As Drake got in his car, he muttered to himself. "Kirk the Kite. Great, just great."

...

Nearly an hour later, Drake found the old cabin Kirk lived in the last time they had talked. To say they "talked" would be a kinder, gentler version of their meeting, the time when Kirk had tried to shoot Drake.

When Drake came to the end of a long dirt road, he saw Kirk standing about twenty feet away, AR-15 in hand. After shutting off the ignition, Drake slowly opened the door, hands in the air. "Don't shoot, mon. I'm not here to jiggle your wires. Just need your help."

Kirk laughed, showing stained teeth. "Last time I saw you, I ended up in jail two years." He raised the automatic rifle and squinted one eye, like he was taking aim on Drake.

"You best git outta here before my trigger finger starts to wiggle some."

"I'm just looking for a tattoo. Man owes me some money, and I'm trying to track his sorry ass. Can I show it to you? Might be your work. If it is, I'll pay you a reward if I can get my money."

To Drake's relief, Kirk lowered the AR-15 slightly. "How much?"

"I'll give you a hundred dollars if I can find him. Can I show you the tattoo? Sketch is in my pocket."

Kirk raised his rifle again. "Any funny moves, your friends'll be coming to your funeral. That is, if you got any."

Slowly, Drake pulled the sketch from his pocket, unfolded it, and held it out for Kirk. "Lay it down on the ground and step back," Kirk said.

After Drake complied, Kirk leaned over and picked up the sketch, never taking his eyes off Drake. Lowering his rifle slightly, Kirk studied the sketch. "Damn good work." He threw the sketch back on the ground. "I can't claim it, though."

Drake picked up the sketch and returned it to his pocket.

"You said this man owes you money?"

Drake nodded.

"I know someone who does this kind of ink for a group of people. Thing is, though, they're rich, at least that's what I hear. You know, not your usual tatters."

"What are they then? A rich gang?" Drake asked.

Kirk shrugged. "Dunno. Just heard it was a group, could have been two, could have been fifty. They all got this tattoo. My friend got paid some serious bucks for doing it. Lot of work in this one."

Drake tried to hide his excitement. "Mind telling me who the artist is?"

Kirk smiled. "Don't mind at all. Name's Alonso. Some call him the Snake."

Drake was caught off-guard by Kirk's sudden willingness to cooperate. "Any idea where I can find Alonzo?"

Kirk pointed a greasy finger down the road where Drake had driven in. "Bout fifteen miles due west."

Drake was battling his frustration at having to pull every tidbit of info out of Kirk. "Got any more specifics?"

"Heard from one of the guys Alonso's headstone was a work of art. Best one in Pinewood, so they say."

Drake knew Pinewood Cemetery was just outside of Madden and was where paupers and other unclaimed remains were often buried. Or the deceased whose families had long since disowned them and refused to claim their remains.

"He dead?"

Kirk threw back his head and laughed. "As a doornail. Now get your sorry ass back in that car and git outta here 'fore I change my mind 'bout killing you."

CHAPTER 32

The call from Jack Johnson was unexpected. But since he had recommended her to the *Palmetto Post*, he probably wanted to ask her how it was going.

"Jack, what a pleasant surprise. How are you?"

"Hi, Enid. Good to hear your voice." Jack sounded tired and his voice raspy. "I know you're busy but you got a minute?"

Enid was starting to feel uneasy. "Of course. I always have time for you. What's up?" She heard a familiar voice in the background, Jack's adopted daughter. "Is that Rachel I hear? Is she home visiting?"

Jack coughed. "She's staying here a little while."

"How's she doing?"

"Good, at least that's what she tells me."

"Is she still dating the hacker? Or are they married now?"

Jack chuckled. "They're both hackers now. Legally, of course. She's working on some hush-hush government project." He paused. "But I'll get to the point. I've been putting off making this call, but Rachel's been after me."

A sense of dread overcame Enid. "Jack, what's going on? Are you alright?"

Another halfhearted chuckle. "I thought I was, but my doctor says otherwise."

Enid told herself to remain calm. "Is your cancer back?"

"Like I said, I know you're busy, but any chance you could get back to Madden for a visit? I can fill you in then."

"Of course. I'll be there in about an hour." When Jack didn't protest or insist she wait until it was more convenient, her fear grew into full-blown panic.

...

When Enid pulled into Madden, a wave of nostalgia, and dread, filled her. Since the distribution center had been built just outside of town, Madden had grown from a sleepy little town to one that was at least bigger and busier. It was no longer a one-traffic-light town. But it was still Madden. And it oddly felt more like home than any other place she had lived lately.

The *Tri-County Gazette's* office was in an old, small brick building on Main Street. Another wave of nostalgia hit her when she saw Jack's familiar pickup truck parked in his usual spot in the gravel-top parking area beside the building.

When she walked inside the newspaper office, an unfamiliar face greeted her. "May I help you?" the woman asked.

"Hi, I'm Enid—"

"Oh, for real? Are you *the* Enid I hear about all the time?"

As Enid struggled for a response, Jack's voice called out from the hallway. "Vivian, yes, this is *the* Enid Blackwell." He walked directly toward Enid and gave her a hug. "God, it's great to see you." He turned to Vivian. "Hold all my calls."

Jack led Enid down the familiar hallway to his office. "You've painted the place," she said. "Looks nice."

"We try to keep it presentable." He motioned to a chair across from his desk. "Please, have a seat. Would you like a cup of tea?"

"No thanks." She studied Jack's face. The lines on his face were deeper and he was thinner, paler, than when she last saw him. But then, it had been a while.

For the next twenty minutes, they shared news and caught each other up on their lives, until Jack leaned back and closed his eyes momentarily. "Life is both wonderful and tragic."

A knot formed in Enid's stomach. She felt like she had been punched in the gut. "Is it your cancer? Is it back?"

Jack smiled slightly. "Yep. Same 'ol cancer, just rearing its ugly head again." He stared off into space momentarily, so Enid just waited for him to continue. "I'm mostly at peace with all this. Got a few months most likely, barring any last-minute pardons from God—or a medical breakthrough."

"Jack, I'm so sorry. I …" At a loss for words, Enid fought back tears. He didn't need for her to fall apart. That would come later, in private. "Is there anything I can do?"

He smiled. "Pray for a miracle." He stared off into space for a few seconds. "And take the paper."

Enid wasn't sure she heard him right. "What do you mean?"

"I mean, this paper is my legacy. As you know, I've tried to find the right buyer, but no one feels right. I wanted to sell it and give the money to Rachel, but she's the one who insisted I talk to you instead. It's yours if you want it, not a sale, a gift."

"But I can't, I mean, we both know I'm not good at running the paper. I tried when you were out for treatment a few years ago."

Jack leaned forward. "My dear Enid. We both know you're not the same person now. If I had any doubts, I wouldn't make this offer." He seemed to be studying her face for a reaction. "Will you at least consider it?"

"I'm honored beyond words, truly. But I can't leave Columbia and come here to run the paper. And if it failed under my direction, I'd never forgive myself."

Jack leaned back in his chair again. "And how is Columbia? Are you and Josh happy there?"

Enid wasn't comfortable baring her soul to Jack as she usually did. He had enough worries of his own. Instead, she tried to keep the conversation upbeat. "It's a great city. Josh has a good future, and I'm hoping things go well for me at the *Palmetto Post*. So far at least, Silas is a great editor to work for."

"But are you *happy*?"

"I think so, I mean, it's all so new. New city, house and neighbors, and jobs." She was anxious to change the subject. "You mentioned once you wanted to go digital with the paper. Is that still the plan?"

Jack shook his head, laughing softly. "Okay, I get the message. But to answer your question, yes, I think it's inevitable. Paper and printing costs are skyrocketing, advertisers are shifting to digital ... well, I could go on and on."

"But won't you lose subscribers?"

"As you know, I made that argument with a potential buyer a few years ago who wanted to go all-digital." He paused. "I was wrong. I mean, yes, we'll lose some of our older subscribers, but the harsh reality is that our older readers are dying off anyway. That's just a cold, hard fact."

"What if I help you find the right buyer?"

"Thanks, but I've made a decision, and Rachel is onboard with it. If you don't take it, I'm closing the paper. She wanted to see you, but she's driving to Charlotte to fly out to an assignment. Said to give you a hug for her." He looked away, his eyes filled with tears. "She'll need you when I'm gone. She has no one else."

The wall that had been holding back tears gave way, and Enid put her face in her hands and sobbed. "I'm sorry. I tried to hold back, but this is just not fair. It's not!"

Jack laughed. "You're telling me, kiddo. It sucks." His smile disappeared. "But it is what it is, and life will go on." He sighed. "Will you at least think about my offer? I happen to know Madden is looking for a police chief, might be a good fit for Josh to come back into his old job and you can take the paper."

Despite her tears, Enid smiled. "You've got this all figured out, haven't you?" She blew her nose into a tissue Jack had handed her. "Josh hasn't mentioned anything about wanting to go back into law enforcement. And besides, the conflict-of-interest issues we had before would be even worse if we came back."

Jack shrugged. "You could work it out. As for Josh, don't you realize he took that job so you could find your way back to what you love?"

"I don't understand."

Another shrug. "All I know is Josh is a lawman. Will always be a lawman. Might be worth a conversation with him. But that's between you two." He stood. "I know you're busy, so head on back. I appreciate you dropping everything to come here. Means a lot."

CHAPTER 34

The next day, Enid's article on Grant Sterling posted online. Jack texted to congratulate her on how well the piece was done. Audrey left a phone message thanking her for doing the article, saying she would make sure Grant saw it also. His bail hearing would be later today, and she was praying he would be released. Enid made a note to follow-up with Audrey later.

Silas said he was happy with the article but was more interested in her doing a story about Cassandra's vision. Josh was right—their lives were destined to be complicated. Enid promised him she would talk to Cassandra.

The most surprising contact came from Lieutenant Albright, an email in which he congratulated her for ignoring the facts and making it look like the police had made a mistake. And then she got a call from Drake Harrow, who wanted to meet with her.

Over her second cup of tea, Enid allowed her imagination to transport her back to Madden. What would her and Josh's lives be like there? Was Thomas Wolf right when he said you can never go home again? But more importantly, could she really give up reporting to manage other reporters, review expense reports, dole out stories and listen to someone groan about being on obit duty? She smiled to herself when she recalled telling Jack not too long ago that she actually missed talking to the families and learning more about their deceased loved ones.

• • •

Investigator Harrow suggested to Enid that they meet at McDonald's on Elmwood and commented that McDonald's is one of the most consistent fast-food joints—Mickey Ds are the same everywhere.

As she sat across from Drake Harrow, he commented on the coffee. "That's the best cheap coffee on the planet." He nodded to Enid. "Sure you don't want a cup? My treat?"

"No, but thanks." She glanced around the eating area, which was nearly empty. The drive-in lines were long, as usual, but only a handful of people were seated inside. "I'm anxious to know what you have to say. Is there an update on Mara Sterling's case?"

Drake took another sip and appeared to be savoring the hot, dark liquid. "Well, yes and no."

Enid studied his expression, which did not reflect his feelings. No doubt his undercover work had conditioned him to manage his expression at all times. Josh had explained that the wrong reaction could get you killed. "What can you tell me?" she asked.

"First of all, Grant Sterling has refused bail."

"You mean he was refused bail?"

"No, he, Sterling, told the judge he didn't want to be released on bail."

"But I don't understand. Why would a financial advisor, of all people, want to stay in jail?"

"Exactly. Only thing I can think of is the man is scared. Whatever is outside the jail is scarier to him than being inside."

"But what explanation did he give the judge and his attorney?"

"He didn't. Just said he wants to stay in jail until he's cleared."

"Doesn't he realize the wheels of justice turn slowly?" Enid asked.

Drake shrugged. "But there's more." He paused as if for dramatic effect. "I think I found the cicada tattoo artist."

Enid made a silent, clapping motion with her hands. "That's great. Where did you find him?"

Drake smiled. "Pinewood Cemetery."

"You mean, outside of Madden?" Enid shuddered as she recalled her terrifying encounter there with the biker gang several years ago while investigating Rose Marie Garrett's murder.

Drake nodded. "That's the one. My contact seemed fairly sure he was the ink artist, said he did that tattoo for a group of people."

"You mean like a gang?"

Drake shrugged. "Maybe."

"So you're telling me Grant Sterling is afraid to leave jail and this tattoo artist supposedly did the same cicada design for a group of people. Is that it?"

"Best I can tell."

Enid leaned back and ran all the information through her mind. "I appreciate your telling me, but what can I do with any of this? It's not confirmed, so I can't report it, and I'm sure you wouldn't want me to anyway."

Drake leaned forward and spoke softly. "Listen, for now, at least, Albright has given me the go-ahead to assist in the Sterling investigation. He's convinced Sterling is guilty of killing his wife and that I'm wasting department time on something frivolous."

"Meaning he could shut you down at any time."

"Exactly."

"But you think I can help you? Is that it?"

Drake sat back and chuckled. "You *are* an award-winning journalist. So I'm thinking maybe you get the scoop for another award-winning story, and I get to see justice."

"Are you convinced Grant Sterling is innocent?"

Drake shook his head. "No, I'm not saying that at all. But I am saying that this feels like a rush to judgment." He shook his head again. "And I can't see him leaving his baby sitting in his wife's blood. Man, if that's what happened, then I'll be the first to condemn him. Just saying we need to check further."

"Well, I can't interview him in jail, since it's not allowed in South Carolina, as you know. But I can give his sister Audrey a list of questions to ask him."

Drake laughed. "See, I know you a smart lady."

"But what about Grant's attorney? Can't he help us? I can get your questions to him."

"Let's not do that. Not yet. It's just that I don't trust anyone else involved at this point, other than you."

Enid hesitated before asking her next question. "Are you concerned about some kind of cover-up or conspiracy?"

Drake smiled and in his best Jamaican Patois said, "Make we jus' keep dis between we fi now."

CHAPTER 35

By the time Enid reached Audrey Sterling, Audrey was already aware that Grant had refused bail and was clearly distraught. Enid told her she needed her help in interviewing Grant, and Audrey reluctantly agreed to meet with her again.

Enid left a message for Josh that she was going to Charlotte to talk to Audrey Sterling. She hated to admit it, but she was relieved when she got Josh's voice mail instead, because he would caution her again against getting in too deep.

The drive to Charlotte was the usual congestion of trucks and cars on I-77. Nearly two hours later, when she pulled into Audrey's driveway, she was surprised to see two news trucks and another car parked in front of the house. Before getting out of her car, Enid put on her dark glasses, hoping she wouldn't be recognized if someone took her photo. She did as Audrey had instructed, going through the backyard to the rear door.

Inside, Audrey had most of the lights off or turned down so that it was hard for Enid to adjust her vision. "I'm sorry, it's just that I'm a bit overwhelmed right now, and being in the dark seems to keep me calm," Audrey said. She turned on the overhead kitchen light. "Let's stay here in the kitchen. Those news people keep trying to peep inside my living room windows."

Audrey settled down across from Enid at the small kitchen table. "How can I help Grant? What can I do?" Audrey picked little bits from the tissue in her hand.

Enid told Audrey about her conversation with an investigator on the case, withholding Drake's name.

"No offense, but why would he need your help? If he's working on the case, why doesn't he do what he needs to?"

"That's a good question, and I understand your hesitancy. But it's not that unusual for the police to collaborate with the press, with the agreement of sharing information. Most of the time, both the police and the press are after the same thing, just getting to the truth. But in this situation, the lead investigator is convinced Grant is guilty, as you know."

"Does this investigator think Grant is innocent?" Audrey asked.

Enid shrugged. "He's just keeping an open mind for now. But more importantly, he's willing to help us."

Audrey pulled at the tissue again, which was now a small pile of bits on the table. "What do you want me to do?"

"By the way, where is Zoe?" Enid asked.

"Because of all the reporters and madness around here, one of Mara's relatives agreed to keep her. She's in good hands."

"That was probably a wise decision. I hate to admit it, but we reporters can be a nuisance at times. I'd like to confront Grant on why he refused bail. Also, I understand he had a run of bad investments. Who was hurt financially in those transactions? Get as many specifics as you can." Enid pulled a copy of the cicada sketch from her folder. "And ask him if he's ever seen this tattoo."

"What is this?" Audrey studied the sketch. "What does it have to do with Grant or Mara?"

Enid took a deep breath. "I need to tell you something. But you must not talk to anyone about this other than Grant."

CHAPTER 36

Josh had a hard time shaking his concern about Enid. As Yogi Berra said, "It's like deja vu all over again." Josh knew Enid would stay with the Sterling story until she got answers. While he admired her tenacity and her skills as a reporter, he worried about her, even if it made him feel chauvinistic at times. She was her own woman, and he didn't want her to change for him. But he wanted her safe.

And now, Larkin's comments about Caleb Thornhill were haunting him. Why had Larkin wanted Josh to be the one to do a thorough background check? There was something about the way Larkin talked about Thornhill that disturbed Josh.

He walked down the hall to see if Tiffany had time for a quick meeting. She was on the phone but motioned him in. As he sat across from her, he realized his own desk always seemed to have a slight film of fine dust on it from the natural deterioration of the bricks and mortar, one of the downsides of the exposed brick walls. But Tiffany's desk was always spotless.

When she ended the call, Josh said, "I'm working on the Thornhill report, but I'd like to ask you a few more questions."

Looking puzzled, Tiffany shrugged. "Caleb and I have known each other for several years, but I can't say I know too much about him. He guards himself carefully." She paused. "Actually, I was thinking about the last conversation we had about Caleb. I apologize if I came off too pushy, but we need to wrap this up as soon as possible."

"I understand. Where is Caleb from? I mean, where did he grow up? I can't find much about him."

"He came here from another state, but I never pushed him for details. He made a fortune somewhere before he moved here."

"How's that? I mean how did he make his fortune?"

"Some kind of tech stocks, as I understand it."

"Has he always been an investor? Is that how he got his wealth?" Josh asked.

"As far as I know, that's what he's always done."

"What about groups he might belong to? I know he's in Intellecta. Any other groups or organizations you're aware of?"

Tiffany laughed and tossed her hair. "You mean like a neo-Nazi group or something else nefarious?" She leaned forward slightly. "Look, I don't do background checks on people I date. Now if I were to get engaged to someone, you bet I'd be checking. But Caleb and I never got to that level. We were just friends."

"I'm not trying to get personal, but if there's something about him that made you back off, it might be helpful to know."

She started to speak, and then stopped, appearing to weigh her response carefully. "Let's just say he was a bit intense for me." She looked out the window momentarily before continuing. "There was this one time, in a restaurant, our waiter spilled a glass of red wine on me. He was apologetic and the restaurant paid for the dry cleaning and didn't charge us for the meal." She paused. "Later I found out from the restaurant owner, whom I knew, that Caleb came back later and demanded that the waiter be fired."

"Did you confront Caleb about this?"

"No, I promised the owner I wouldn't say anything. It almost seemed as if he was afraid of Caleb."

"So you stopped seeing him after that?"

"Not abruptly, but I started noticing little things that made me realize we were not a match made in heaven."

"I won't use this information, but it's helpful."

Tiffany stared intently at Josh, which made him uncomfortable. "If you're wondering if I have doubts about his temperament and whether it might hinder his political career, then put that thought to rest. I don't know a nice politician. The job requires them to go for the jugular." She pushed her chair away from her desk. "You're concerned about Caleb, aren't you?"

Stealing Larkin's line, Josh said, "Maybe I'm just jealous. He's handsome, rich, charming, and mysterious. What's not to hate about that?" When Tiffany didn't react, he continued. "Why did you recuse yourself from this background check? Were you concerned in any way about what you might find?"

Tiffany looked down and examined her perfectly manicured nails. "I just felt our client might doubt my ability to be unbiased, since he's aware of my past relationship with Caleb."

"Well, I know you're busy but just one more thing. To your knowledge, has Caleb always had the same name?"

Her jaw tightened slightly. "Same name? I mean … yes, as far as I know. What are you getting at?"

"I'm just saying that I can't find anything about him other than the last fifteen years."

Tiffany stood and straightened her black silk trousers. "Well, I know you'll find whatever you need because you won't stop looking. That's why I hired you. Anything else on your mind?"

Taking her cue to leave, Josh stood. "I'll keep you posted."

CHAPTER 37

When Audrey walked into the Richland County Detention Center, she realized she wasn't as mentally prepared for this visit with Grant as she had thought. Some of the people there were crying, some were cursing the authorities. It was as if she had entered the gates of hell. Pulling her shoulders back and taking a few deep breaths, she reminded herself how important her mission was today. She was determined to get information that might help the authorities find the real killer.

Visitors at the detention center are separated from prisoners by plexiglass partitions and talk through phones. When Grant came out and sat down across from her, she barely recognized him. Even though he had only been there a few days, he looked thinner and for the first time she noticed the gray in his temples. Most of all, he looked hopeless and defeated, and that's what concerned her the most.

"How are you?" Audrey asked Grant, and then realized it was a stupid question.

"I've been better. How's Zoe?"

"She's fine." She didn't tell him Zoe cried a lot, often saying "da-da." No need to add to Grant's misery. "But we miss you." She paused. "I need to ask you some questions."

"There's nothing else I can tell about what happened. I don't know anything. Don't you believe me?"

Audrey couldn't stop the tears and hastily wiped her eyes with the back of her hand. "Of course I do. Can you just trust me on this?"

Grant shrugged. "What do you want to know?"

"Are you happy with your attorney?"

Another shrug. It broke Audrey's heart to see her brother so resigned to his situation. "He's okay."

"We'll get you another one, if you're not happy with him."

Grant rubbed the back of his neck. "I don't think, I mean, he's fine. Is that what you came here to ask me?"

"No, I was just curious." Audrey unfolded the copy of the cicada sketch. "Have you ever seen this?"

Grant sat up straight in his chair. "Where did you get that? Put it away."

"Grant, what's wrong. Where have you seen this?"

He leaned forward and lowered his voice. "It's just an insect. I'm sorry I overreacted. This place doesn't exactly bring out the best in people, including me."

Conflicted about how to proceed, Audrey reminded herself she was there on a mission. "I need to know. The authorities need to know."

"Where did you get that sketch?"

"There's a reporter helping us, helping you, by trying to find out who the real killer is. She gave it to me."

He stared at the sketch. "But how did she get it?"

"Look, I know this is going to sound crazy, and maybe it is." Audrey took a deep breath. Did she really want to go down this path with Grant in his mental state? Again, she reminded herself of her mission. "We can discuss it further when you're out, but a woman who has a gift of seeing the future saw Mara's murder. Before it happened."

Grant smiled for the first time. "Can my life get any crazier? Now you're telling me someone saw Mara's …" He stopped and cleared his throat, and the smile disappeared. "Saw the murder *before* it happened?"

Audrey nodded. "Yes."

Grant's jaw clenched. "So why didn't she stop it?"

Aware of the one-hour visitation time limit, Audrey pressed on. "I'll fill you in later. Please let me ask you a few more questions. I'm not one hundred percent sure of all this myself. What do we have to lose?"

Grant lowered his head. "Go on."

"You recognized this sketch. Where have you seen it?"

When Grant looked back up again, Audrey was alarmed at the fear on his face. "It's all my fault," he said.

"What is? How could you be responsible?" Audrey could feel sweat trickling down between her shoulder blades.

Grant put his face in his hands momentarily before continuing. "I made a bad business decision, a big one. And it caused some people to lose a lot of money." He paused. "The wrong kind of people."

Confused, Audrey wasn't even sure what to ask. "Are you saying they were criminals?" And when he didn't answer she added, "How did you get involved with these people?" Audrey wanted to shake him by his shoulders, to bring him to his senses. Surely he was just confused. "Is that why you're afraid to get out of here?"

Grant locked eyes with her. "Promise me you'll let this go. Think of Zoe. Keeping her safe is all you need to focus on." Grant hung up his phone and called for the guard.

Audrey sat there alone momentarily, shaken by Grant's reaction to the sketch. *What have you gotten yourself into?*

CHAPTER 38

As Drake drove down the road, he found himself humming Garth Brook's song "I Got Friends in Low Places." *Ain't that God's truth,* he thought, recalling his mother's often used expression. Working undercover for years introduced Drake to some of the worst offenders: killers, rapists, drug dealers—you name it and he had met them. And had probably shared a beer or two with them.

Today he was going to meet with one of the good guys, a fellow undercover cop. At least he used to be a white hat guy. Sometimes, when you spend too much time with scum, it rubs off on you. You lose sight of decency, of your humanity. But he had no reason to believe Travis was anything other than the good cop he had known since they were rookies together.

After leaving the paved county road, he followed Travis' directions down several dirt roads. Eventually, the camper trailer by the pond that Travis had described came into view.

As Travis instructed, Drake waited in the car until he saw Travis open the door and wave him in.

Inside the camper, Drake had to adjust his eyes to the dim light. Glancing around, he saw clothes strewn on the floor and a half-empty bottle of Jack Daniels on the chipped laminate counter that separated the tiny kitchen area from the rest of the camper.

"It ain't the Ritz, but it's home." Travis embraced Drake in a hearty man hug. "How you been, man?"

"Mi good, mon. How 'bout yuh?"

Travis laughed. "I've missed your crazy accent."

Drake pushed a pair of soiled jeans aside and sat on the stained cushion of the built-in sofa. "Good thing is, the women love the island talk too."

"Rightly so, man. You here as Whistler today or someone else?"

"I'm on loan to the Richland County Sheriff's Department for a few months. Just doing some work on a case."

"That means you must be up for a promotion."

"Not likely. Bowman County just can't afford much training. You know how it goes."

Travis shook his head. "Don't I ever, man. But you said you need my help. What's up?"

"You still working the gangs around here?"

"I'll be pulling out soon. Been here too long. Things are starting to get dicey."

Drake pulled up a photo on his phone. "I'm working a homicide and this sketch came up. Recognize it?"

Travis took the phone and spread the image so he could study the details. "Whew, man. You don't want to mess with them." He handed the phone back to Drake.

"Is this a gang symbol?"

Travis pulled up a flimsy wooden stool and sat in front of Drake. "I wouldn't call it a gang. More like a secret society."

"What's your involvement with this secret society?"

Travis ran his fingers through his hair. "Drugs and money, they run together, as you know. I got hooked up with this gang that was bringing drugs into Bowman County on auto transport carriers. Can you believe that?"

"I'd believe anything about the ingenuity of scum."

"The carriers loaded up the cars with drugs and carried them state to state."

"So this is their symbol, like a Mason kind of thing?"

Travis got up to pour a cup of coffee. "Want a cup?"

"Nah, I'm good." Drake felt the familiar sensation in his gut. That feeling he got when he was onto something important. He reminded himself to be patient, to let Travis tell him, whatever it was, at his own pace. There was no hurrying him up, Drake knew from experience. That kind of patience was critical to working undercover. Try to rush things and you might get yourself killed.

Before sitting down, Travis added a splash of milk from a carton sitting on the counter next to the bottle of Jack. "Ever heard of Cicada 3301?"

"It came up in some research. What's it about?"

"Well then, you know it was a group of uber intellectuals who solved puzzles. Lots of them were brilliant, I mean like high IQ geniuses."

"But I thought they disbanded years ago. And I wasn't aware they were involved in anything criminal."

"The group fizzled, and you're right. Far as I know, they were on the up and up. Just bored brainiacs."

"So how are they—"

Travis held up his hand to interrupt Drake. "Wait, let me finish. One of the members went by the code name Orion."

"As in Orion the Hunter?"

"That's right, after the constellation Orion. You see, Orion eventually got bored with Cicada 3301 and started his own group of friggin' geniuses. Umbra."

"Umbra?"

"It's a physics term meaning the darkest part of a shadow or the moon. This Umbra group is brilliant, but they use their brains for taking revenge or gaining control."

"Why haven't I heard of them?" Drake asked.

"I told you they are brilliant. And mostly not from around here. But they're working their way into our local crime scene."

"You've connected with them?"

"Indirectly. I was hanging with a gang who ran protection on the auto carriers. One of them got drunk and told me they were hired by Umbra." Travis lowered his head. "Found the stupid son of a bitch a couple weeks later with his throat slashed."

Drake leaned back against the camper wall and exhaled. "Whew. That's some scary shit."

"And you'd bes' not cross 'em."

"So Umbra is running the auto transport gig?" Drake asked.

"Let's just say they're financing it. And raking in big returns," he added.

"So this Umbra gang or group, they fund themselves by trafficking drugs and they're big on revenge?"

Travis shrugged. "That's all I know." He waved his arm around the camper. "I need to get back home, hang out with people that aren't scumbags and killers. If you're aiming to go after Umbra, you make sure your life insurance payments *are up to date.*"

CHAPTER 39

The next day, Larkin called Josh and asked him to meet at Larkin's home. Josh agreed and got directions.

Driving through the posh neighborhood, Josh realized that though it was not far from his own residence, it was light years away in terms of social status. The area felt like old money, the kind that was passed down from generation to generation. Not too many young people on their own could buy into a neighborhood like this.

Larkin's house was a large two-story with white-painted brick and black shutters. The yard was magazine-worthy, not like his own that still needed a serious raking.

As Josh got out of the car, the front door opened and Larkin stood there with a cup of coffee in his hand. "Welcome to my humble abode. Come on in."

Josh didn't see anything humble about it, but then it wasn't the governor's mansion Larkin had lived in for eight years. They settled into Larkin's home office and made small talk over coffee for several minutes.

"Thanks for seeing me today," Larkin said.

"You're our client, so why wouldn't I meet with you?"

Larkin nodded and smiled. "How's the investigation going on Caleb?"

Josh tried not to show his frustration. First Tiffany, now Larkin. "I'm working on it, but there's not a lot of information. It's like the guy materialized out of nowhere about ten years ago."

"I knew you'd dig deep." He paused briefly. "And I figured you'd hit a brick wall at some point."

"I'm no politician, as we both know. But it doesn't make sense for your PAC to fund a guy you apparently have reservations about."

Larkin set his cup on the mahogany side table. "If we hadn't worked together, and if I didn't know your history as an undercover cop, I would give you a polite but dismissive answer. But I trust you. I can still trust you, right?"

"I think we've been through enough together that you don't have to ask that, but yes. And I have to ask that we keep this meeting between us. Tiffany and I have a tenuous relationship right now, and she would demand to know what we talked about."

Larkin chucked softly. "That's a fair trade. But the stakes aren't quite the same. If I told Tiffany, at worst you'd get fired. And that's highly unlikely. Despite what you may think of her, she's a fan of yours. She says you keep her grounded."

"And what are the stakes for you if I were to talk?" Josh asked.

Larkin put his fingertips together, tapping them gently. "Politics is all about power, you know that. And power is all about money."

Josh knew Larkin well enough to know he expected Josh to stay quiet and listen, so he did.

"Caleb has the potential to be a powerful politician, and despite my reservations about him at times, if he uses that power and his intellect responsibly, he can do a lot of good for our state." Larkin tapped his fingertips together again. "He's brilliant, as you know. Far smarter than you or I."

"Does that scare you?" Josh asked.

"At times, yes. He's always ten steps ahead of me and everyone else."

Josh shifted in his seat. "Is that why don't you trust him?"

Larkin went over to his desk drawer and pulled out a manila folder. He held it out to Josh. "Read this."

Josh took the folder. "What is this?" He saw the photo of a man in several articles. "Is this Caleb?"

Larkin looked out the window to the front lawn, appearing to be deep in thought. A moment later, he replied, "That's what you need to find out."

Josh looked at the articles again. The name was Howard Whitaker. "If it's not a younger Caleb, they could be twins."

"I just got this information yesterday from someone who made me swear not to reveal it to anyone, and in particular, not to tell Caleb I had it. I was hoping you had perhaps discovered this information on your own during your background check. But then, Caleb is a clever man."

"Did this person tell you how he got this information or why he gave it to you?"

"He wouldn't tell me anything else. I can tell you, my informant is a private citizen, not a lawman or a politician. He knew about the PAC I work for and that Caleb is someone we're interested in supporting."

Josh flipped through the copies of newspaper articles. He scanned them quickly and saw the name of Howard Whitaker in each of them. Whitaker was a suspect in a severe beating, a murder, and an extortion scheme. But he was never caught. One thing that caught Josh's attention was the reference to Whitaker being an "evil genius." Josh returned the papers to the folder and closed it. "Why is the location redacted in each of these articles? It's like your guy didn't want anyone to trace them."

"I have no idea."

"And your informant didn't tell you how this person is connected to Caleb or why it would matter?" Josh asked.

Larkin shook his head. "It may be nothing. It may be something."

"Is it possible this is actually Caleb? That Howard and Caleb are the same person?"

Larkin shrugged. "I have no idea."

"And if I find something that's detrimental to Caleb, you know I can't ignore it."

Larkin chuckled softly. "Once a lawman, always a lawman. All I ask is that you keep me and the PAC out of it. And make damn sure you watch your back."

CHAPTER 40

Drake sat through Lieutenant Albright's morning meeting, which seemed to drag on forever. Overtime was capped, budgets were tight, and cases needed to be closed. The usual stuff.

Drake checked his phone to make sure it was turned off. Ever since he had been reprimanded severely when his cell phone rang during a meeting, he was careful not to get on the wrong side of Albright again. Drake needed him to write a good report to Drake's superior in Bowman County.

Once the meeting had ended, Drake sat at his desk to tend to some overdue reports. It was nearly an hour later before he realized his phone was still turned off. As soon as he turned it on, several messages filled the screen. He didn't recognize the number, but that wasn't unusual in his line of work since many of his confidential informants used burner phones. But these messages weren't from a CI. Each mentioned "Red Stripe," Travis' nickname for Drake. When they were rookies, Drake complained about not being able to buy his favorite Jamaican beer in Bowman County. And when Drake and Travis both went into undercover work, they agreed Red Stripe would be their way of calling the other one for help, their SOS.

Drake tried to call the number that the messages were sent from but didn't get an answer or a prompt to leave a voice message. He grabbed his jacket and keys and left to go find Travis.

...

While driving, Drake realized he had not told anyone where he was going, so he called in and told them he was checking a lead. He didn't give a specific location, in fact, he didn't even have an address. All he had were GPS coordinates.

When he arrived at Travis' RV by the pond, he waited for Travis to come to the door and wave him inside. That was their agreement, for safety. But there was no sign of Travis, although his pickup was parked beside the RV. Drake considered blowing the horn, but if Travis was in the middle of something with one of the gang members, Drake didn't want to interrupt him. Then again, Red Stripe was a clear message, a call for help.

Drake approached the RV cautiously, with his hand on his holstered gun. He tapped on the door. "Travis. It's me." No response or any noise from inside the RV. "Travis."

Drake glanced around, saw no one, and gently pushed on the RV door. It moved slightly but stopped. He pushed a little harder, but something was blocking the door. "Travis, I'm coming in. You alright?"

Drake put his weight against the RV door and forced it open. Even in the dim light, he could see what was blocking it—a man's body. He drew his gun and shoved hard enough to get inside the RV. Travis' body was lying on the floor, face up, in a pool of blood. His throat had been slashed.

Even before the loss of his friend registered, Drake's first thought was that this crime scene looked eerily like Mara Sterling's crime scene photos. And if that was the case, there would be no prints or other forensics at the scene. The killer was no amateur gangbanger.

CHAPTER 41

Enid had been summoned to a meeting with Silas, a meeting she had been both expecting and dreading. He wanted an article on Mara Sterling's murder, one of the primary reasons he hired her. And she had virtually nothing she could offer at this point, at least nothing that every other newspaper wasn't already reporting. Perhaps Silas wanted to give her a different assignment. Or fire her.

"Hi," she said, trying to be cheerful when she walked in the small conference room where Silas was waiting.

A brief smile was all Silas offered before jumping into the conversation. "I've got a busy morning, and hopefully you do too. So I'll be brief."

"Look, Silas, I—"

Before she could finish, Silas raised his hand. "I'm not here to criticize you. I know you're trying to reconcile your conflict of interest with that fortune teller and the newspaper article you're working on. I'm trying, and will continue to try, to be patient. For a while at least."

Enid relaxed her shoulders a bit. "Thanks for your trust in me."

Again Silas raised his hand. "But I do need something. You mentioned in one of our updates that there was once a secret group that I can't remember the name of now."

"Cicada 3301," Enid said.

"Yes, that one. It has nothing to do with any of this, but it might make a good filler while you're working on the Sterling story. Think you've got enough for a piece?"

Enid nodded. "I think that would make a good article. I'd like to find a former member, or at least someone who may be familiar with the group. If I can't find a source, I'll just do the history and perhaps even pull in some other secret groups."

Silas slapped his hands on the table. "Good. When can I get it?"

"A couple days, if you can wait. I'll have to do some digging to provide enough details."

Silas stood. "Good. I've got to run." Nearly out the door, he turned back. "How's Jack, by the way?"

"He's hanging in there. I'll tell him you asked about him." Enid's uneasiness returned. Before leaving the office, she stopped by to see the office manager and to let her know she'd be working at home the rest of the day doing research for the article.

. . .

On the drive back home, Enid's thoughts were on Jack, not the article. She felt bad about refusing his request for her to take over the newspaper. He rarely asked for her help, yet he had helped her so much. But first, she knew she had to focus on what would make her and Josh happy. She needed another conversation with Jack to put it all to rest. But now, she needed to write this article and restore Silas' confidence in her to produce a good story.

After putting her notepad and phone in the office, she went to the kitchen and made herself a cup of tea. She liked working from home, and running a newspaper would be a big adjustment in her work environment. And did she really want to go back to Madden? She missed it at times, but was moving back a good idea? And trying to commute from Columbia every day would be time consuming. And what about Josh? Some days he seemed to enjoy working with Tiffany. But on other days, he clearly missed working in law enforcement. He hadn't seemed overly interested in returning to Madden as its police chief when Pete talked to him. Or was he masking his feelings, putting on a brave front for her?

She shook her head slightly to toss out all these random thoughts. *Time to get to work.* First, she did an extensive online search, but there were only a few articles from years ago, 2012 through 2014, that came up referencing Cicada 3301.

She then went to the Intellecta website and was surprised there are more than 50,000 members in the United States. She submitted a request for an interview with a local member, if there was one. She stressed in the request that she needed to talk to them as soon as possible and that if requested, she would keep the name anonymous in her article.

On a whim, she called the *Palmetto Post's* researcher, a smart young woman who was probably Intellecta worthy herself and left a message. "Hi, this is Enid. I'm doing an article on Cicada 3301, specifically those whose members were also Intellecta members. See if you can find any information about the connections between the two groups."

CHAPTER 42

Drake looked around the RV and took a few photos on his phone. Other than the signs of a struggle and a few things tossed around, there were no obvious clues. Was it a coincidence that Travis had given him information about Orion and the Umbra group just before he was killed? He considered the number of lowlife bums Travis would have associated with in his undercover work. Anything could have gone wrong, including a drugged-up thug looking for crack or anything else to get high on.

That's what Drake kept telling himself as he looked at the contacts on his phone until he found the number for his commanding officer in the Bowman County Sheriff's Department. There were two numbers in his contacts: one for routine calls and a second one for situations like this. He called the second one.

"Hey, it's me, Drake. Travis has been killed. I'll give you the coordinates." He relayed the GPS numbers. "I'm at the scene now but I'm getting out. Call me later."

The only answer he got was "Copy that." But it was all he needed. After he ended the call, he glanced around again and wiped his prints off the RV door. Feeling foolish, he pulled on one of the latex gloves he always carried and checked for a pulse on Travis. "Rest in peace, mon. Drink a Red Stripe fi mi when yuh reach paradise."

It might be an hour or so before someone from the sheriff's office got to Travis, and Drake didn't have the time to wait, nor did he want to wait for Travis' killer to come back.

He said a prayer over Travis' lifeless body and left, making sure everything was left just as he had found it.

. . .

What were the odds? Drake kept asking himself that question on the drive back to Columbia. What were the odds that soon after Travis revealed information to Drake about Umbra, Travis was killed. Had someone been watching Travis? Or him? And what were the odds that Travis was killed in the same manner as Mara Sterling?

What if anything did the two victims have connecting them? One was an upper middle-class wife and mother living in a nice neighborhood. The other was an undercover investigator who was entrenched in the low life world of drug dealers, killers, and worse. Drake rubbed his temple in an attempt to lessen the pounding.

He needed to talk to someone. But Albright? Drake didn't want to put his commanding officer in Bowman in a situation of having to lie to Albright. The only way to play this was upright.

On the drive back to Columbia, he kept thinking about the best way to reveal all of this to Albright. No matter what Drake thought of him, he still needed a good report from his CO.

CHAPTER 43

When her cell phone rang, Enid was surprised to see the caller was Grant's sister. "Do you have a minute?" Audrey asked.

"Of course. Is everything okay?"

"I'm not sure. And I don't know who else to talk to."

Enid heard Audrey weeping softly. "I'm glad you called. Have you talked to Grant?"

"Yes, I met with him and asked the questions you gave me."

Enid felt her pulse quickening. "Is that what's upsetting you?"

The was a moment of silence before Audrey replied. "Grant is all the immediate family I have left." She paused. "And I don't want to lose him."

"What happened?"

"When Grant and I were just kids, we went for a walk through the woods behind our house. Normally, we didn't walk far, and we were forbidden to go anywhere near the railroad tracks at the edge of the woods. But one day, we were feeling mischievous and decided to walk the tracks. We'd seen a movie about hobos and hoped we might see one."

"What happened?" Enid asked

"A man approached us and grabbed Grant from behind. I was screaming, and Grant was struggling to get away. Finally, I picked up the biggest rock I could find and hurled it at the man's face. Grant and I played softball with the neighbor's kids, and I was the star pitcher. It came in handy that day. I hit the man square in the forehead. When he let go of Grant and grabbed his head, we ran as fast as we could. Thankfully, he didn't follow us. But I'll never forget that look of fear on Grant's face. And I saw it again today, especially when I confronted him about the tattoo." She wept again. "Grant is terrified of something or someone. But he wouldn't tell me what. He told me to stay out of it." She cried louder now. "But I can't. He didn't do it. I know it."

"I'm sure this is all distressing for you. And I'm sorry for your pain. And for Grant's. If he's innocent of killing Mara, then who could he be protecting?"

"I think it's me," Audrey said. "Me and Zoe."

"I'm sorry, I don't understand. How will telling the truth put you and Zoe in danger?" She heard Audry sobbing. "Try to relax. I'll do some checking around and see if I can get any updates. Just try not to worry." But Enid knew as soon as she said it that Audrey wasn't going to get any relief until this nightmare was over.

. . .

Enid called Drake and left a message for him to call her as soon as he could. She then turned her attention to writing an article on a break-in at a local soup kitchen, the same place she had met Theo, the father of a missing girl, several years ago. One break-in was hardly newsworthy, but it was one in a string of church break-ins over the past six months. Thankfully, no one was hurt and nothing of value was taken.

The kitchen was trashed, which led the police to assume teenagers were the likely culprits.

For the most part, she was looking forward to working for the *Palmetto Post*, but she had to admit she missed writing some of the articles she used to complain about when working for the *Tri-County Gazette* in Madden. Writing about nothing but crime now was giving her a distorted view of the world, much as someone in law enforcement begins to suspect everyone because that's all they deal with. She'd have to find a way to remind herself of the goodness in the world and that there are decent, law-abiding people.

Just as she wrote the last sentence, her phone rang. "Drake, thanks for calling me back. Can we talk about the Mara Sterling case for a few minutes?"

"No. I mean not on the phone. Meet me at McDonald's." With that, he ended the call.

Thirty minutes later, she was sitting across from Drake, watching him wolf down a burger and fries. "Sorry," he said. "I haven't had anything to eat and I'm starving."

"Take your time. While you eat, I'll fill you in on why I called."

Drake stuffed a couple fries in his mouth and nodded.

"Audrey Sterling, Grant's sister, visited him in prison, and then she called me."

Drake took a took long pull on the straw in his sweet iced tea. "Go on."

"She said Grant was terrified, and she thinks he's staying quiet to protect her and Zoe."

"Zoe's the kid, right?"

Enid nodded. "Audrey is convinced Grant is innocent, but she is his only family and certainly biased." She paused to allow Drake to eat the last bite of burger. "Do you think he's innocent, and please don't say policeman don't have opinions, only evidence."

Drake threw back his head and laughed. "That's crap. Of course we have opinions, but we have to push them aside and focus on evidence." He appeared to study Enid's reaction and then lowered his voice. "Are we totally off the record?"

"Of course."

"I think she's right. He's not the kind of person, as far as I can tell, to be sadistic. And leaving your kid beside her dead mother, now that's pretty damn sick." He wiped his mouth with a napkin. "Sounds like he knows something on someone who's pretty dangerous." He leaned back in the booth. "I'm going to tell you what I've found out but if you print any of this …"

"I won't. You've got my word. As long as you'll give me something official when you can."

"And I expect quid pro quo from you. Let me know when you get something." He wiped his mouth again and continued. "It's still Albright's case, and he's convinced Grant is guilty. Anyway, I tracked down one of my buddies who is familiar with that cicada tattoo."

Enid sat up straight. "Seriously? Can I talk to him? Off the record of course. At least I'll be ready when it's okay to print."

Drake shook his head. "You can't do that. He's dead."

"Dead? You mean …?"

"After he met with me, he left me a code that we had agreed on, an SOS of sorts. But when I got to him, he was killed. Throat slashed."

"Just like Mara."

"Exactly."

"So what did he tell you about the cicada tattoo?"

Drake took a long sip and put the empty cup on the tray. "I think you know about the Cicada 3301 group from more than a decade ago. A secret group of brilliant dudes who worked on puzzles. I don't get it, but then I'm nowhere near a genius."

"So he thinks they killed Mara?" Enid asked.

"No. But there was a group that emerged from Cicada 3301 that called themselves Umbra. The original group, as far as we know, just solved puzzles, and they didn't get bug tattoos. But Umbra, this spin-off group, Umbra, are the ones with the tattoos. And they are bad news."

"In what way? What is Umbra's purpose?"

"My contact said it's revenge and control. He also said the leader goes by Orion."

"The hunter?"

"Yep."

"Do you think Umbra killed your undercover contact?"

"'Mi sure 'bout it, beautiful lady."

CHAPTER 44

Ironically, Tiffany's background research firm didn't hire dedicated researchers. That is, not the kind who banged away at keyboards all day. Instead, the firm's business model relied on face-to-face evaluations and talking to people who knew the targets of their investigations.

At times, Josh felt they were missing opportunities by not focusing more on cyber searches, particularly in these times when people put their whole lives online for everyone to see. But then again, the targets of their investigations were, for the most part, savvy enough to keep their private lives to themselves. Their social media accounts were mostly photo ops, showing them being seen at the right places with the right people, the people who could advance their political or business careers. If one of their targets was stupid enough to post a photo of themselves drunk at a party, then it was mostly over for them other than the wringing of hands.

But Josh had learned about the dark web mostly from his former assistant Roo, Enid, and Pete. Josh dabbled in the dark web some, but he wasn't comfortable snooping around because he wasn't skilled enough to cover his tracks. If he did stumble onto something, the subject of his search would likely be able to trace the search back to him.

But he had exhausted all conventional searches for Howard Whitaker. It was time to call in reinforcements. He informed the office manager he was going to work from home and then put everything he thought he might need in his leather backpack.

When he got home, Enid was sitting in their office. "Hi, babe." He kissed the top of her head, letting his lips caress her auburn tresses, smelling slightly of lavender. "Mind if I talk to you about something?"

She took his hand his hers and glanced at the time on her laptop. "You're home pretty early. What's up?"

"I need you to help me or connect me with someone who can." He threw his backpack on a nearby chair and took off his jacket. "Since you offered to help me with research, well, I'm here for help."

"I don't go messing around in the dark web, but I can connect you with Rachel."

"Jack's adopted daughter?"

Enid nodded. "She and Tommy are both white hat hackers."

"What's that?" Josh asked.

"White hat hackers typically work for the government or large organizations to intentionally try to hack into their networks. That way, they can find any vulnerabilities and fix them."

"That's pretty neat. Do you think she'd help me?"

"I'm sure she would, and I'd love to talk with her. Tell me what you need."

"Well, you know I'm working on a target, Caleb Thornhill. I had an interesting talk with Larkin, who is actually the one who ordered the background check for the PAC. They want to back Thornhill but need to make sure there are no surprises in his background for reporters like you to dig up."

"What do you know about him so far?" Enid asked.

"I've done all the usual checking with people who know him, although there aren't many. And I've done the basic online searches. No one is particularly close to him, but those who work with him say he's aloof and brilliant, an Intellecta in fact."

Enid stiffened. "Intellecta?"

"Yeah, you know—"

"I know what Intellecta is, it's just that, well, this story I'm working on, the husband is an Intellecta."

"Huh, that's odd. I mean, how many can there be?"

"Over 50,000 in the US, apparently. But go on."

"I also need info on Howard Whitaker."

"How is he connected to your target?"

Josh pulled out the folder Larkin had given him and handed it to Enid. "Here. See for yourself."

She skimmed the articles. "Larkin gave these to you?"

Josh nodded.

"And you think this Thornhill guy you're doing a background check on is connected to Howard Whitaker?"

Josh shrugged. "Could be. That's what we need to find out."

...

Enid tapped on Rachel's number in her contacts and hoped it was still good. She hadn't talked to her in a while.

"Enid, oh my gosh, it's so good to hear your voice. How are you?"

For the next few minutes, they caught up on the highlights of their respective lives. Rachel was still single but seriously involved with the white hat hacker whom Enid had known as Tommy Two when he helped her find Theo's missing daughter. "What's he go by now?" Enid asked.

"We both have dozens of code names, depending on the project. His real name is Andrew."

"Any plans for a wedding for you and Andrew in the future?" Enid recalled the timid and distraught young woman she had first met years ago. She sounded so confident now, so happy.

Rachel laughed. "You sound like Jack. Let's just say you'll definitely be on the invite list, but don't rush out and buy a new outfit to wear. Not yet."

"Okay, I'll try to wait patiently. But seriously, I hope he's the right one for you." Enid paused. "Can I ask you how Jack's doing? I mean *really* doing?"

"You know how private he is about his health. But I will say, it's not looking good. He's getting weaker by the day."

Enid's shoulders tensed. "I can't bear to hear that. And I know how close you two are. I'm so sorry—for both of you. Is there anything I can do?"

"He told me he offered you the paper. And that you refused it."

"Well, I wasn't that emphatic, but, Rachel, you know I'm not an editor or an administrator."

"For what it's worth, I think you should take it, you know, carry on the legacy. If he sells it to someone, they might destroy what he's built."

"I didn't dismiss Jack's offer as casually as you might think. I've been giving it a lot of thought. But surely you're aware of what's happening to local newspapers." Enid continued, "How do you get your news?"

"I have several online sources I use."

"Exactly. People are streaming news, not reading papers, and most online papers don't focus on local news. All this cord cutting and steaming is having a detrimental impact on local journalism."

"But the *Tri-County Gazette* has a good subscription base. It's profitable," Rachel said.

"Most of those subscribers are older readers. Young people like you don't read local news, even online. The statistics are dire. It's not just a couple of newspapers shutting down—it's a significant portion of them. One study says we've lost nearly a third of our local papers in the last two decades. That's a lot of communities losing their voice, their watchdogs, every single week. That's going away."

Rachel sighed. "But isn't that all the more reason to try to save the paper?"

"While I cherish local reporting, staking my future on an eroding industry ..." She paused, searching for the right words. "I just can't help but feel like I'd be boarding a sinking ship. I have to think about our future, mine and Josh's. Frankly, I can't build my life on that kind of uncertainty. I've had too many years of that."

"Listen, I get everything you're saying. And you're right, you have to do what's right for you. But you've always told me the most important thing for you is finding the truth." Rachel sighed. "Things change, you know that. Don't you want to be part of that change? When the pendulum swings back, and people realize they've lost their local news, you can be a part of that shift. Just promise me you'll give it some more thought."

"I will, I promise," Enid said. "Now, do you think you might help me with some research?"

"I'll try. What 'ya need?"

"I'm helping Josh with a confidential background check on someone. We've done the usual Google search, driver's license, and other common databases."

"Do you think he's using an alias?"

"That's what we need to find out. He's running for some kind of political office. We're still working on keeping our professional lives separate, so I don't quiz Josh about his targets. I don't know much more than the target's name, Caleb Thornhill."

"What specifically am I looking for? Dirt? Scandal?"

"I need for you to check the dark web for his name and also for Howard Whitaker."

"Who's that?" Rachel asked.

"I'm not sure exactly. Josh was given some newspaper articles in confidence that show Whitaker was involved in criminal activity and was a suspect in several serious crimes years ago. The guy looks a lot like Thornhill, but younger."

Rachel spelled the names to be sure she had them correct and repeated a summary of Enid's request. "I'm on it. I'll let you know the results. Shouldn't take long. You may want to send me a copy of those articles. Might be something in them that will help the search."

...

As soon as Enid ended the call with Rachel, she got a response from the Intellecta organization about her request for an interview. The message contained the name and email address of a person who handled their public relations and had agreed to talk to Enid. She might be able to pull an article together for tomorrow's edition if she got enough information.

Enid replied with a request for the woman to call at her earliest convenience and was surprised when her phone rang several minutes later.

Enid thought the woman sounded "normal," and then silently laughed at herself. Did she think geniuses should sound different than ordinary people? "I appreciate your calling me so quickly."

"My pleasure. What kind of article are you writing?" the woman asked. "By the way, I'm Monica."

Enid explained that she was working on a background story about Intellecta as a companion to another article. Monica gave her the usual information: who is eligible, how you apply for membership, how many members, and other details. Most of which was on the Intellecta website. "May I ask you if your organization has ever encountered members who use their genius for nefarious purposes, and if so, how did Intellecta handle it?"

"You're a crime reporter, so I guess when you report on these kinds of things you suspect everyone of something."

Sensing that she had offended the woman, Enid tried to explain. "I wasn't implying that. My apologies. I can't go into the details of the crime, but I'm reporting about a person who is in jail, accused of murdering his wife, and he's a member of Intellecta."

"Oh my, that's terrible. I hope you don't pull Intellecta into that story. Surely our organization is not involved in any way."

"We will only reference Sterling's membership, but no inferences will be made that Intellecta is in any way involved."

"Did you say Sterling?"

"Yes, Grant Sterling. It was in all the national papers, so you probably recall that name."

"And he's accused of killing Mara?"

Enid felt the hairs on her arm stand up. "Do you know Grant Sterling? And Mara?"

Monica's voice was trembling. "I don't read the papers much. Too depressing. But yes, I know Grant and Mara." She corrected herself. "Knew Mara. I can't believe she's dead."

"May I ask how you know them?"

"As long as you don't print this."

"Agreed," Enid said.

"Intellecta has several people who talk to the press, but I was asked to call you because your message said you were in Columbia, South Carolina, and I used to live there, in fact grew up there. Grant and I became members of Intellecta at about the same time, and we developed a camaraderie of sorts. And since Mara loved to entertain, they used to invite me to their home for dinner. In fact, those dinners were one of the things I miss the most about Columbia. I don't miss those famously hot summers though."

"I'd like to get a few more details about Intellecta, the organization, and then if you don't mind, I'd like to ask you some off-the-record questions about Grant. I can't go into all the details, but his sister is adamant he's innocent, and I'm just trying to get to the truth. Would that be okay?"

"I don't feel comfortable talking about Grant without his permission. But ask me anything you want to know about Intellecta."

"Are you familiar with Cicada 3301?" Enid asked

There was silence on the line.

"Monica, are you there?"

"Yes, I'm sorry. It's just that ... I mean, I've heard of them and I've heard some of our members may have participated, but I don't know enough to give you facts. I can't help you."

Enid could tell there was no point in pressing Monica further on this topic, so she just continued to ask more about Intellecta until she felt she had enough for a decent article. After thanking Monica for the information, Enid asked, "Now, off the record is there anything you can tell me about Grant that will help clear him?"

After a brief silence, Monica said, "Sorry, it's just that this is all so much to take in. Mara's dead. And Grant is in jail. I just can't wrap my head around it."

"Anything you tell me about Grant or Mara will not be printed without your permission. Understand?"

"I don't know what I can tell you. I never witnessed any major disagreements between them. Just small husband-and-wife kind of spats."

"What kinds of things did they argue about?"

"Well ... are you sure we're off the record?" Monica asked.

"Yes, I promise. I'm not recording anything, just taking a few notes no one else will see."

"Alright." Monica sounded nervous. "Like I said, I liked Mara. She was everything I'm not. The perfect host, an extraordinary cook. And a loving wife and mother." Monica gasped. "Oh, no. What about Zoe? Is she okay?"

"She's fine. Staying with relatives."

"Good. I never got to meet Zoe, because I had moved by the time she was born, but Grant sent photos often. He's a proud dad."

"And what about Mara? Any indications from Grant that he was unhappy with her?"

"He said she was 'perfect,' that was his word. But I know they argued about how much money Mara spent. She liked the best of everything. He sent photos of their gorgeous kitchen renovation. But I sensed he was worried about money at times."

"But he is a financial advisor. Surely he knows how to manage his own affairs."

Enid waited but Monica didn't respond. "Is there anything else you can tell me about Grant and Mara?"

"No, that's all."

Enid detected a chill had settled over the previously cordial conversation. Knowing she would likely never talk to Monica again, Enid decided she had nothing to lose with the next question. "Was Grant faithful to Mara?"

"Why would you ask that?" Monica asked, her voice louder.

"The police allege he was involved with someone."

"Grant was a good man and a loving father. He gave Mara *everything* she wanted. No matter how hard it was on him."

CHAPTER 45

Drake sat across from Albright in his office. "From what you've told me, you've had quite the time lately," Albright said. "I mean chasing down undercover cops. Getting one of them killed."

Drake's jaw clenched hearing the lieutenant accuse him of causing Travis' murder. But he'd learned the best thing to do when Albright was in one of his moods was to shut up and listen. No matter how difficult it might be.

Albright continued, "When you asked me about doing some additional investigation, I didn't know you were going to run your own show." He slammed his palms down on the desktop. "What the hell were you thinking?"

Drake waited briefly to make sure he didn't interrupt Albright. "Sir, I apologize but I was checking out some information on that tattoo."

"What tattoo?"

"The one …" Drake stopped short. "It's in the Sterling file."

"You talking about that woo-woo vision your crackpot fortune teller saw?"

Drake knew no matter how he answered, it was a no-win situation. "The copy of the sketch is in the file. As I told you earlier, I just wanted to be sure we checked it out."

"You from Jamaica, that right?" Albright squinted at Drake.

"Born there but left when I was a teenager." Now Drake was really irritated. "Sir, may I ask what my birth country has to do with this conversation?"

Albright laughed. "Now don't go getting all civil rights on me. Just wondering if you were raised to believe that a woman, out of the blue, sees a murder before it happens. And then we go chasing our tails, when we could be doing something meaningful on the other *dozens* of pending cases."

Drake was considering his response when Albright's desk phone rang. "Yeah. When?" he slammed the receiver down. "Someone shanked Grant Sterling. He's in ICU." Albright glared at Drake. "Well, what are you waiting for? Go check it out. Tell them you want a statement when he's awake."

Drake stood. "Yes, sir. Any restrictions on my investigation, since, you know, I seem to have stepped over the line with Travis."

Albright pointed his finger at Drake. "Don't get smart with me. Just find out what the hell's going on."

...

Drake went to Richland Memorial Hospital. When he asked at the nurse's station where he could find Grant Sterling, she pointed to a room down the hall where a deputy was standing at the door. "You can't talk to him now. He's in and out of consciousness."

"He going to make it?" Drake asked.

The nurse shrugged. "Who knows. He's lost a lot of blood."

"I'm just going down to talk to the deputy." As Drake walked the short distance down the hall, he could feel the nurse's watchful glare behind him.

"Hey, mon, how you be?" Drake asked the deputy. "Don I know 'ya?"

"Hey, Drake. It is Drake, right?"

Drake dropped the accent. "Yeah, it's me. How you been? Haven't seen you since the academy."

The deputy shrugged. "Okay, I guess. Still chasing bad guys."

"And they be chasing us too, hey?"

The deputy smiled and nodded toward the room door. "You here to see this guy?"

"Yeah." Drake glanced around. "Any way I can get a few minutes with him?"

"I don't know, man. My orders were that only medical personnel get in. Besides, I think he's still unconscious."

"I get it." Drake reached into his pocket and pulled out a copy of the cicada tattoo. "I just need to know if the dude who shanked him had this tattoo."

"That some kind of bug?"

"Cicada, so I've been told." Drake glanced down the hallway again. "Five minutes, tops. Come on, man."

The deputy shifted his weight back and forth a few times and looked toward the nurse's station. "Two minutes. And if I tap on the door, you need to get out quick or I'll be in big trouble."

Drake gave him a light punch to the arm. "You're top shelf, mon. Thanks." Drake glanced around again before stepping inside the room. Sterling had numerous monitors attached to him, and an IV pierced his arm.

Drake spoke softly, barely above a whisper. "Grant, can you hear me?"

No response.

Drake touched Grant's arm lightly. "If you can hear me, I need to know who did this." Again, no response, but Drake thought he heard a slight moan. "Grant?" He held the copy of the cicada tattoo in front of Grant's closed eyes. "If you can hear me, I need to know if the man who shanked you had this tattoo?"

Drake waited momentarily and then decided to give up and leave. He'd have to wait until Grant was fully awake, if he made it. Drake was folding the sketch to return it to his pocket when Grant's eyes fluttered slightly. Drake quickly unfolded the image and held it up in front of Grant.

Grant's eyes opened slightly, and Drake heard the monitor's beeping increase. He glanced at the screen. Grant's blood pressure was rising, and the nurse would soon be in. "Grant, I've only got a minute. Look at this tattoo. Did the man who stabbed you have this?"

Grant's eyes darted around the image, taking it in. Drake thought he nodded slightly, but maybe he imagined it. Drake put his hand on Grant's left arm, the one without the IV, and tapped Grant's index finger. "If you mean yes, raise your finger."

Drake held the image in front of Grant's face again and watched as Grant's finger raised slightly. His eyes were now fully opened and tears streamed down his face. Drake pulled a tissue from the box and dabbed at Grant's face. "I know this is upsetting. But I appreciate your help. We'll take it from here."

Grant's finger raised slightly again before he closed his eyes. Suddenly, the monitor alarm sounded. "Shit," Drake said softly to himself. He stuffed the copy of the tattoo in his pocket just as the deputy tapped on the door and opened it slightly. "Get out of there."

CHAPTER 46

Still reeling from his narrow escape from the hospital, Drake drove to Elmwood Cemetery and parked his car. Being among the dead was comforting to him somehow. He had been raised to talk to the deceased, so they were like old friends. Not these dead people specifically, as none of his relatives or friends were buried here.

Drake had discovered Elmwood not long after being transferred to Columbia. He was fascinated with the ornate mausoleums and often wondered how much money you had to have to be buried in one. Not that he wanted to be buried above ground. He was superstitious about things like that. But he respected the beauty of the structures and the wealth they showcased.

Sometimes when he went there, he walked through the confederate soldiers' burial section. He tried to imagine what the Civil War must have been like. War was stupid, and especially one in which more than 700,000 soldiers were killed. The confederate soldiers buried here and throughout the South fought for what they thought was right. Did they even understand they were fighting to preserve slavery? He preferred to think the confederate soldiers were just doing as they were told.

Drake sometimes felt like one of those soldiers, just following commands, even stupid ones at times. But then he reminded himself that even during those times he had saved lives and righted some wrongs. Surely those things tipped the scale and made his work, his life, meaningful.

By the time he walked back to his car and started the engine to leave, he had a new sense of resolve: he had to find the man or men with the cicada tattoo. More than ever, Drake was convinced Grant Sterling did not kill his wife. Before leaving the cemetery, Drake tapped a familiar name from the list of contacts on his phone. "Enid, can we meet?"

. . .

Enid waited for Drake at the local McDonald's, which had become "their" place to compare notes. She knew better than to invite him into their home. Josh had stressed to her that for undercover investigators, work was work and home was home. Keeping that separation between the two was critical.

As soon as Drake walked in, she knew something was wrong. The happy-go-lucky facade was gone. "I'm going to get a Coke. You want anything?"

Enid shook her head and held up her iced tea. "I'm good."

Drake sat down in the booth across from her and took a long sip from his straw. "Man, that's good. Would be even better though it if was a Red Stripe." After another deep draw, he pushed the cup aside. "Thanks for meeting with me. I'm not sure why I called you, but you're a good listener. And I wanted to update you and compare notes."

"Something's bothering you. What's wrong?"

"Might as well jump in headfirst. Sterling was stabbed in jail. He's in serious condition. May even be dead by now."

"Grant? Stabbed? By whom? How? Why?" Enid asked.

Drake glanced around McDonald's dining area. "Wonder what it's like to be normal? You know, like Josh is now."

Enid wasn't sure how to answer that. "You mean normal because he's not in law enforcement?"

Drake's head dropped slightly. "You know, I shouldn't be talking to you about all this. It's police stuff. But Josh has made it clear he's out of the business, and I can't blame him. And you and I compared notes once, and I'd like to do it again." Then added, "Off the record, of course."

Enid felt a familiar uneasiness. "Before we talk, may I ask you a question about Josh?"

"Me? You want to ask me about your husband?" Drake's familiar smile had returned. "Sure, mon. Go for it."

"Do you think Josh is really happy being out of police work?"

"Whoa! Now that's a loaded question. And why you ask me somethin' like dat?"

Enid couldn't help but smile when Drake slipped into his childhood accent. "I promise not to tell him what you say."

Drake took another long sip and appeared to be thinking deeply about her question. "That's hard to say. Sometimes, yes. But other times ...." He held out his hands, palms up, and shrugged. "But know this, pretty lady, he's head over heels in love with you. And that makes everything else okay with him. Get it?"

Enid didn't reply, but Drake's response confirmed her own impression. Josh was a lawman through and through. And he wasn't telling her about his worries. She took a deep breath. "So tell me more about Grant."

Drake filled her in on the few details he had. When he told her about Grant's reaction to the drawing and his "yes" finger response, she felt a chill spread throughout her body. "Is it possible the man who attacked Grant also killed Mara?"

"I dunno," Drake said. "I'll see if I can find out anything from the warden about this tattoo and any prisoners who might have it. But my informant said it was a group of people, so we're not dealing with one person."

"I have some updates too." She told Drake about her conversation with Monica from the Intellecta organization. "I think she knows something. Or maybe I'm reading too much into the conversation, but I think maybe she had more than a casual friendship with Grant. Maybe not recently, but when she lived here. She may be the affair Albright referenced."

Drake shook his head. "Dunno. But that affair allegation came from an anonymous tip, and I don't think it's been verified."

"But wasn't that one of the key allegations against Grant?"

"Grant doesn't have a good alibi. Claims he was out of town but no one can verify his story. I don't think he did it, but he could be hiding an affair."

"Monica also hinted about Grant's money troubles. What kind of financial advisor has money problems?"

Drake shrugged. "Perhaps the kind who get involved with a group of killers."

Enid sipped the last of her iced tea. "Look, Drake. I think you need to talk to Josh. It might be good for both of you. Anyway, I need to write this story on Mara. Silas has been good about letting me write all around it and collect color, but he's getting impatient."

"Color. What kind of color?"

Enid smiled. "That's what news people call background information, quotes, anecdotes, and things that add color to a news story, you know, to make it more interesting to readers."

"Ah, good to know," Drake said. "Color. I like that."

"Anyway, let me know as soon as you get some on-the-record information I can use."

As she stood to leave, Drake put his hand on her arm. "You be careful. I don't know what we're dealing with, and if you go poking too close, you might be in danger. Don't risk your life for a story."

CHAPTER 47

Josh packed his laptop and a few folders in his backpack and told the office manager he was going to work from home the rest of the day. When he pulled into their driveway, he was relieved to see Enid's car.

"Hi, it's me," he called out as he walked inside.

Enid met him in the hallway. "This is a nice surprise," she said, giving him a hug. "You finished for the day?"

"Still working," Josh said. "Remember when you offered to help me?"

"Sure. How can I help?"

"I'm hitting brick walls. Of course, I shouldn't be talking to you about a client, but –"

"This about Caleb?"

Josh nodded.

"You haven't liked him from the start, have you?"

Josh squared his shoulders. "I don't dislike him."

Enid laughed. "Yes, you do. What bothers you about him?"

"Let's go to the office and talk. It might help me to get my concerns off my chest."

Josh followed Enid down the hallway into the small bedroom that had two desks facing opposite walls. Josh's desk was all wood, as was his antique banker's chair. Enid used an off-white Ikea table with a rolling set of plastic drawers beneath it. This set-up was a far cry from the lavish office her ex-husband had designed for her in their Charlotte home not long before their divorce. But a fancy office couldn't make up for the problems in their marriage.

"Have you talked to Tiffany about your concerns?"

"Tried to, but they were together once, and I think she still has feelings for him."

"You mean, like *lovers* kind of together?"

Josh nodded. "Larkin says he knew she'd give the assignment to me to avoid the appearance of bias. And he wants me to dig deep."

"He told you that or you assumed that?"

"His message was clear."

"Caleb Thornhill sounds like an actor's name. Or a pseudonym of some kind. Do you have a place of birth or date of birth?"

"He said he was born in 1984."

"So he's around forty or so. Does he have a middle name?"

"If he does, I don't know it."

"That's odd, don't you think? That you wouldn't have that information?"

"I asked Tiffany, and she just shrugged. She just wants me to do a superficial background check and close this file as quickly as possible."

"How can I help?"

"Can you check the Intellecta records? See if Caleb is a member?"

Enid turned to look at Josh. "That's odd. Grant was a member of Intellecta. I just talked to someone there about him." She looked at the Intellecta website but member information was restricted. "I'll get our research assistant to do it on her own time. She loves to help solve a mystery, and I'll throw her a few dollars for extra help. She's one of those Gen Z types who thinks email belongs in the same museum with horses and buggies." Enid tapped the text on her phone.

"I was wondering, have you thought any more about Jack's offer?" Josh asked.

Enid rubbed her temples. "Even if I wanted to take the paper, I can't see how it would work. I sure don't want to work in Madden while we're here." She paused. "Unless you're considering the police chief job."

"Would you like for me to?"

She reached forward and took his hands in hers. "I admit there are times I miss our life in Madden. It felt like home. But the best solution is for Jack to find a reputable buyer." She released his hands. "Are you truly happy doing background checks on executives and politicians?"

Before he could answer, Enid's phone pinged. It was a reply from their research assistant:

CT was a past member of Intellecta. Left his chapter in NC years ago. My source says he left the organization with another man to form their own group. I don't have that name. Need anything else?

When Enid shared the text with Josh, he asked, "How do we know it's the same Caleb Thornhill?"

"How many geniuses with that name do you think are in the Carolinas?" Enid looked at the text reply again. "This story I'm doing on the Sterling murder case, is it a coincidence that the Cicada 3301's members were geniuses and that Drake said the cicada was a symbol used by a group of people called Umbra who were intent on revenge?"

Josh ran his hand through his hair. "I have no idea where you're going with all this."

Enid shook her head. "Neither do I."

"Are you suggesting my target Caleb Thornhill is involved in your subject's murder?"

"You don't like him, and your instincts are usually spot on."

Josh laughed. "Maybe I'm just envious of him. But even if Caleb was part of your secret group, why would he put himself in the limelight for scrutiny? Surely he knew any involvement would come out."

Enid made some notes on a legal pad. "Agreed." She sat up straight and turned to Josh. "Why not just ask Caleb about it?"

CHAPTER 48

The next day, Josh sat at his downtown office desk, thinking about his conversation with Enid. Surely there was no connection between Mara Sterling's murder and his target, Caleb Thornhill.

Confronting Caleb was something he'd do without hesitation as a law officer. But this work had its own set of norms and rules. And confronting someone with that kind of accusation could get him thrown out of the firm. Some days, that prospect seemed attractive. But he was making good money, had good benefits, and most of the time he convinced himself his work made a contribution to society by potentially uncovering information that could harm the community. On those lofty days, he could force himself to conform and be the kind of employee Tiffany expected. On other days, like today, he felt helpless, trapped by rules he didn't understand—or like.

Tiffany had asked Josh to come to her office, and he knew she was impatiently waiting. He glanced at the time on his phone and gathered his notepad, the folder on Caleb, and a pen before dashing down the hall to her office.

The door was open and she motioned him inside. "Thought you were going to stand me up," she said.

"Sorry, I let the time slip by." He sat down and pulled his chair up closer to her desk. "You wanted an update on Caleb."

"We need to wrap this up. It's gone on too long. Had I known …" She glanced out the window and then back at Josh. "This work is not the same as law enforcement. I admire your tenacity in doing these background searches. And I have no problem telling our clients we've done a *thorough* job." She laughed, tossing her hair over her shoulder. "But unless you have something on Caleb we need to discuss, I'm going to tell our client he's good to go."

Irritated at being dressed down, Josh doodled on his pad to steady himself. "Our client seems wary of Caleb also."

"And your point?" The edge in Tiffany's voice was unmistakable as she drummed her nails on the desk.

"My point is that I asked our own client about Caleb, and he wasn't able to give me much information."

Tiffany frowned. "Well, that's not unusual. That's why people hire us."

"Of course it is, but in this case, our client has concerns and can't find anything, not on their own and not from us. That's a big red flag in my book." He hesitated but then decided he might as well go for it. "I need to know how deep your bias toward Caleb runs."

Tiffany's reaction wasn't what Josh expected. Instead of being angry, she laughed as though she had heard the funniest joke ever.

"May I ask what's so funny?" When she didn't respond, Josh added, "Do you think it's funny that I questioned Caleb's background or is it because I questioned your integrity?"

Tiffany took a tissue from her desk drawer and dabbed it under her eyes. "Probably more of the latter. And I'm not surprised Larkin is in the dark." She threw the tissue into a small trash can under her desk.

Now that she was talking, Josh decided to just let it play out. He studied her face as he would any other suspect's body language and expressions.

"Caleb and I were a brief, uneventful item a few years ago. It began after a political meeting at a hotel and too many glasses of wine." She paused momentarily, as if recalling every detail. "Caleb is a handsome, wealthy man. What's not to be attracted to? But he's emotionally unavailable, as they say. No compassion."

"Are you saying he's evil?" Josh asked.

"No, not at all. Just saying that he wasn't a great lover. Too fixated on the mechanics and not the emotion."

"Is that why he's still single?"

Tiffany didn't respond immediately, instead rubbing her temples. "He said that growing up, he never learned to show emotions. But then he stressed that he did care about me, about others in his life. We just agreed to be friends and let it go at that." She put her palms on her desk, spreading her fingers. "So that's it. I can't tell you what I don't know." She smiled. "In fact, I was hoping you'd uncover something at least interesting. You see, he's an enigma to me as well."

"I'd like to do that, dig deeper. But I can't do it if you don't give me time."

"Another couple of days. That's it," Tiffany said as she glanced at the time. "I have another meeting in a few minutes."

"Just one last question," Josh said. "Who is Howard Whitaker?"

Tiffany's shoulder slumped slightly. "Where did you get that name?" And then she held up her palms toward Josh. "Never mind. He's Caleb's half-brother. They've been estranged for years, according to Caleb."

Josh tried to contain his frustration. "Why isn't that in the file? It would be helpful to talk to Whitaker, even if he only gives us sibling rivalry tales."

"Howard disappeared many years ago, according to Caleb. No one knows where he is. Besides, he has nothing to do with Caleb. I'm sure of it."

Josh stood to leave. "Maybe not, but I'd like to talk to him."

CHAPTER 49

"Can you come to Madden?" Rachel's voice led Enid to believe her request was about more than just relaying information from her research.

"Is everything okay there?" Enid was afraid it was about Jack and had been mentally preparing herself for such a call.

"He's about the same, although he's going to Duke Cancer Center to participate in some experimental treatment."

"I can be there in a couple hours. There're a few things here I need to wrap up. That work?"

"Sure. I'm not trying to be mysterious, but I don't want to talk about this over the phone," Rachel said.

Enid knew that one of the pitfalls of the kind of white-hat hacking Rachel did was that you became paranoid, convinced that nothing was truly private. "Where should I meet you?"

"Jack's at home, so let's meet at the newspaper office." Enid tried not to read too much into Rachel's request and pushed it out of her mind so she could finish an article she was writing on a series of local parking lot muggings. The world was becoming more dangerous every day.

...

"Hi, Vivian. It is Vivian, right?" Enid asked when he saw the woman sitting at the front desk of the *Tri-County Gazette*.

The woman's face lit up, looking pleased that Enid remembered. "Yes, that's right. How are you, Ms. Blackwell?"

"Good thanks, I'm supposed to—"

"Sorry to interrupt, but Rachel is in Jack's office. We were expecting you." Then she added in a more subdued tone. "He's not coming in today."

"Thanks." Enid walked down the hallway, pushing aside memories of working with Jack. His office door was open and Rachel was sitting across from the empty desk chair.

"I'll sit here. You can sit in Jack's chair."

Enid smiled at Rachel's obvious ploy but didn't say anything. "I hope you haven't been waiting long."

"Just got here. Thanks for coming. We can go to lunch afterwards, if you like. Sarah's Tea Shoppe has added some yummy menu items."

"Is Theo still cooking soup for them?"

"Yes! His soups are to die for."

"Lunch would be nice." Enid settled back into Jack's chair. "I'm anxious to know what you found out."

"Well, one thing I've learned from you about journalism is not to bury the lede. So I'll jump right in. Howard Whitaker is not a good guy. And before I say more, it goes without saying you *cannot* tell anyone where you got this information. It was sealed years ago."

"Sealed? Why?"

"Whitaker went into WITSEC, the witness protection program, about ten years ago."

"Do you know why?" Enid asked.

Rachel nodded. "Apparently he started a group whose purpose was to get even."

"Get even? You mean like revenge?"

Rachel nodded.

"Revenge for what?"

"I didn't get specifics, but the case he testified in was something about running drugs across state lines."

"And does anyone know where he is now? Enid asked.

"As you know, the files are sealed. WITSEC works hard to protect the whereabouts and new identities of their subjects." Rachel sighed. "But it doesn't matter. He took off one day, didn't tell his case manager where he was, and hasn't been heard from since. That was about a year ago. Apparently, he went underground, hiding who knows where. But," she added, "he has a relative whose name is …" She did a mock drum roll on the desk. "Caleb Thornhill, the other person you asked me about."

"Caleb is related to Howard?"

"Half-brothers, from what I could tell."

Enid leaned back in Jack's chair. It was a wooden banker style chair like Josh's and squeaked every time she moved. "Interesting. The target of Josh's investigation is related to a person who was in witness protection but disappeared. Did you find out anything else about Caleb?"

Rachel shook her head. "His name is in Howard Whitaker's file but that's it. He has no history, no background. It's like he just appeared about ten years ago. Poof." She waved her hands in the air for emphasis.

"That's about the same time Whitaker went into WITSEC. Do you think Caleb's identity is fake? Is that what you're saying?"

Rachel shrugged. "Dunno. But Caleb doesn't have a police record anywhere that I could find. In fact, he's too clean." She leaned over to the shredder behind Jack's desk and put her notes in the slot. "There. No trace of this conversation. You ready for that lunch now?"

. . .

The first thing Enid noticed when they walked into Sarah's Tea Shoppe is that very little had changed. She was looking around, taking it all in, when she heard, "Ms. Enid," how are you?" That came from Sarah, the owner. "We've missed you. Are you back in Madden now?"

They exchanged hugs. "No," Enid said. "Just visiting with Rachel."

"Well, lunch is on me—for both of you. So happy to have you here, even if only for a visit."

Enid and Rachel sat at one of the tables against the wall, and it wasn't long before Sarah reappeared. "Today's menu is on the chalkboard." She pointed to the wall. "Just tell me what you want."

After placing their order, Enid unfolded the white linen napkin on the table. "Hardly ever see these anymore in a restaurant," Enid said. "I still use them for special meals."

"No, that's for sure. I can't imagine myself washing and ironing those things," Rachel said. "But it is nice."

Enid noticed the light had gone from Rachel's eyes, and her brow was furrowed. "How is Jack, really?"

Rachel shrugged. "Okay, I mean all things considered. We're hopeful this new experimental drug will work." Her voice trailed off. "If not, I guess we just enjoy him while we can." She shook herself, as if to cast off those thoughts. "I promised myself I wouldn't get sad." She forced a faint smile. "How are you, that is other than being busy chasing bad guys? Sometimes it's hard to remember you're a reporter, not a cop."

Enid laughed. "Sounds like something Jack would say. I'm fine. I appreciate the information you gave me, and if you find out anything else on Caleb Thornhill, it will sure help Josh. He feels like he's chasing an enigma."

Rachel dumped a packet of artificial sweetener in her tea glass. "I know this stuff is poison, but I can't drink straight tea." She stirred the glass vigorously. "Josh is in a totally different line of work. How's that's working out?"

"Everyone keeps asking me if he's happy. I think we're both struggling a bit to figure out what our new life is. It'll just take some time."

"You know, Madden is looking for a police chief. I heard they were going to ask Josh."

Enid smiled. "Pete's already been in touch."

"See, if Josh took that job and you took the paper, then you'd both be doing what you love."

Enid placed her hand on Rachel's. "I love the paper, but not running it. I covered for Jack once before, and honestly, I hated it."

"But what if you hired someone to manage it and you just edited and wrote?"

Enid didn't want to encourage Rachel's fantasies by admitting that she had already considered that option. But was that what she really wanted? "Josh was police chief here years ago. It might seem like a step backward to come back."

"But Madden isn't the same as it was then. It's bigger, got more people, and more crime, for sure."

"That's what Jack said. "But I'm sure if Josh is interested, he'll tell me."

CHAPTER 50

On the drive home, Enid couldn't shake the feeling of dread that had overcome her. Probably all the talk of Jack's cancer and Josh's future was making her uneasy. She glanced down at the instrument panel and realized she needed to get gas.

At the next exit, she pulled off the highway and into a service station that sold a gas brand she had never heard of. She decided to get just enough to get her back to Columbia.

There were four gas pumps, and she was the only customer. Maybe for a good reason. She got out and unscrewed the gas tank cover, and when she turned to reach for the pump, she saw two pickup trucks pull into the station. One pulled to the side of the building and the driver appeared to be going inside. The other driver parked away from the pumps and got out to walk toward her. He looked agitated. Was this some kind of road rage? While she was lost in thought, had she cut someone off? She didn't recall seeing this pickup at all. But then she had been thinking about other things at the time.

She hastily tried to put the pump back in place, while keeping an eye on the man approaching her. Suddenly, someone grabbed her from behind. She couldn't see him but could tell he was tall and strong. He had an arm around her neck, and she was unable to get free. "Let me go," she managed to say. She glanced toward the service station but no one was coming to her aid.

Her attacker held her tight while the man from the truck approached. He put his finger in her face. "I hear you've been asking too many nosy questions. You let us take care of Grant Sterling, and we'll leave you alone. But if you keep meddling in what's none of your business, Miss Reporter Lady, someone will be reporting on you." He spit on her face. "Got it?"

"Why?" she asked.

The man in front of her threw back his head and laughed. "Why, she asks." He leaned in close, put his mouth to her ear, and whispered. "Because I *said so.*"

Enid studied the man's face. He had on Ray-Ban sunglasses and a knit hat pulled down so that she couldn't see his hair color. A few brown and gray strands peeked from the back of his cap. His face was smooth, the face of a man who took care of himself. But not that young.

Suddenly, the man holding her pushed her against the car. "Go home. Have some babies, and if you file another story on Sterling, I'll be back. Capisce?"

Enid filed that info away in her memory also. He was educated enough to know at least one Italian word. The man leaned against her with his face close to hers. "Get outta here. You've been duly warned."

The men drove off before Enid could crank her car with trembling hands. She chided herself for not getting a license plate number for either vehicle. Instead of heading left toward the interstate, both vehicles turned right, down the two-lane road that was devoid of traffic.

After taking deep breaths for a few minutes, she was able to calm herself down. She had not been injured, only threatened. Their message to her was clear, but what wasn't clear was why. What had she stumbled onto that had them rattled?

Her last published article was about the emergence of cicada broods in South Carolina. Silas had wanted it to lay some background for when they were able to report on Cassandra's vision. The article didn't make any mention of Grant Sterling or Mara's murder, but the Cicada story must have triggered their reaction.

Her cell phone rang, giving her a jolt. Audrey Sterling's name appeared on her screen. When she answered, Audrey began speaking before Enid could say anything. "Enid, this is Audrey. You've got to drop this story about Grant. I don't know why but ..."

Enid could hear her sobbing. "What's happened? Did someone threaten you?"

"I can't talk now. Just promise me you'll drop this story." The call ended.

Puzzlement had now replaced Enid's fear, and her hands had finally quit trembling. What was going on? First the two thugs had told her to back off, and then Audrey. That could only mean one thing: she was hitting close to home—even if she didn't understand how.

CHAPTER 51

Drake was working on a report for an assault on a homeless man on Main Street when his phone rang. A distinctly Southern female voice said, "Is this Detective Drake Harrow?" The way she said "DEE-tech-tiv" made him smile.

"Yes, ma'am, I'm Investigator Harrow. How can I help you?"

"I have a message for you from Mr. Sterling, one of my patients."

"Grant Sterling? Are you at the hospital?"

There was a long pause before she replied. "I shouldn't be involved in something like this, but he made me promise to call you. The deputy stationed outside the room gave me your number."

"I understand and appreciate your help. What is the message?"

"I should tell you Mr. Sterling passed earlier today. It was so odd. He seemed like he might recover, and then ... but I shouldn't be telling you all this."

"I'm sorry to hear about his passing. Go on, please."

"It was the oddest message. He was only barely conscious so he just gave me a few words before he said, 'tell Drake Harrow, with police.'"

Drake was getting impatient. "Ma'am, what was the message?"

"He said something that sounded like umbrella emerged. I assumed you'd know what that means."

"Are you sure he said umbrella?"

"I can't be sure. Like I said, he was barely able to talk."

"But you're sure he said 'emerged'?"

"Yes, at least I think so. I told him he needed to rest, so I didn't quiz him too much. He seemed to be a nice man. You hate to lose any patient, but especially the kind ones."

"What made you think he was kind? I'm just curious since he couldn't carry on a full conversation."

"His eyes. You know they say the eyes are the mirror to the soul. He had kind eyes. I could tell even though he was teared up most of the time."

"Did he seem afraid to you?"

"Afraid? I'm not sure. I just thought he was in pain." She lowered her voice. "I hear he was accused of murdering his wife. There's no way. I can read people, and that man was no murderer. I've got to go now. Tell his family I'm sorry for their loss."

After the call ended, Drake sat staring at the notes he had taken. Umbrella? Emerged? What was Sterling trying to tell him? Was it related to the group of men Travis had mentioned? Umbra. That's what it was! Umbra, not umbrella. And then he remembered Enid's story about the cicada emergence in South Carolina this year. Coincidence? He didn't believe in them.

He pulled up the *Palmetto Post* website and there was the article under local news. He skimmed it quickly to refresh his memory. Apparently, South Carolina was one of several states that would experience a rare phenomenon this year with the emergence of two broods, broods thirteen and fourteen. The last time the two broods had emerged together was in 1803, when Thomas Jefferson was president.

Was that what Sterling's message was about? Umbra? Was he trying to tell them Umbra had emerged? And if so, what could that mean?

He was jolted from his thoughts by another phone call, but this one was on his private cell phone. "Enid, what's up?"

"We've got to talk," she said. "I'm headed into Columbia and will be there in about twenty minutes."

. . .

Enid left a message for Josh. "Can you meet with me and Drake at McDonald's? We need to compare notes."

When Enid walked into McDonald's, she was surprised that Josh was already there. She went to his booth and leaned in to give him a kiss. "Thanks for coming."

"I've learned that tone of voice before, and you only use it when you're scared or pissed off. I don't think I did anything, so what's going on?" Josh asked

"Am I that transparent? Anyway, I'm not mad. Well, maybe I am, but not at you. And I was scared, but I'm okay now." When she saw the inevitable questions coming, she held up her hand. "Let me get something to drink first, and then Drake should be here. I want you both to hear this." She left Josh looking puzzled while she went to the counter to order.

When Enid returned to the table, Drake had arrived. Enid waited a few moments while they were talking. "Uh, excuse me? I think I called this meeting."

"Sorry, it's just that Josh's me mon, and I don't get to see him much," Drake said. "You sounded upset when you called. What happened?"

Enid was glad she was sitting across from Drake instead of Josh. She didn't want to see Josh's face when she told them about the encounter at the gas station.

When she told them about the threats from the men in the pickups and about Audrey's call to her, Josh turned around as far as he could in the tight quarters of the booth. "I can't believe you've gotten yourself into another dangerous situation. Is it just in your DNA to be reckless?"

Josh said to Drake. "Sorry to drag you into an *ongoing* conversation between us." He nearly spat it out.

"I understand," Drake said, looking directly at Josh. "You worry about your wife, and you should." Then he looked at Enid. "But she's a professional. She has to do her job, just like I have to."

"Thank you, Drake," Enid said. "There's more I need to tell you. I had Rachel do some covert checking on Howard Whitaker, the man named in the article Josh was given."

Under the table, Josh put his hand on her thigh and patted it. Enid knew it was a small gesture of apology. "And what did you find out?" Josh asked.

"Howard Whitaker and Caleb Thornhill are half-brothers."

"I just found that out from Tiffany earlier today,' Josh said. "Go on."

"Howard was in WITSEC for a while but then disappeared," Enid said.

Drake's left eyebrow shot up. "Witness protection? Why?"

"That I don't know."

Josh pulled a pen from his pocket, a holdover habit from his law enforcement days, and began scribbling notes.

"And I need to tell you something," Drake said to Enid. "Sterling is dead. Died early this morning. But here's the interesting part. One of his nurses delivered a message he gave her right before he died."

Enid's hand flew to her mouth. "Oh, no. Poor Audrey and Zoe."

Drake nodded and continued, "Sterling told her to tell me that umbrella emerged. But I think he was saying Umbra."

"What is that?" Josh asked.

"Travis told me that a man who went by Orion formed his own group of geniuses who called themselves Umbra. I think that's what Grant's message was referring to."

"Umbra is the darkest side of the moon or a shadow," Enid added.

"That's right," Drake said. "My informant told me about the group, said they were a bad lot." He cleared his throat. "That was right before he was killed."

Josh turned toward Enid again. "You are *off* this story. Now."

Enid knew this would be a much longer discussion when she and Josh were alone. "We can talk later."

Drake leaned back in his seat. "I think it's time for me to talk to Caleb Thornhill about his brother."

CHAPTER 52

What Josh really wanted to do was to follow Enid home, grab her, and hold her tight to protect her until she agreed to drop the story on Mara Sterling's murder. But that could wait until tonight. Besides, he needed time to think. What right did he have to demand that she refuse a story?

But now Josh needed to talk to Tiffany. It suddenly occurred to him that while he was worried about getting Enid fired from her job, he might very well get himself fired. Why wasn't life simple any longer? All he wanted was for him and Enid to be happy, to live in a place where they could put down roots and call it home. And for both of them to do work that fulfilled them. Of course, that's what most people wanted. He and Enid were not unique, but most people's professions didn't put them in these kinds of situations.

On one hand, he admired Enid's dogged pursuit of the truth. Without reporters willing to take those risks, where would the world be? But this was his wife, the love of his life, and he couldn't take comfort in lofty ideals. Enid had been threatened. And it terrified him.

Pushing those thoughts aside momentarily, Josh realized he had not considered how to approach Tiffany. When he called and demanded to meet with her immediately, she sounded annoyed. She was the boss, after all. But he needed to have a showdown conversation with her about Caleb. Years of law enforcement and undercover work had honed his instincts. But he had gotten rusty and missed the signs along the way. How much did Tiffany know about Caleb and Howard?

By the time he pulled into his reserved parking spot, he had calmed down slightly. Nothing good would come from storming into Tiffany's office demanding answers. Taking the stairs instead of the elevator would at least give him a few more minutes to compose himself. *Take a deep breath.*

When Josh opened the door onto their floor, Tiffany was talking to a man in the hallway by the elevator. Josh knew he was either a client or a prospective one because Tiffany behaved differently when interacting with people who were paying the firm.

While it was a different kind of admiration than he felt for Enid, Josh respected Tiffany's single-minded pursuit of the firm's success. She had boundaries as to how far she would go to keep a client, but he had seen her turn away only a handful of people since working with her. And most of those were the ones who couldn't pay the firm's hefty fees.

When the man Tiffany had been talking to got into the elevator, she turned to Josh. "Well, well. You sounded a tad upset." She motioned with her hand. "Come on into my office and let's talk about what's bugging you. I've got a client meeting soon, so we need to get to it."

Settled in the chair across from Tiffany's desk, Josh began. "We need to talk about Caleb."

A scowl spread across Tiffany's face. "So it's Caleb again. Why do you dislike him so much?"

Without considering the consequences of his reply, Josh said, "Why do you like him so much? So much that you're willing to risk the firm's reputation on defending him?"

Tiffany put both palms on her desk. "Whoa. That was pretty cold." She paused briefly. "I'll answer that question but first tell me what prompted your demanding to meet with me immediately? Something must have set you off."

Not wanting to jeopardize Drake's investigation, Josh weighed how much he should tell her. "I've come across some information about his half-brother, Howard."

"But we're not doing a file on Caleb's brother."

"Pardon me for being blunt, but you're dodging the question. How much do you know about Whitaker?"

Tiffany let out a big sigh. "I know Howard got involved with some kind of weird group and disappeared." She shrugged. "But Howard is not our target," she repeated.

Losing his patience, Josh raised his voice. "You told me to *always* look at the family of our targets." He pointed his finger. "*You* said that." He stopped and took a deep breath. "Sorry for the outburst, but I'm losing my patience with all of this." He waved his arms around the office, as if "this" was a lot more inclusive than just Caleb. Was that how Josh felt?

Tiffany sighed. "No apology needed. I don't know much about Howard's case, and Caleb told me Howard had moved away and they had lost contact."

"And have you ever heard of Umbra?"

"Who?" Tiffany asked.

"Not who. What. It's a group."

"Can't say that I have."

Josh couldn't tell if Tiffany was being truthful, and that annoyed him about himself, about his fading instincts. "It seems that Howard probably started the group he testified against."

"Well, that sounds somewhat mysterious, but unless you know Caleb himself is involved in something illegal, or that appears illegal, then I don't think that negatively impacts his report. Do you?"

"I want to confront Caleb about this."

Tiffany put her fingertips together, tapping them several times. "I see. Well, I'm happy to set something up for all of us to meet."

"I want to meet with him alone," Josh said.

Tiffany leaned forward. "Do you not trust me?"

"I have information that I can't share with you. Not yet."

"But you're going to share it with our target." It was an accusation, not a question. "And what do I tell our client? That Caleb shouldn't get the PAC's support because my employee says Caleb's brother once got involved in something that we don't know much about?"

Josh didn't want to tell her that their client, Bob Larkin, was the one who tipped him off to Howard Whitaker. "I don't think it's wise to talk to our client just yet. I need more information from Caleb first."

Tiffany slapped her palms down on the desk again. "Fine. Do what you have to, but I want this file closed and your report on my desk by the end of the week. Is that clear?" She seemed to be waiting for Josh to react. "And then we can talk about whether your lack of trust in your boss is a barrier to our working together." She glanced at the Apple watch on her wrist. "I've got to get ready for this meeting."

CHAPTER 53

The clock was ticking on the deadline for the report, but Josh's instincts told him to wait until tomorrow to contact Caleb. Everything Josh learned today had his nerves on edge, and he needed to have a clear head when he talked with Caleb.

The weather had turned cool, so sitting outside to talk with Enid wasn't an option. Besides, the piles of leaves scattered around the yard reminded him he had not helped around the house very much since they moved in, and he felt guilty.

Much to his surprise, Enid was not at her desk working when he got home. That was unusual. He looked in the kitchen and in their bedroom. With panic setting in, he called out, "Enid, where are you? Enid?"

Finally, he glanced out the kitchen window, still dirty with a film of tree pollen, and mentally added cleaning the windows to his growing list of household chores. He exhaled a loud sigh of relief when he saw Enid outside talking with their neighbor Sophie. They were laughing and both were smiling.

He knew Enid missed being anywhere long enough to make friends again. A pang of guilt stabbed at him, until he reminded himself that taking the job with Tiffany was his attempt at putting stability back in their lives. Had he crossed the line in his meeting with her today? If so, he'd soon be looking for a job. With her extensive contacts and connections, she could blackball him, making it impossible for him to find a job in Columbia. How could he ask Enid to move again?

When Enid walked in the back door and into the kitchen, Josh was still staring out the window, lost in thought.

"You're home early. Everything okay?" she asked.

He nodded. "How's Sophie?"

"She's fine. Still can't find the right job here."

"Want a glass of wine?" Josh asked.

"Does that mean you want to talk?"

Laughing, Josh replied, "Oh, no. Don't tell me I've ruined the thought of having a glass of wine. Do I always put the two together, wine and serious talk?"

"Quite often. But I'd love a glass. We can sit in the living room. Too breezy outside."

"I agree. You get some cheese and crackers, and I'll pick a good bottle. Red good tonight?" Josh asked.

"I noticed a bottle of pinot noir in the pantry that someone gave us. Want to try that?"

"Sounds good."

A few minutes later, when they were settled on the sofa, Josh poured them each a glass and then proposed a toast. "To fulfillment."

"That's an odd toast."

"It's been an odd day." Josh filled her in on his meeting with Tiffany, unsure how Enid would react when he told her he may have gone too far and put his job in jeopardy."

"Well, that's good news."

Josh thought perhaps she had misunderstood him. "How is putting my job on the line and dressing down my boss good news?"

"Well, we've still got boxes to unpack, and if you lose your job, there's no point."

Josh processed her comments briefly before responding. "Are you saying I can't find another job in Columbia?"

Enid brushed a cracker crumb from her mouth. "Would you want to?"

This conversation wasn't the one he had in mind. "I can't answer that. Not yet. And I'm not sure what the answer is. Or should be. So can we hold that thought until later? I may be overreacting to Tiffany. She can be a bit overbearing at times, but she seems to be fair." He took another sip of wine. "And I told her I was going to confront Caleb about Howard."

"What are you going to say to Caleb?"

"I want to know more about this group, Umbra. And if and how Caleb is involved with it and with Howard. Tiffany says they're estranged, but I want to hear what Caleb has to say. Drake is talking to him from a legal standpoint, but I want to find out more about Caleb the man."

Enid tucked her legs beneath her as she repositioned herself on the sofa. "Is it possible Caleb had something to do with Mara Sterling's murder?"

Josh exhaled deeply and leaned his head back against the sofa. "That's the big question, isn't it? But surely if he was involved, he wouldn't be seeking such a public profile. Running for a political office exposes you, eviscerates your private life. Why would he put himself in such a vulnerable position?"

"Does he have a cicada tattoo?"

"Well, I can't very well ask him to open his shirt when we talk. That would be inappropriate at the very least. But I can ask him what he knows about the group his brother formed and their tattoo symbol. And if knows anything about whether the timing of the emergence of Umbra is in some obscure way related to the historical cicada emergence we're about to experience here. Perhaps, like Sterling's message to me, Umbra the group is active again. And tying their rebirth to that of the actual cicadas may be a symbolic act. Of course, Caleb may, as Tiffany said, know nothing about Umbra or Howard's activities."

"But you don't believe that, do you?" Before Josh could answer, Enid's phone rang and she glanced at the screen. "It's Silas, my editor. Mind if I answer this?"

Josh motioned for her to take the call, and he got up and went to the kitchen. He heard Enid say emphatically "no" to Silas. Josh wanted to stay and listen but respected her privacy and busied himself straightening up.

A few minutes later, Enid joined him. "What happens if we both lose our jobs?"

"What happened?" Josh asked. "Want to talk about it?"

"Not much to say really. Silas is understandably impatient about the Mara Sterling article and wants me to run a story about Cassandra's vision. Of course, I said no."

"What will you do? Do you really think he'll fire you?"

"I need to warn Cassandra. It won't be hard to find her, so if I don't do the story, he'll get someone who will."

CHAPTER 54

The next morning, Enid planned to contact Cassandra, and Josh was going to confront Caleb. It should be an interesting day. Josh decided to set up a folding table in the living room to work from so he wouldn't bother Enid in their small, shared office.

Enid looked around the room, surveying the few items of furniture. Somewhere along their last couple of moves they had sold or given away most of their things and become nomads, wanderers in search of purpose and stability.

She sat at her computer, trying to figure out how to write a story that would satisfy Silas yet not betray Cassandra or Drake. She had promised Cassandra not to do a story until the man with the cicada tattoo who had brutally murdered Mara Sterling had been caught. But what if the vision was only symbolic, as Cassandra said some visions were. If that was the case, why had Drake uncovered the group with the same symbol?

Her head was aching and her fingers hovered above the keyboard, paralyzed not by a lack of words, but by the weight of them. Each keystroke felt like a deliberate choice, a conscious acknowledgment. Journalism was not just her job; it was her creed. *The truth, always,* she whispered to herself, a mantra that had guided every story. Today it echoed in her mind, a hollow ring.

She leaned back, closing her eyes, listening to the hum of a lawnmower in a nearby yard. Otherwise, the morning was unusually quiet, as if time were standing still, waiting for her to take action. The article she was hired to write gnawed at her conscience. It would be a lucrative scoop for the *Palmetto Post* and would undoubtedly propel her career forward. But at what cost?

Enid thought of Josh's easy smile, his unwavering support through all they had encountered together. He loved her, not just for her successes but for her relentless pursuit of what was right. As a former lawman, he was driven by the same principles, even as he had left that career behind.

And she thought of Cade, her ex-husband. She admired Cade's ability to maneuver through the corporate entanglements of the news world. He had once expressed concern that the major newspapers were no longer owned by news professionals but by big business and investors. Yet, he had managed to maintain his integrity and rise to the top of his profession. He could play the game; she obviously could not. Or didn't want to.

With sudden clarity, she realized the truth she sought in her work was no different from the truth she needed in her life: unvarnished and unyielding.

So she began to type, not the article she was supposed to write, but a resignation letter. Perhaps it was time to find her truth elsewhere, beyond the headlines and the bylines. In her heart, she knew the stories she needed to chase were not just out there in the world, but also within herself, waiting to be acknowledged and shared.

When her cell phone rang, Enid was startled out of her deep thoughts and yanked back into the stark reality of what she was doing. She assumed the call was from Silas, as their last conversation had been disturbing for both of them.

But the screen showed an unknown number. When she answered the woman said, "Enid Blackwell? This is Olivia."

For a moment, Enid was confused, as the name didn't register. "Olivia?"

"Grant Sterling's executive assistant, former assistant that is."

"Oh, yes, we talked at your office. I'm sorry, how can I help you?"

"Can we meet somewhere. Not at the office."

"Of course. Would you like to meet at the newspaper office?"

"Oh, goodness no. Definitely not. There's a Drip coffee shop in Five Points, near uptown Columbia." They agreed to meet in an hour.

. . .

"Thanks for meeting with me," Olivia said. "I hope this wasn't too out of the way for you."

"It's not far from my house, actually," Enid said.

"I'm sure you were surprised to hear from me. I was still shaken up about all that's happened when you came to the office asking about Mr. Grant's business."

"I understood that you were just trying to make sense of a senseless situation. And I'm sure the police were grilling you also."

Olivia nodded. "I didn't lie to you, or to the police, but there's more that I need to tell you."

"Do you want me to report on whatever you're going to tell me?"

"Oh, goodness no. I just ... I don't want Grant's legacy to be tarnished, for Zoe's sake."

Enid felt a sense of dread coming on. More critical information she couldn't report on. When we met earlier, you said some of his clients had lost millions in bad investments. Did any of them threaten him as a result?"

Olivia looked around the room, twirling a paper napkin between her fingers. "Yes. That's why I didn't say more."

"What's changed now?"

"I can't sleep. And I can't stay in this place, I mean Columbia, any longer. Too many bad memories here." She paused to take a deep breath. "Grant got connected with a man with political ambitions. I think Grant knew him through a group for highly intelligent men. It's like Mensa."

"Was the group Intellecta?" Enid asked.

"Yes. Are you familiar with it?"

"I just recently learned of it. Go on."

"Well, Grant and this man had met years ago and they hit it off."

"Was he one of Grant's financial clients?"

"Yes, for years. It was a mutually beneficial relationship. Grant got numerous referrals from him, and in turn, made him a lot of money. The man was thinking of running for some kind of state office and was building his wealth, you know, to build his reputation."

Enid felt her chest tighten. *Don't jump to conclusions. Columbia is the state capital, so there are politicians and wanna-bes everywhere here.* "Can you give me the man's name?"

Olivia stared at Enid for a moment, as if she wasn't sure what to do. "Caleb Thornhill."

Enid gripped her hands together under the table. "Do you suspect Thornhill had something to do with Mara's murder?"

"No." She paused. "And yes. You see, Mr. Thornhill introduced Grant to a group of investors, and ..." Olivia's voice cracked. "They were his downfall. Nothing good happened after he got involved with him."

Enid thought of Drake. "You've got to go to the police."

Olivia shook her head. "No, I can't. You see, they ... when they broke into Grant's office and stole records that tied the group to Grant, they threatened to come back and kill me if I told the police. That's why I'm leaving town." She cleared her throat. "But I had to tell someone. Maybe you can give the police this information from an anonymous source."

"Tell me all you know and I'll see what I can do. I won't disclose you as a source, but they may not take me seriously without proof."

Olivia slipped her hand into the pocket of her cashmere cardigan and pulled out a small object that looked like a unicorn. "This is the only thumb drive I had with me. It belongs to my granddaughter, so there're a few children's stories on it I wrote for her. You can just erase those. I have copies." She handed the thumb drive to Enid. "They didn't take everything when they broke in."

Enid put the drive in her purse. "Does the name Umbra mean anything to you?"

Olivia's eyes widened. "Yes, of course. That's the group that Grant got involved with. And I believe they killed Mara—and him.

CHAPTER 55

While Enid was out of the house, Josh sat at his makeshift desk in the living room and tried to contact Caleb Thornhill. He left messages at his office number and on his mobile number. Josh had decided to be honest with Caleb about his background check and tell him he had found the connection to Howard Whitaker, Caleb's half-brother.

While Josh was looking back through his notes on Caleb, his cell rang. Bob Larkin's name appeared on the screen.

"Josh, I just wanted you to know I've asked Tiffany to close the background check on Caleb and send me the bill for what we owe the firm."

"Is there something wrong with the work we've done?" Josh asked.

"Goodness, no. Sorry I didn't explain myself better. Caleb called me yesterday and told me he wants to drop his political ambitions."

"Did he explain why?"

"Just that he's changed his mind. He apologized for the inconvenience, time, and effort he cost everyone but asked us to 'drop it.' Those were his words, 'just drop it.'"

Josh's mind was reeling, full of questions. "Have you ever had that happen? I mean a candidate just tell you to drop it?"

"It's not that uncommon. Once people realize the scrutiny they're under, they often decide it's not worth the exposure and hassle for their family. Some would rather drop out than to see themselves as the headline of an embarrassing news article."

"By the way, a lot has been going on, and I didn't get back to you on that article you gave me to check out," Josh said. "Howard Whitaker is Caleb's half-brother, and it appears Howard may have been involved in illegal activities."

"Interesting. Perhaps that's what prompted Caleb to drop out."

"Just so you'll know, Caleb is already on the county law enforcement radar, so they'll likely bring him in for questioning," Josh said.

"Well, good luck with that. Caleb told me he's going away for some R&R up in the Blue Ridge Mountains. Says he rented a cabin near a trout stream, off the grid, so no need to try to reach him."

Josh didn't take Caleb for the outdoors type. "You have no way of contacting him?"

"Nada, nothing."

"I need to tell the investigator on Mara Sterling's case." Josh immediately regretted saying anything.

"Why, is Caleb involved in a murder investigation?"

"Let's just say his name has been coming up in various ways."

"Well, I'm happy to cooperate with the authorities, but I don't know anything other than what I've told you." He paused for a moment. "I got the impression from Tiffany that things may not be working out for you there."

Josh felt like he'd been punched in the stomach and was unsure how to respond. "We're working it out."

"Well, I've still got connections with SLED and other law enforcement agencies in the state, if you're interested."

Another brief silence. "You're a lawman, Josh. You can't wash it off like mud. It's part of your DNA."

"So what are you saying, that I should quit and go back to being a cop?"

"I'm saying that I've made mistakes, many of them, and I'm blessed to have reached a point in my life where only one thing matters. Know what that is?"

"Happiness, I suppose."

"Close. But it's contentment."

"What's the difference?" Josh asked

"Think of it like this. Happiness is like those bright, sunny days we chase after in the middle of winter. They're brilliant and beautiful, but they're fleeting. Happiness is like that—it comes from moments or things that happen to us, like a great piece of news or a fun day out.

"And contentment?" Josh asked.

"It's more like a deep river that flows regardless of the weather. It doesn't depend on the conditions—it's steady and sustaining. It's not about a burst of joy or a perfect moment; it's about a deep-seated peace that comes from accepting life as it is, finding a balance. It's about striving to be at peace with what you have, who you are, regardless of life's ups and downs."

"So you're saying I should go back to law enforcement and be content with that."

Larkin laughed. "You're making contentment sound dull, like you're giving up. But it isn't about settling. It's about building something lasting inside you. Contentment just quietly fills you up, makes you whole, even when things aren't perfect."

Josh thought of Enid and their life together. *We were content once.*

CHAPTER 56

As Enid reviewed the contents of the thumb drive Olivia had given her, she felt guilty in a way for looking at it. It wasn't intended for her eyes. But then, she didn't want to waste Drake's time if it turned out to be nothing useful—or maybe even blank.

But immediately upon opening the files on the drive, she realized how invaluable this information would be to the investigation. She made a copy of the contents on another thumb drive, only to be sure it wasn't lost somehow or destroyed. She put the drive with the copy on it in the toe of her dress black heels, the ones she couldn't stand in for very long and rarely got worn. She returned the shoes to their box on the top shelf of the closet. *If the wrong people knew I had this information, I could be in real danger.*

After leaving a message for Drake that she had to deliver something to him as soon as possible, she called Cassandra. They hadn't talked in a while, and Enid needed to warn her that Silas might run an article about her, or at least about her vision, with or without Enid's writing it.

Within a short time, Drake returned her call and they agreed to meet at the main Richland County Library. He was concerned that they had been seen together too often at their usual locations—McDonald's or Lizard's Thicket on Elmwood.

Enid drove the short distance to the library. She smiled when she saw Drake. Because of his size and distinctive dreadlocks, he would be easily remembered. No doubt he was right about changing their meeting place.

"Find anything good to read?" she asked.

"Nah, no time to read, sadly," he replied. "But they got a lot of good books here. I may retire and just stay here all day, every day," he said, laughing.

"There are some who do that already," she said, nodding toward a few men dozing in chairs in one of the reading areas. They found an unoccupied table away from everyone where they could talk privately.

"I remember when libraries wouldn't let you talk out loud, so I find myself whispering when I'm in here," Drake said.

Enid smiled. "Me too." She reached into her tote bag and handed him the thumb drive.

"A unicorn?" He examined it, turning it over. "Ah, wait, I see. It's a drive. Very cute."

"I think you'll find it even more appealing when you see what's on it."

"Care to elaborate?"

Enid glanced around. "Not really. Just call me after you've looked at it. I made a copy for safekeeping."

"Must be important for you to go to that trouble. Can you tell me where you got it?"

"Grant's executive assistant and office manager."

"She know you're giving it to me?"

Enid nodded.

"Then I'll be in touch." He rose to leave. "By the way, I want to thank you for your help. It's not often I say that to a reporter. But you're different. Josh is lucky to have you."

"Thanks, I appreciate that. But I'm lucky to have him also."

"That man loves you more than anything in 'dis world. He'd die for you, without question. But dat kind of devotion make a man vulnerable."

. . .

Enid was nearly home when she got a return call from Cassandra, and they agreed to meet at Cassandra's home. The address Cassandra gave her was in the Rosewood area, not far from where she was. Enid put the address into her phone map.

Cassandra's home was a small, two-bedroom cottage just off Rosewood Drive. All the homes were neatly kept. Enid felt a pang of envy when she saw a home much like the one she had rented in Madden. Were those really the good old days or was she selectively remembering only the good times? After all, she had nearly been killed there, had been kidnapped, and she had put others in danger. Suddenly, she saw Cassie's face in her memory and tears sprang to her eyes. She blinked and refocused her thoughts on how she could explain to Cassandra about the article Silas wanted to publish.

Enid pulled into the narrow driveway and before she got to the door, Cassandra greeted her from the small porch. "I'd suggest we sit outside but it's a little breezy, don't you think?"

Enid nodded. "Thanks for seeing me." She followed Cassandra inside. "Your home is beautiful. So welcoming."

"Thanks. Please, have a seat over here. It's the most comfortable chair."

Enid sat in a mid-century chair upholstered in a turquoise geometric print, and Cassandra sat across from her. "Can I get you a cup of tea?" Cassandra asked.

"No, I'm fine, but thanks. I just wanted to give you a heads-up. My editor at the *Palmetto Post* wants to print an article about the vision you had. I've told him repeatedly that we can't because it might jeopardize the case, but he's insistent that we print it as coming from an anonymous but reliable source."

"I see. Well, that will definitely make life more interesting," Cassandra said. "Have you told Drake, I mean Detective Harrow?"

So Cassandra and Drake were on a first name basis now. "No, but I know they're making good progress on the case."

"What did you tell your editor?"

"I refused." Enid paused. "But he may go ahead with it anyway."

"News is an interesting industry," Cassandra said.

"How so?"

"There's always a pull between the truth and what will sell. I guess we'll have to wait and see what he does."

"You could sue the paper for violating a confidentiality agreement, although there's nothing in writing to back it up."

Cassandra put her fingers to her temples and closed her eyes.

"I'm sorry to cause you distress," Enid said. When Cassandra didn't reply, Enid asked, "Are you in pain?"

Cassandra shook her head and rubbed her temples again. When she opened her eyes, she stared at Enid. "It will all be fine. And you and your husband will be fine also."

"Did you just have a vision about me?" Enid asked.

Cassandra nodded. "Usually, I have to be in closer proximity to the person I'm reading, but this vision came through clearly." She paused briefly. "I did see death, but I sensed it was symbolic. But the road to resurrection may be difficult."

"I'm not sure what to make of that," Enid said.

"You are looking for something that doesn't exist. And you can't align your beliefs about life with its realities. This will bring about the death of something dear to you."

"Are you sure it's not a person who will die?"

Cassandra smiled slightly. "As I've said, I'm never absolutely sure of any of my visions. But I usually have a sense when it's real death."

"You mean like Mara Sterling's vision?"

Cassandra nodded. "Yes, exactly like that."

"Is there anything I should do or change?" Enid couldn't believe she was getting caught up in Cassandra's vision and reminded herself that it could all be imagined . . . or even a hoax. But Cassandra's sincerity ruled out the latter. She believed what she was saying, even if it wasn't real to anyone but her.

"Look inside and chase your own truth now."

Enid froze when she heard Cassandra talk about the very thing she had thought about earlier. All she could do was nod. "I'll keep you updated on the article and try to give you a heads-up. That is, if I'm not fired before it hits."

Cassandra just smiled. That all-knowing smile that made Enid feel emotionally naked.

• • •

Instead of going home, Enid drove to the *Palmetto Post's* office. She had no idea if Silas would be in, or even if he would talk to her. And she hadn't talked to Josh. But this was something she had to do.

"Hi, Enid. What brings you in today?" the office manager asked.

"I'd like to talk with Silas, if possible."

"Is he expecting you?"

"No, I mean I don't have a scheduled meeting with him. Can you see if he's got a minute?"

Moments later, Enid heard Silas' voice as he walked down the hallway. "Of course I'll make time for you. Come on back."

Enid followed him, now losing her nerve. What was she thinking?

Instead of going to his office, Silas directed her into the conference room. "My office is a mess, so let's meet in here." He sat down on one side of the table and motioned for her to take the seat directly across from him. Instead of asking why she wanted to meet, Silas just sat quietly, waiting for Enid to speak.

She took a deep breath and again questioned herself. Did Cassandra's vision push her in a direction she wasn't ready to take? No, this was an overdue conversation. So she began. "Thank you for meeting with me without an appointment. I'm ... I'm not exactly sure where to start."

Again, Silas just waited for her to speak.

"I know you hired me to do the article on Mara Sterling's murder. And at first, I thought it was serendipitous that I had met with Cassandra and had some knowledge of the situation before you hired me. I thought it would be an advantage. But it's been a curse."

"Are you too close to this story?" Silas asked.

"I don't think that's it. It's just that I promised Cassandra I would help her, not write about her."

"So you feel more loyalty to her than to the paper or to me?"

Enid felt like she had been slapped in the face, and it stung. *The truth sometimes hurts,* her journalism professor had told her. "Yes, I guess I am."

"That makes you a good person, Enid Blackwell." Silas took a dramatic pause. "But a lousy reporter."

Enid felt sick to her stomach. She took pride in her work, and now Silas had called her "lousy."

As if sensing Enid's reaction, Silas added. "I mean for this story. You know I love your work. That's why I chased after you, why I hired you."

"But you regret it now?"

"No. But I can't have my reporters letting their personal feelings prevent them from reporting the news." He sat back in his chair and appeared to be studying Enid. "I don't have to lecture you on the state of the news industry. Hell, it's common knowledge, we're being overtaken by bloggers and pseudo-reporters. And probably AI before too long." He smiled. "And I'm sure the print papers feel the same about us online papers. The industry has a voracious appetite. When Ted Turner founded CNN in 1980, he revolutionized the news industry. Print couldn't keep up with 24/7 broadcast news, and now broadcast news can't keep up with online reporting. And online papers can't keep up with bloggers and podcasters. It's a vicious cycle, and whoever gets the story out there first wins."

While Silas had not said anything Enid didn't already know, his words hit her like a boulder rolling down a hill, unstoppable. "I remember writing obituaries for Jack's newspaper and complaining about it constantly," she said. "But I wrote about things that people really care about, not what we tell them to care about. I miss those days."

Silas leaned forward, putting his hands on the table. "I know you do. But you can't raise your hand and ask the world to stop on your account."

Enid took another deep breath. "Maybe I can. Or I can try to help in my own way."

Silas ran his fingers through his hair and exhaled a loud sigh. "When are you resigning?"

CHAPTER 57

Enid felt sick to her stomach as she waited for Josh to return home that afternoon. What had she done? And how would she contribute to their income? Silas didn't seem like a vindictive person, but he could blackball her so that no one else would hire her. And she wouldn't blame them. There were limited opportunities in Columbia for news reporters.

What would she tell Josh?

In a brief moment of deja vu, Enid recalled a similar conversation with Cade, her ex, when she wanted to leave her bank job. He thought she was crazy. But Josh isn't Cade.

"Hi, Enid, I'm home."

She pushed her concerns aside and went to the kitchen to greet Josh. "Hi, Babe." She studied his face. "What's wrong?"

He opened the refrigerator and grabbed a bottle of filtered water, got a glass from the cabinet, and poured. "Let's go sit on the porch for a change. I need some air, and it's not too chilly today."

"Sounds good. I'll grab something to drink and meet you out there." She searched the refrigerator and found a carton of almond milk. Not what she really wanted, but drinking wine when she was upset didn't seem like a wise choice. She poured a glass full and went out to the porch. "It is nice out here this evening," she said as she settled into the rocker beside Josh. "Want to talk about your day?"

"You don't look too cheerful either. Is everything okay?"

She managed to smile. "You go first."

"Well, Caleb Thornhill is in the wind."

"You mean disappeared?"

"I mean he's not in Columbia any longer, as far as Larkin knows."

"Have you asked Tiffany if she knows where he is?"

Josh took a long drink of water. "No. I know this sounds awful, but I don't trust her to tell me the truth. Not about Caleb."

"Do you think they're still an item?" Enid asked.

Josh seemed to consider the question before he replied, "I honestly don't know."

"But your instincts are great. What's your gut tell you?"

Josh laughed. "That it needs food! Why don't I make some pasta for us tonight?"

"That would be nice." She looked across the front lawn of their rented house. A house, not a home, she realized. "Do you miss law enforcement?"

"Why do you ask?" He set his water bottle on the floor beside his rocker and took her hand. "Do you miss working for Jack?"

Enid felt her world tilting on its axis. She had to be honest with Josh. Otherwise, what did that say about their relationship? "Yes, I do." Then she added. "I miss reporting about things that people care about." A pause. "And that's what I told Silas today."

Josh just squeezed her hand.

"He needs me to write about Cassandra's vision, but I can't. I think he may go ahead with the story anyway. It's too newsworthy to ignore, and I agree. But she came to me for help."

"So here we are again, in a new place trying to figure out who we are."

"I know who *we* are, as a couple. That's never in question for me. But I just don't know who I am. Not anymore. I need, no I *want,* to be an equal partner, so I need to settle down and work. Just work, not question things, not try to save the world."

Josh laughed softly. "But that's who you are. And what I love about you. So did you quit today?"

Enid nodded. "Are you upset?"

"Hell, no. Are you?"

Enid laughed. "Hell, no. But I am concerned about what I'll do. I'm a reporter, but now that I've left the *State* newspaper and the *Palmetto Post*, I'm afraid no one will hire me."

Josh picked up his water bottle and drank the last bit. "You know, it's funny we're having this conversation. I've been thinking a lot about when we met, the life we had."

"Are we just remembering the good stuff and romanticizing it?" Enid asked.

"Perhaps. Maybe you should go back with the AP, like you did when you and Cade worked there."

"No way. I'd have to start at the bottom again, and I'd have no input into what assignments I'd get. That never crossed my mind as an option."

CHAPTER 58

Drake was annoyed that Albright kept putting him off every time he asked to meet with him. After an hour of waiting, Drake walked by Albright's office. He was sitting at his desk and for a minute Drake thought the man was asleep.

Drake walked in. "Sir, I'm sorry to interrupt you, but I really do need to talk to you."

"So you've said."

"I've got the information to solve Mara Sterling's murder."

"Is this another insect vision?"

Trying to hide his annoyance, Drake continued. "I need to share something with you."

Making a huffing noise that made him sound like a horse, Albright said, "I guess we can talk now. Shut the door."

Drake closed the office door and sat in the chair across from Albright's desk. "Sir, I have obtained files from the woman who worked for Grant Sterling as his executive assistant and office manager."

Albright's right eyebrow shot up, giving his face a comical look. "What kind of information?"

"There's a group called Umbra—"

"Who?" Albright asked.

"Umbra. It's the darkest side of the moon."

Albright made another horse-snorting noise. "You and your wild theories."

"One of Grant Sterling's clients, Caleb Thornhill, recommended Sterling to a group, the Umbra group. They were trying to raise money for various, let's say, projects they wanted to pursue. Sterling had made Thornhill a lot of money on his investments, so Thornhill recommended him to the group."

Suddenly appearing to be interested in something he could grasp onto, Albright interjected, "And he lost money for them, I'll bet. It's usually about love or money. Was this Caleb fellow part of that Umbra group?"

"There's no indication he was a member of the group. But Sterling had an excellent reputation, an uncanny record for making big money for his clients. According to his assistant, the one who gave us this information, Grant didn't want to get involved with them, had a bad feeling about them. But they offered him a big bonus in addition to his commission. And according to the assistant, Mara Sterling liked to spend money. They had just done extensive renovations to their house, and Grant needed cash. So he agreed to work with the group."

"My second wife was like that. That woman could spend some money. Go on."

"Anyway, the start-up tech company Grant invested their money in had big returns at first but then flopped, and the group lost a fortune. According to the information I have, Sterling warned the group up front that they could either win big or lose big, but they wanted in anyway. Caleb himself opted out, as he had already made a fortune in real estate and other investments and wasn't interested in taking this kind of risk."

"Well, hell, nobody likes to lose money, but they don't go killing their investment advisor." The right eyebrow shot up again. "You are, I suppose, going to tell me they murdered Sterling's wife. Why not kill him?"

"Well, it appears the group killed Mara Sterling as revenge on Grant Sterling and then had him killed in jail."

"That's cold," Albright said. "Killing a man's wife and leaving the kid beside her body. Damn. But then why kill Grant also if they had already taken their revenge on his wife?"

"They must have thought he would talk to the police about their group and his suspicions that they were some kind of nefarious group. That's probably why his office was broken into after Mara Sterling's murder. But the assistant knew Grant kept a copy of important information in a hidden safe." Drake held up the unicorn thumb drive. "That's what's on here."

Albright looked out the small window in his office. "You know, the world is changing too fast. It's too mean. Hard to trust anyone."

"I hear that, sir." For the first time since he had begun reporting to Albright, Drake felt sorry for the man and the demons that haunted him.

Albright stared outside for another moment and then looked back at Drake. "So what about this insect tattoo thing? What that just random, irrelevant information?"

"No, sir. I think this group also killed Travis, my undercover friend. When we met before he died, he told me about this group that used the cicada tattoo as its symbol."

"Damn weird symbol, if you ask me. Damn weird. What's the cicada connection with this group?"

"Not sure. Still trying to figure that out."

"Do we know who the leader of this group is?"

"I believe it's Howard Whitaker, Caleb Thornhill's half-brother."

"Bring 'em both in. Let's see what they have to say."

CHAPTER 59

"What about the vision story?" Josh asked. "The whole Cassandra thing is too good to ignore."

"If she agrees, I'll find a way to get it published," Enid said. "Maybe as a freelance article later. We'll see. Drake promised me an exclusive when this is all over."

"What about Grant's assistant? Is Drake getting someone to cover her?"

"Olivia is leaving town to go someplace safe but promised to let us know where she is. I don't think this group knows she had a copy of Sterling's notes, so she's not too worried. But she knows she'll be a witness if and when they arrest the killer or killers."

Josh kissed her on the cheek. "I've got to go into the office today and clean up the Caleb mess with Tiffany. So just stay close to home and let me know where you are."

Enid gave him a hug. "I love you, but you're starting to hover. I'll be fine." She took a step back. "Are you resigning today? If so, I'll plan a pity party meal for us tonight, to celebrate our freedom."

"Like Janice Joplin said, 'Freedom's just another word for nothing left to lose.' I'll see what Tiffany has to say first. Besides, I may not have to resign. She may fire me."

After Josh left, Enid settled down at her desk to make some notes and collect her thoughts. She still had a few assignments to complete for the *Palmetto Post*, and Silas was generous enough to let her finish them. He was a good man, and he was absolutely right about the state of the news industry. It was a ferocious beast that had to be fed constantly.

All her life, Enid had been an overachiever, so backing off, especially from a news story, wasn't her nature. But she reminded herself she was standing up for what she thought was right.

Enid rubbed her temples and focused on organizing her research for the articles. Unable to concentrate, she called Rachel's cell phone and was surprised when she answered.

"Hey, Enid, what's up?" Rachel asked.

"Could you do me a quick favor?"

"Sure. Is it legit, or do I need to cover my tracks?"

"I just need to know if you can find something about a group called Umbra." She spelled it out for Rachel. "Anything about what the group stands for, who its founders are, that kind of thing."

"Is this about the same thing you had me look for before? That Caleb guy?"

"Yes. And I hate to ask more of you, but can you do it right away? Things are moving fast on this case. I'm sure Drake, the detective, is also looking for information on the group, but I'd like to know for myself."

"Sure. Give me thirty minutes or so and I'll call you back."

Determined to finish her articles, Enid looked at her research notes again. A noise at the back of the house startled her. If it was Josh, why was he coming in the back? He hadn't had time to meet with Tiffany. Maybe it was Sophie from next door. But she had never come to visit, other than talking to Enid over the fence.

Enid looked at the calendar. It was recycling day. Maybe Josh had forgotten to push the big green container to the curb and they were going into the backyard to get it. But she had never known them to do that.

She went to the kitchen to look out the back window and gasped. The back door had been pried open. Bits of splinters from the wood door were scattered across the floor. *Stay calm.* They didn't have a landline, and her cell phone was in her office. She tried to back up quietly while keeping an eye on the kitchen door. If she could just get to her phone to call 911. Or maybe she should just run out the back door for help. Where was the intruder now?

Suddenly, a hand covered with a black latex glove grabbed her from behind and began dragging her back down the hallway. She was unable to scream or even get her teeth on the hand to bite down.

And then her cell phone rang. It was in her pocket after all. Then she remembered she had kept it nearby for Rachel's return call. The momentary distraction caused her attacker to loosen his hold slightly, and Enid took the opportunity to bite his hand as hard as she could. And then she pushed her weight against the man, causing him to step back. She hit him in the groin with every bit of strength she could muster and pulled away to get to the open kitchen door. She only had moments to escape.

Then there was a loud thud and a moan, and her attacker, dressed in black commando gear, was on the floor. He appeared to be out cold. Sophie was standing in the hallway with a baseball bat. "Are you okay?" she asked Enid.

"Sophie, I . . . how did you get in?"

"I used to check the house for the prior tenants when they traveled. I've been meaning to give you the key and kept forgetting. Sorry."

Enid dropped onto one of the kitchen chairs. "Are you serious? Thank goodness you had it. But how did you know someone was inside?"

"I didn't. Not actually. But I was outside giving Kibo some of his favorite treats when I saw this guy in black hanging around your back door. I started to call out to him to see what he wanted, but I thought maybe he was a repairman you had called, and I didn't want to be a nosy neighbor. But then I got worried. I mean what kind of repairman dresses in all black? So I grabbed my bat and the door key and came over just to be sure. When I knocked and you didn't come to the door, I came in."

Enid jumped up and embraced Sophie. "Thank you, thank you. I don't know what would have happened if you hadn't."

Sophie grinned. "I guess being the star hitter on our women's softball team back home came in handy after all. But you looked like you were taking care of yourself pretty good." She glanced back at the man on the floor. "Let's call the police and an ambulance. I hope I didn't kill him." She kicked his leg lightly. "Or maybe I do."

CHAPTER 60

Drake was sitting in the living room and had just finished taking statements from Enid and Sophie when his cell rang. He stepped outside to take the call, and when he came back inside, he looked at Sophie. "He's got one helluva headache and a mean concussion, but he'll live."

"Who is he?" Enid asked. "Do we know yet?"

"They're running his prints," Drake said. "You're both lucky." He pointed a finger at Enid and then at Sophie. "And stupid."

"What was I supposed to do?" Sophie asked.

Drake shrugged. "I dunno. Like maybe call 911?"

Sophie muttered something Enid couldn't understand.

"Drake, come on, she's a hero." Enid said. "Give her a break."

Drake turned to Sophie. "I be pulling yo' leg, girl. You done good. Remind me not to ever piss you off."

Enid put her hand on Sophie's arm. "You saved my life. I can't thank you enough."

Josh ran in through the open front door and grabbed Enid. "Are you alright? What happened?" He then looked at Drake. "I just got your message and got here as soon as I could."

Enid, Sophie, and Drake filled Josh in on what had happened. By the time they finished, Josh's hands were shaking. "I was afraid something like this might happen. How did they find out about you?" he asked Enid.

"I don't know. But we need to warn Grant's assistant. She hasn't contacted me yet so I don't know where she is." Enid looked at Drake. "She knows she'll likely be a witness and promised to stay in touch. I believe she will."

Enid's phone rang. "Maybe this is her." She glanced at the screen. "No, it's Rachel. I asked her to check something for me. I'll call her back later." Then Enid's phone pinged, indicating an incoming text. "It's from Rachel again," Enid said. "She found Umbra's manifesto on the dark web."

Drake threw his hands up in the air. "You can't be mess'n 'round there. It's no man's land. Contract killers, traffickers, and worse."

"Calm down, Drake," Enid said. "Rachel knows what's she's doing." Enid tapped on the phone and downloaded a document Rachel sent. After reading it, Enid forwarded it to Drake. "I've sent it to you. It explains a lot."

Drake's phone pinged and he opened the text from Enid and read Umbra's manifesto aloud.

...

We are Umbra, the unseen hand and the silent balancer of scales. Born from the dark side of a failing society, we stand where justice fails and the rule of law falls silent. We are the response to the cries unheard, the pain unavenged, and the wrongs unredressed.

The judicial system, once a bastion of fairness and order, has become a puppet theater where the strings are pulled by the affluent and the powerful, leaving the common man a mere spectator in a rigged performance. Crimes go unpunished, and victims are left in the ashes of forgotten corners. The police, guardians of peace, now wade in corruption and incompetence, more concerned with protecting their own than serving justice.

Umbra was formed as an answer—an ultimatum to a society that has turned its back on its own. We do not seek to replace the laws but to enforce the principle upon which they were founded: that each action must meet its consequence, that each injustice must see retribution, and that the scales must be balanced.

Umbra does not recruit; it recognizes its own. To those who wield power without accountability, consider this a warning. We are watching, and we will act. To the silent sufferers, the overlooked, and the downtrodden—take heart. Justice moves in the shadows, and its name is Umbra. We are the balance. We are the consequence. We are Umbra.

...

A silence fell across the group, as though the air had been sucked from the room. It was Drake who spoke first. "These be very bad people, this Umbra." He looked at Enid. "You are lucky, indeed."

Enid nodded. "Yes, I am. And I think I know why they targeted me."

"Why's that?" Josh asked.

"That article on the double brood cicada emergence in South Carolina. Silas knew about Cassandra's vision and he thought it would be good to have it on record as something to reference later when we were able to report on the killer's tattoo. And, if the vision turned out to be a hoax, then the emergence story was just local news."

"I still don't understand," Josh said.

"I get it now," Drake said as he tapped on another text message. "I had the officer at the hospital get a photo of the attacker's back." He turned the phone around so they could see the photo. A large cicada tattoo covered his back. "They assumed when they saw Enid's article that Grant had told her something about Umbra. And before Grant died, he told the nurse to tell me 'Umbra emerged.' I guess Grant assumed we'd figure it out from his notes."

Enid suddenly felt chilled and wrapped her arms around herself. "How many more of them are there?"

Drake shrugged. "We may never know. These shadowy, underground groups are difficult to track. The dark web makes a perfect hiding place."

"I figured out something else," Enid said. "I think I understand why Umbra chose the cicada as its symbol."

"And?" Sophie asked.

"The cicadas go through a cycle. They emerge in large numbers when the soil reaches a certain temperature. And they come out at dusk to avoid daytime predators. After they emerge, they shed their exoskeletons and mature into adults."

"Why do they make that noisy sound?" Sophie asked.

"The males have an organ that produces a sound to attract females, and the females flick their wings in response. That's why you have that loud noise."

"So then what happens?" Josh asked.

"After the mating, the females cut slits into tree branches and lay their eggs in the cuts. But the adult cicadas live only a few weeks after emerging, because their main purpose is to reproduce."

"So the baby cicadas are all orphans?" Drake asked.

"The eggs hatch about six to ten weeks later and the baby cicadas fall to the ground and burrow into the soil. They stay there for either thirteen or seventeen years, depending on their species. They live on sap from tree roots and then emerge when it's their time to restart the cycle."

"Is there a new cycle of cicadas that emerge each year?" Sophie asked.

"What I described are periodical cicadas. There are also annual ones that emerge each year with life cycles of two to five years. They are not synchronized like periodical cicadas, and some of them mature and emerge each year."

"That's amazing, and some good research," Drake said. "Not that I can use it in my report. Imagine me trying to explain visions and cicada cycles. I'd be the laughingstock of the department."

"You're right, but the cicada cycle does explain the Umbra group's emergence. They stay underground until something occurs that they feel they have to make right. They take care of it and then disappear for a while."

"But you know Howard Whitaker is involved, right?" Josh asked Drake.

"Well, not really. Turns out Whitaker is one of many identities the man has," Drake said. "The attacker isn't Whitaker, but we'll know more about the guy soon, probably by tomorrow."

"Do you think Whitaker is the founder of Umbra?" Josh asked.

"Whitaker's history, like his half-brother Caleb's, only goes back so far."

"But why would Caleb risk the exposure of running for political office and people digging into his past?" Josh asked. Before anyone else could respond, he answered himself.

"Unless he was sure Tiffany's firm wouldn't dig too deep. He had enough history to satisfy most people."

"But not you," Enid said.

"And how many of them, these Umbra thugs, do you think are out there?" Josh asked Drake.

"No idea," Drake said. "Might as well ask me how many of those cicada bugs are coming out this year."

"So do you think they'll keep coming after Enid?" Josh asked.

"I don't know, but my guess is they'll go back underground, for now at least. Too much exposure for them. And while they wanted to eliminate Enid because they thought she had figured them out, which in a way she did, it's not worth the risk to them now. They might be evil, but they're also smart."

CHAPTER 61

The next day, Josh left early to meet with Tiffany, since he had been unable to see her the day before. Enid's near attack still had him rattled. And he was angry. Very angry—and worried.

When he arrived at the office, Tiffany was at the coffee machine. "Buy you a cup?" she asked.

"No, thanks. We need to talk."

She looked at him with a surprised look. "Okay then. Let's cut through the niceties and go to my office."

Josh handed her a typed note, which had only a few paragraphs.

"What's this?" she asked.

"My resignation. Effective immediately."

Tiffany sighed. "Well, come on in and shut the door."

She sat at her desk and skimmed the paper. "No notice? You must be upset. What's going on?"

"Don't be flip about this, as if you are clueless about me leaving." He took a deep breath to steady his nerves. "What was the plan? To have me whitewash a report on Caleb Thornhill so you could tell Larkin he was squeaky clean? Are you and Caleb still seeing each other? And where is he, anyway?"

Tiffany held up her hands. "Whoa. That's a lot of demanding. And why do I have to answer any of those questions?"

"You don't. But I need to know if you think I'm so stupid I wouldn't figure out what's going on."

Tiffany ran her fingers through her long hair and leaned back in her chair, closing her eyes. When she opened them again, she looked like she was about to cry.

"Do you love him?" Josh asked.

"No. I . . . We're just friends. Okay, friends with benefits. I have no knowledge of anything illegal or shady Caleb has done. I mean that. You're not the only person in this room with integrity," she said, raising her voice. "He has a brother, Howard, who got into some trouble years ago. Caleb wanted to distance himself from Howard, so Caleb changed his name. But Caleb wasn't involved with him."

"Really?"

"Sarcasm doesn't become you, but I understand your skepticism."

"You know he wasn't involved because he told you he wasn't? Or because you did your own background check?" Josh thought he saw Tiffany's cheeks redden slightly. He continued. "Did you know someone attacked Enid yesterday?"

Tiffany sat up straight. "What? No. Is she alright?"

Josh was comforted to see that she was genuinely surprised. Did he really think she was involved? He wasn't sure at this point. "She's fine. Thanks to our neighbor."

"Are you insinuating that Caleb had something to do with it?"

"The police are investigating. Too early to tell." He paused. "Do you know where Caleb is now?"

"No, I mean, he said he'd be in touch but I haven't heard from him in more than a week. I can't believe that you think he's involved. Or even worse yet, that I might be."

Josh wanted to tell her about Umbra, and his suspicions about Howard Whitaker's possible involvement in Mara Sterling's murder. But he knew better. "The investigation is ongoing. We'll know more later."

Tiffany picked up the resignation letter on her desk. "I'm not going to try to talk you out of leaving. You clearly have trust issues with me, and I can't have employees who think I'm covering up a crime."

"I'll finish the report on that last assignment and get it to you by tomorrow. There's nothing else left for me to close out. Except the report on Caleb, and I'll give you what I've got. But there's no conclusion to it," Josh stood.

Tiffany, still seated at her desk, said, "I wish you and Enid all the best. We'll get your final paycheck cut so you can have it tomorrow." She pushed the resignation aside, as if dismissing it. "Do you have another job? I can give you references. Despite our disagreements, I have the utmost respect for you. You're a good investigator."

"I appreciate that, but I need some time to figure out next steps." Josh hesitated and then added. "You need to be careful. I'm not as trusting of Caleb as you are."

Josh left the office, not looking back. When he got to his car, he called Drake. "Can we talk?"

CHAPTER 62

Since Drake was in the neighborhood, he agreed to make an exception to his self-imposed "rule" of keeping work and home separate and offered to stop by Josh's house.

When Drake arrived, he accepted Enid's offer of coffee and a piece of the pastry she had gotten at the bakery, so they all sat at the small kitchen table.

"Thanks for coming by," Josh said. "I know you're doing your best to push for more info, but have you found out anything about Enid's attacker?"

Drake shoved the last bite of pasty into his mouth. "That was mighty good." He wiped his mouth with a napkin. "Actually, I was going to call you. We've identified the man. His name is Rex Watson."

"That sounds familiar," Josh said.

"He was arrested when you were sheriff of Bowman County. Aggravated assault on a bank manager who wouldn't give him another loan. Tried to stab him in the parking lot after work, but a security guard stopped it."

"And I remember that story in the *Tri-County Gazette*," Enid said. "Jack wrote it himself. But you don't think that man came after me because Josh was sheriff when he was arrested?"

"Nah, no reason to think Watson made the connection with either of you. Thugs like that have a way of popping up over and over if they stay in the same area long enough."

"But there is a connection," Enid said.

Josh nodded. "Yes. Revenge."

Drake shrugged. "Perhaps," and then said to Enid, "That Umbra Manifesto you turned up on the dark web lays out the group's intent on revenge. I guess Watson found them and was attracted to their mission, seeing he had his own revenge to dole out. According to his arrest record, Watson was given a suspended sentence for community service. Ha, what a joke."

"I thought the group was formed by Intellecta members. Do you think Watson is a genius like the rest of them?"

"Very doubtful," said Drake. "I'm guessing that after the group was founded, the recruits were just foot soldiers, hotheads who wanted to get back at folks."

"Was Watson able to give a statement?" Josh asked.

Drake shook his head. "Not yet. We've got an APB out for Howard Whitaker and for Caleb Thornhill."

Josh rubbed the back of his neck and turned his head to the side to stretch. "Tiffany swears Caleb is not involved."

Drake shrugged. "We'll see. So have you quit?"

Josh looked puzzled. "How'd you know about that?"

Drake laughed. "I didn't, mon, but if anyone be ready to quit, it be you!" His smile faded. "So what happens now for you two?"

Enid looked at Josh and then said, "I don't know, but we'll figure it out."

Drake glanced at a text message on his phone. "Well, I've been summoned into Albright's office for a meeting. Can't wait," he said, smiling. As Drake stood to leave, he said to Josh and Enid, "Follow your heart."

. . .

After Drake left, Enid and Josh were still sitting at the kitchen table. Finally, it was Josh who broke the silence. "How could I have missed it?"

"Missed what?" Enid asked.

"I knew Caleb was too slick to be real, but I didn't think he was a killer."

"And we don't know that he is. Let's not jump to conclusions." Enid took Josh's hand in hers. "What's really bothering you?"

He squeezed her hand. "I'm fine. Between your attack and my confrontation with Tiffany, I'm just a little unsettled."

"Did it go that bad with her, your conversation with Tiffany?"

"I was pretty harsh and acted more like an arresting officer than an employee."

"Are you finished with the work you committed to do for the firm?" Enid asked.

"Yep, all tidied up. What about your work with Silas?"

"I've been thinking about it, and I'd like to do the article on Cassandra for the *Palmetto Post*, if he'll allow me to keep her real name out of it. She doesn't need that kind of attention."

"I think that's a great idea. It will bring you closure and give him the story the paper wants."

CHAPTER 63

Drake sat across from Albright and waited, wondering which one of Albright's rules he had broken. And what the punishment would be.

"I won't mince words," Albright said. "I'll just get right to it."

Drake braced himself mentally for what was about to come.

"You know, when you came to me, asking to get involved in the Sterling case because some fortune teller had a vision of a bug tattoo, I thought you were crazy." Albright laughed. "That's putting it mildly."

"I agree, it was unusual." Drake said. "But I thank you again for letting me pursue that angle."

"I was convinced, as you know, that Grant Sterling killed his wife. Spouses kill each other all the time. Been happening since the dawn of time. That plus that the anonymous tip that he was seeing someone, which maybe he was. Maybe the caller was a jilted lover wanting to get even. Who knows. But he didn't have a confirmed alibi for the time of the murder either. I guess I've been doing this too long, think everyone's lying."

Drake was amused that Albright said he wanted to get right to the point but seemed to be meandering all around what he wanted to say. "You don't have to explain sir. Just glad we finally got to the truth." Drake was mentally planning how to explain the damaging report Albright was likely to send to Drake's commanding officer back home in Bowman County. There would be no commendation from Albright and no recommendation for a promotion. He then realized Albright was speaking. "I'm sorry sir, I was just—"

"It's fine. I was just saying that I'm pleased with the work you did. It took courage to open yourself up for possible ridicule and failure." To Drake's astonishment, Albright Held out his hand to Drake. "Congratulations."

"Thank you, sir, but we haven't completely solved the case yet."

"You will, I'm sure of it. And then I think you'd better plan on going back to Bowman County and taking that promotion you deserve." Albright's expression changed. "You know, it's hard to admit you're wrong. But I was, about Grant Sterling and about you."

"I ... I'm not sure what to say."

"Go on now, get out there and wrap this one up. I need to talk to Grant Sterling's sister and bring her up to date."

Drake numbly walked back to his own desk, unsure that he had heard Albright correctly. What he wanted most right now was to go out and have a few Red Stripes with his buddies, but it would be much later today before that was possible. In the meantime, he had two calls to make.

When he got to his desk, the dispatcher called him and said the hospital was looking for him. Enid's attacker was awake.

. . .

When Drake arrived at the hospital, the head nurse on Watson's floor warned Drake to keep his questioning short. Watson was weak and still recovering.

Drake pulled up a chair beside Watson's bed. "I'm Investigator Drake Harrow, and I assisted Lieutenant Albright on the Mara Sterling case. He tells me you understand you are under arrest, you've been informed of your rights, and you've waived your right to an attorney. Is that correct?"

Watson closed his eyes and nodded.

"I need for you to say it," Drake said.

"I don't need no attorney. I didn't kill that woman."

"But you attacked a reporter in her home, and you're being charged with assault and attempted murder. Do you understand that?" Drake asked.

"Nosy bitch. All reporters can go to hell as far as I'm concerned. They don't report important stuff, like corrupt men who steal your money and get away with it."

Drake decided to take a different approach. "I saw the tattoo on your back, your group's cicada symbol. Was the reporter's article, the woman you attacked, was it her article that made you angry?"

"She wrote that story about us, you know, my tribe, so I had to shut her up."

Drake couldn't believe what he was hearing. "She wrote about a cicada double brood emergence, about insects, not about you or your little group of hooligans," Drake said.

Watson's eyes narrowed to mere slits. "She knew."

"I understand that's the symbol for a group called Umbra. You're a member, I take it."

Watson's hands were handcuffed to the bed rails, and he clenched his fists open and closed several times. "What of it?"

"I read the group's manifesto. Interesting shit. The group was formed to take revenge on people."

Watson remained silent.

"Is that why Mara Sterling was killed? Revenge on Grant Sterling?"

"Told you I had nothing to do with that. I didn't have no dealings with that man or his wife."

"But Howard Whitaker did, didn't he?" Drake asked.

"You'd have to ask him."

"I plan to. Any idea where he is?"

Watson laughed. "Far away from here, I'm pretty sure."

"Do you know his half-brother Caleb Thornhill?"

"Who?"

Drake repeated the name. "He's one of those Intellecta guys too, like his brother." Drake tried not to laugh when he asked the next question. "You one of those geniuses too?"

"Yeah, right. I'm a friggin' genius. Can't you tell?" Watson pulled against the handcuffs. "You gonna arrest that bitch that hit me with the baseball bat?"

"You can file a complaint, if you like, but it sure looks like self-defense to me. I mean, you were there to kill the reporter and her neighbor stepped in. Am I right?"

"We're done here. I need my rest," Watson said.

CHAPTER 64

The next morning, Josh started to get dressed and then he realized he had nowhere to go. *Is this how retired people felt?* He looked over and saw a note from Enid on her side of the bed. She had gone to the *Palmetto Post* office to talk to Silas about writing the final article, the one about Cassandra's vision.

After showering and getting dressed, Josh went into the kitchen for a cup of the coffee Enid had made before she left. When his phone rang, he assumed it was Tiffany's office manager telling him his check was ready since it was already mid-morning. But he recognized the number as being from Bowman County.

"Joshua Hart?" a woman's voice said.

"Yes. Who is this?"

"I'm Nora Caldwell, the mayor of Madden."

"Mayor? What can I do for you?" Josh tried to hide his surprise.

"I'd like to meet with you, and with your wife, if that's possible."

Now Josh was really confused. "May I ask what this is all about?"

Caldwell laughed. "I apologize for being mysterious, but I'd really rather talk to you both at once. I can come to Columbia if you'd prefer."

"No, I think a short road trip would do us both good. And I'd like to see Madden again. Enid says it's grown quite a bit."

"Yes, it has. Are you both available tomorrow? The mayor's office is now in the new town government building. It's been built since you were police chief. I'll text you the address."

"By the way, are you by any chance related to Franklin Caldwell?" Josh asked.

"Yes, he was my grandfather. Did you know him?"

"Only by reputation. Everyone said he was a great mayor."

"Thanks. He was a good man, and he left big shoes for me to fill. But I try."

After the call ended, Josh decided not to interrupt Enid, as she was probably still meeting with Silas or working at the office. When his phone rang again, Josh saw that this call was from Pete.

"Hey, Pete. You running SLED yet?"

Pete laughed. "I'm not sure I'm ready for state law enforcement. Just barely figured out how to be a police chief."

"Don't be modest, I hear you've done a great job."

"Yeah, well, you see, that's why I'm calling," Pete said. "I kinda gave your cell number to the mayor. I probably should've asked you first. Hope you're not upset."

"Well, I was wondering how Mayor Caldwell got my cell number. But it's okay. She's summoned me and Enid to Madden for a meeting tomorrow. Like to fill me in on what that's all about?"

"Well, I think she'd rather tell you herself."

"Come on, Pete. If I'm dragging Enid to Madden, I'd like to know what it's about." Josh was silent for a moment. "What have you done, Pete?"

Pete snickered softly. "Might have suggested you're the best man to replace me. Just meet with her before you say no. You shouldn't turn it down."

"But why does Enid need to be there?"

"That I'm not privy to. Maybe the mayor, being a woman and all, just wants to be sure your wife is included in the discussion." Pete said. "Look I've got to run, but let me know how it goes. Remember, don't say no right off the bat. Promise?"

Josh laughed. He missed Pete's youthful enthusiasm. His going to work for SLED was a big loss for Madden but a good career move for Pete. "Yeah, sure."

CHAPTER 65

After leaving the hospital, Drake called the number Enid had given him for Cassandra. He was surprised when she answered. "Hey, this is—"

"Yes, Drake, I know who you are."

"Did you have a vision?" Drake laughed, but when Cassandra was silent, he added. "Sorry, I didn't mean to offend you."

"No offense taken. I get that all the time. Besides, I was going to call you."

"Oh? What about?" Drake asked.

"I'm going to move out of state, and I wanted you to know where you could find me, you know, for anything related to the case."

"I imagine you're ready to get away from here. Are you worried about the killer coming after you, because if you are, I can try to get someone to watch your place until we get this guy."

"Do you know who he is?"

"We think so, but we have no idea where he is. I've talked to one of his fellow thugs but didn't get much out of him." Drake paused. "Mind if I ask where you're going?"

"I'm going home, back to the Appalachian mountains. I need to make peace with being a seer. I think of it as a curse, but I want to learn how to use it to benefit people, like my grandmother did."

"How will you do that?" Drake asked.

Cassandra laughed softly. "Honestly, I have no idea. But there's a mountain woman who does spiritual work who has agreed to help me figure it out. I'm trying to accept that this ability was given to me for a reason."

"That's very noble of you. I mean that," Drake said. "I know a university professor who's doing some research on psychic abilities, and he may want to talk with you. Would you be willing to do that?"

"Yes, I would do that. Thank you for being respectful. Some people, especially in law enforcement, are not only skeptical, they're hostile toward me, as if I'm trying to con someone. It's very disheartening at times."

"I'm sure it is, but as I told you, my grandmother in Jamaica was an Obeah practitioner, so I'm about as open-minded about your abilities as anyone could be."

"Drake, may I ask you a question?"

"Of course."

"Do you think I should have told Mara about my vision?"

He exhaled a long sigh. "Whew, that's a tough question. Like you said, you're not a hundred percent accurate, and you could have really messed up her head if you were wrong. But you did the right thing going to Enid Blackwell after the investigator disregarded your statement. She's good people. And the sketch Sophie did for you has been invaluable."

"Thank you for saying that. I'll text you my new address. I won't be leaving for a couple weeks. I need to say goodbye to Enid and Sophie as well. There's one more thing."

"What's that?" Drake asked.

"I've been having some brief flashes of images lately. One man is attacking the other one. But the vision doesn't last long, and I don't know exactly who the people are. Just two men."

"Do you think it's related to Mara's murder?"

"I honestly don't know. I've stopped seeing clients for a while because my visions are difficult to interpret right now, very sketchy. I just can't relax until this is all over."

"I get it," he said. "Maybe I'll come see you up in the mountains, you know, when this is all over. I mean just a friendly visit. I'm not trying to—"

"I'd like that. I really would."

CHAPTER 66

After dinner, Josh said, "I need to tell you about a call I got today."

Enid scraped the plates and put them in the sink. "That sounds intriguing."

"Does the name Nora Caldwell mean anything to you?"

"I've heard that name. I think Jack mentioned her. She's on the town council, I think."

"Actually, she's now the mayor of Madden, Franklin Caldwell's granddaughter. He was the mayor before I moved there."

Enid stopped what she was doing and stared at Josh. "Why did the mayor of Madden call you?"

Josh shrugged. "She didn't tell me, but she wants to meet with both of us. She offered to come here, but I thought you might enjoy a little road trip to Madden tomorrow."

"Tomorrow? Are you serious?"

"Yes, but if it's not convenient, I can call her back and reschedule."

"And you don't know what this is about?"

Josh rinsed a plate. "It would be nice to have a dishwasher again."

"Don't change the subject, Joshua Hart." Enid smiled and slapped at him with her dishtowel.

"I have a suspicion that it is about the police chief's job."

"And?" Enid asked.

"I think I told you Pete told me about throwing my name in the hat and suggesting the mayor call me."

"Is that something you'd really like to do? I mean, would it be enough for you?"

Josh pulled the plug and let the water drain from the sink. "Let's sit back down and talk about it." He pulled out a chair for Enid. "I can't honestly answer your question because I don't know myself. I decided not to spend too much mental energy on it until I talk with her."

"But why does she want me there?"

"Now that, I have no idea. Maybe she wants you to be my deputy."

Enid playfully slapped Josh's arm. "You're giddy today. Especially for someone who just quit his job."

"Wait a minute, you quit too, so we're both awfully cheerful for two unemployed people."

Enid leaned over and kissed Josh and ran her hand through his hair. "Maybe we're just happy we have a chance for a real re-do." She kissed him again. "And we have each other. That's enough for me." She leaned back in her chair. "At least until I get hungry and we can't buy food."

"I don't know what I did to deserve you. So are we good to go tomorrow?"

"No reason we can't. By the way, I had a good conversation with Silas this morning. He jumped at my offer to write an article on Cassandra's vision and to keep her identify safe."

"And I'm sure he tried to talk you out of leaving," Josh said.

"He apologized if he caused me stress, you know, pressuring me for the article on Cassandra. I assured him that was not why I was leaving."

"So then why are you leaving?"

"I'm not sure exactly. I feel both liberated and a little sad. I just know it's time for me to find out who Enid Blackwell really is." She paused. "You know, this all feels like deja vu, but yet different. When I left the bank to go back into journalism, I was confused, had no confidence, and my marriage was falling apart. But this time, while I'm not sure what's next for me, for us, I'm not scared."

CHAPTER 67

When Enid and Josh arrived in Madden at the new town hall, they went to the conference room on the first floor, as Mayor Caldwell had instructed. "This is a nice building," Enid said. "Madden has really grown since we lived here."

Josh opened the door to the room and they were both surprised to see the mayor and Jack Johnson sitting together on one side of the table. "Jack, I didn't know you were going to be here," Enid said.

Josh looked at Mayor Caldwell. "I wasn't aware either," he said.

Caldwell stood up. "Please, have a seat." She motioned to the two chairs across from her and Jack. "I apologize for the secrecy. I didn't want you, either of you, to think we were ganging up on you."

"But you are, aren't you?" Josh asked.

Jack cleared his throat. "Let me add my apology. When Nora said she was going to meet with Josh, I told her I had tried to get Enid to take over the paper." Then looking at Enid he added, "And I told her you refused because you and Josh were building a life in Columbia, where both of you had new jobs."

"Jack, that's not the only reason I turned down your offer," Enid said.

Jack held up his hands in surrender. "I know, I know. You said you're not an editor or administrator."

"And I'm not," Enid said.

Mayor Caldwell then said, "When I heard Josh was leaving his job, I pounced on the opportunity to talk to you." She looked at Jack and took a deep breath. "So Jack and I put our heads together and decided to offer you a package deal."

Enid looked at Josh then back to Caldwell. "I think we all know Josh is overqualified for the police chief job here."

Mayor Caldwell smiled and walked over to the credenza. When she sat back down she pushed a dish covered in aluminum foil across the table toward Josh. "Miss Emma said you always liked her pies, so she asked me to give this to you."

Josh smiled. "I hope it's apple. That's my favorite."

"It is," Caldwell said.

"Okay," Enid said, "so Josh gets a pie and what do I get?" She held up her hand when Jack tried to speak. "Wait, hear me out. I think we need to put all of our demands on the table."

Josh turned slightly to look at Enid and grinned. "I agree." Then he leaned in toward her and said in a low voice. "What are our demands?"

"How much bigger is Madden now than it was when Josh was police chief?" Enid asked.

Caldwell glanced at Jack. "I'd say it will soon be double the size. The distribution center added a lot of growth and we have a manufacturing plant breaking ground soon that will hire several thousand people."

"Then you should offer Josh twice what he made years ago."

Mayor Caldwell remained silent and expressionless.

"Well then," Jack said to Enid. "What are your demands for yourself?"

"That you continue to work for the paper, at least while you can, to onboard me."

Jack laughed. "Onboarding. Now's that a corporate term if I've ever heard one." He shook his head and laughed again. "Go on."

"I'd like to make it a semi-weekly paper, with Sunday and Thursday issues, and coverage for only Bowman County. The main focus, of course, will be the town of Madden. The other two counties now covered by the *Tri-County Gazette* can be absorbed elsewhere by the other papers." She paused and then added, "Eventually, I'd like to make it a tri-weekly and then a daily paper. That is if I manage not to run it into the ground first."

Josh turned fully around in his seat to look at Enid. "Are you serious? You want to run the paper?"

Enid looked around the table at each person: Josh, Caldwell, and then Jack. "No. But I don't want the paper to go under either, or for it to be sold to someone who has no ties to Madden." She held up a finger for emphasis, "Oh, and there's one more thing." She looked at Jack. "I write the obituaries."

...

On the ride back to Columbia, Josh and Enid were silent for several miles. Josh spoke first. "Well, I must say, that was a surprising conversation in many ways."

"If this is not what you want to do, then we can always back out." She paused, looking out the side window. "But I sense this is exactly what you really want."

"I can't let you take the paper on my account, unless it's what you really want," Josh said.

"As I said to you last night, it's time for me to find out who Enid Blackwell really is. I also meant what I said about not wanting the paper to fail or to fall into the hands of a corporate buyer who has no interest in the town or its citizens."

"You're starting to sound like a crusader," Josh said. "Is that how you see yourself?"

"Honestly, I'm not sure. But Madden has given me a lot, and so has Jack. I owe this town and its newspaper a great deal." She grinned. "Besides, I might enjoy being the boss for a change." She looked out the window again. "I've missed this area. Although it's changing quickly. I hope the growth doesn't destroy its character." She looked back at Josh. "So was I right? Did you really want the job but you hesitated because of me?"

Josh smiled. "Yeah, but it was the pie that sealed the deal. Miss Emma makes great pies. But she's second to you. Not making pies, I mean. But you're the absolute best thing in my life. Thank you for … for just being you. I love you."

Josh's phone pinged, signaling an incoming message. "My phone's there in the console. See who that's from. Maybe Nora and Jack decided I'm not worth twice the salary."

Enid picked up Josh's phone. "It's from Bob Larkin. He has something he needs to give you. Wants to drop by."

"Tell him to stop by in about an hour. That should give us time to get home."

Enid sent the text response and replaced the phone in the cup holder. "Wonder what Larkin wants to give you that's so urgent?"

"No idea," Josh said.

CHAPTER 68

Josh and Enid were surprised to see Larkin's car in their driveway when they arrived. "He must really be anxious to deliver whatever it is," Enid said.

Enid invited Larkin to come inside. "Can I get you anything?" Enid asked.

"No thanks, I'm fine. And I apologize for showing up like this. I've got to go to a dinner this evening, and I didn't want to miss seeing you." He handed a large mailing envelope to Josh. "This is for you. From Caleb."

Josh looked at the mailing label, which simply stated, "Hand Deliver to Joshua Hart." Josh turned to Larkin. "Any idea what this is all about?"

"None whatsoever." Larkin looked at the envelope, as if waiting for Josh to open it.

"Why didn't he just give it to me himself? Or mail it to the office?" Josh asked.

Larkin shrugged. "Like I said, I'm just the delivery person. A courier dropped it off a few days ago, but as you see on the envelope, Caleb requested a specific delivery date." He glanced at the Piaget watch on his wrist. "Well, I guess I've done my job, so I'll head out now."

From the front door, Enid watched Larkin back out of the driveway. "That was so odd." She shut the door and sat down across from Josh who was just holding the envelope. "Why didn't you open it while Larkin was here? Do you think it's about him?"

Josh broke the seal and opened it. "I guess there's only one way to find out." He pulled out a letter, several pages long, as well as copies of several newspaper clippings.

"I'll get us a glass of wine," Enid said. "We can celebrate our new life in Madden while you figure out what's going on with Caleb."

When Enid returned from the kitchen with two glasses of cabernet sauvignon, Josh was holding the envelope's contents on his lap and was staring into space.

She set the glasses on the coffee table. "What's wrong? You look like you've seen a ghost."

Josh just handed her the contents. "I need that drink." He sipped on his wine while Enid read the letter and skimmed the newspaper articles.

"I'm not sure what to say. In some ways, this sounds like a goodbye letter."

"I think that's exactly what it is." He reached for the letter. "Here, let me see it again."

Dear Joshua,

I hope this letter finds you and your beautiful wife well. Perhaps I should have told you how much I envied your life together. I had hoped that one day, I would have a similar fortune. However, life is fleeting and cannot always be managed as we'd like. But I'll get to the point.

You were right to question me, my background, and my suitability for political office. Looking back now, I wonder why I thrust myself into the spotlight, as I should have remained in the shadows. But I wanted to give back to the world for a change instead of merely taking and achieving, which is what I've done for many years. All those things I spoke about were very real to me: better education, affordable housing, health care, among other idealistic promises all politicians make. But I meant every word. It's important that you understand my sincerity.

As you've likely discovered in your thorough background check, I was a member of Intellecta, an organization for high-IQ individuals. Its mission, while noble, left a lot to be desired. Why have all that intellect organized if it didn't contribute meaningfully to the world? So, I began a spin-off branch called Orion, named after the warrior. I wanted Orion to go to war against poverty and injustice—all those things I mentioned. One of Orion's members was Howard Whitaker, my half-brother. In our younger years, we could have passed for twins, both in appearance and in our shared ideals. But as our appearances changed, so did our respective ideologies.

I'm sure you probably hit a brick wall looking into my past. Howard and I had the same mother and grew up with different last names. I assumed the surname "Thornhill" about fifteen years ago, hoping to make a clean start. There's no point in telling you my prior name because I had no arrests or other legal blemishes, other than being related to Howard. He was my downfall. It was as if he couldn't let me go, and my association with him was my albatross. When Howard testified against some powerful men involved in drug trafficking, he disappeared for years. But then Mara Sterling was killed, and Howard showed up again. I never asked him if he did it, but I know he's capable of such things.

I left Orion years ago, as, like most organizations, it became embroiled in internal competition and infighting. A few years later, I learned that Howard had taken the code name Orion and formed his own group called Umbra. Aptly named, Umbra represented the dark side of genius. But its members were not geniuses—just men focused on retribution and personal revenge. I can only apologize for Howard's actions. Although I had no part in Umbra, I wanted you to understand Umbra's origins and, sadly, its evil intent, as well as Howard's part in it.

If your lovely reporter wife reads this, I hope it will help her understand why her article on the cicada emergence in South Carolina hit closer to home than she may have realized. And I fear it may have put her in danger. That image she used in the article was, as you now know, Umbra's symbol. And it made her a target.

You see, over the past year, Umbra has also emerged after being underground and dormant for years. Despite the financial support of many high-profile individuals you would likely recognize, Umbra suffered a major financial setback when their investments failed. I'm sorry to say I'm the one who recommended Grant Sterling as an investment advisor. The group asked for my advice, but I wanted nothing to do with Umbra. I knew Sterling was a successful and knowledgeable wealth advisor from our work together over the years.

When Umbra pressured Grant to find them a high-return investment, he was reluctant, and rightly so. As you know, a basic investment principle is that the higher the potential return, the higher the risk. But Howard and Umbra had been laying low to plan something big and needed big money to finance it. I don't know what their plans were. I didn't want to know. I never meant to put Sterling or his family in danger.

Do I need to connect the dots for you? I imagine not, and that by now, you have figured out that Umbra, whose mission is revenge, killed Mara Sterling. Targeting Grant's wife, instead of him, should tell you something about the depravity of the group.

You can tell your investigator friend at the police department that I have no idea where Howard is now, or any members of Umbra for that matter. They have gone underground again, much like the next brood of cicadas. They are adept at staying hidden until they choose to emerge again to take revenge.

Despite his hatred of me, Howard never targeted me, as you might think he would. Perhaps it was because he knew that witnessing my own brother's descent into depravity was torturous enough. He took pleasure in it, and I suffered silently while showing the world the facade of a promising politician with high ideals that I will never achieve.

All I can do is offer my heartfelt apologies for all the pain the Sterling family and everyone else involved has suffered. I should have come clean earlier, but I was foolish enough to think I could distance myself from Howard and Umbra and pretend they did not exist.

May you live a long and happy life.

Sincerely,
Caleb

CHAPTER 69

The next day, Josh's cell phone rang and Drake's name appeared on the screen. "Is Enid with you? She needs to hear this too," Drake said.

"She's right here. I'll put you on speaker. Have you found Howard or Caleb?"

"Like Caleb's letter said, Howard has vanished. We've got all the law enforcement agencies looking for him. Not a trace so far. But there's something else I need to tell you. I just watched them wheel Caleb away on a gurney in a black body bag."

"Can't say I'm surprised," Josh said. "Not after reading that letter."

"Well, here's the thing," Drake said. "We won't know the cause of death until we get the forensic report, but I'm not so sure it was suicide."

"Why's that?" Josh asked.

"I'm going to send you a photo that will answer that question."

"Where did you find him?" Enid asked.

"A deer hunter found his car off Highway 21, on an old road that cut through the woods."

"Probably went there right after he wrote that letter," Enid said. "How much of this can I print? I owe Silas one last article."

"I've explained to Albright that you helped solve this case and that we owe you an exclusive. Of course, his first response was 'hell no,' but then he agreed. But you can't use the letter or mention anything about Howard. And you can't include specifics about the cicada symbol. All that will be evidence if, and when, we find Howard Whitaker."

"Thanks. I'll write it and send it to you before I give it to Silas. That way, you can omit anything you think I shouldn't include."

"Perfect," Drake said. "By the way, I hear you're both going back to Madden. I'm headed back home myself in a few weeks. We'll have to do a BBQ, or whatever it is normal people do."

Josh laughed. "Normal doesn't fit any of us, but I like the idea of getting together. Stay in touch and let us know when you're back in Bowman County."

"We'll all miss Pete, but he's perfect for SLED. And you're perfect to take his place. "Dem musta give yuh a helluva deal," he said, slipping back into Patois.

After the call, Enid looked at the time. "I've got to get ready for my interview with Cassandra."

"I'm headed out, so the office is yours," Josh said. I've got to wrap up a few things with Tiffany, and I need to let her know about Caleb. She really liked him. And I have to give her credit. She saw the good in him, and I didn't."

Enid put her arms around Josh's neck. "Don't be hard on yourself. You had every reason to be suspicious of Caleb. It's just so sad though." She pulled away. "Oh, did Drake send you the photo?"

Josh picked up his phone. "Oh, I forgot." He tapped on a text from Drake, looked at the photo and then at Enid.

"What's wrong?"

He turned the phone screen so she could see it. "Take a look."

Enid stared at the image. Caleb's body lay face down, bare from the waist up. The tattoo outlined in black was stark against the pallor of his skin. The edges of the large cicada image showed no signs of healing and revealed fine lines of dried blood. She put her hand on her heart. "Oh my, does this mean—"

"I don't think he gave himself that tattoo."

CHAPTER 70

"Thanks for agreeing to this last interview," Enid said to Cassandra who was seated across from her desk in the home office. "As I mentioned to you, Silas is agreeable to keeping you anonymous. And considering that Howard Whitaker still hasn't been apprehended, keeping your identity safe is essential."

"I appreciate that. I guess Drake, I mean Investigator Harrow, mentioned to you that I'm moving back to the Appalachian region."

Enid detected a slight blush on Cassandra's cheeks. "Yes, I'm happy for you, that you've got a plan for making peace with your gift. And Drake also told me about setting up a meeting with a professor at the university who is studying people like you. I think that's great." Enid smiled. "He's a good man. I hope you two stay in touch."

"Yes, I hope so, too."

Enid handed Cassandra a copy of the photo of Caleb's body showing the cicada tattoo.

Cassandra's hand flew to her mouth. "Oh my. Who is this?"

"It's Caleb Thornhill."

"Was he involved in Mara's murder also?" Cassandra asked.

"It doesn't appear he was. They're still investigating Caleb's death and whether it was suicide."

"It was murder," Cassandra said, matter-of-factly.

"Is there anything you saw that would help with the investigation?" Enid asked.

Cassandra shook her head. "Probably not. But that could have been the vision of the two men I saw. Just now, when I saw the photo, I saw a man being driven down a narrow road. He was drugged and then put in his car. Someone else was driving." She shook herself, as if to get rid of the vision. "That's all I saw. It was very sketchy. No way I can identify either of them."

"You need to share this with Drake. It might be of help somehow."

Cassandra nodded.

"How is your client work going these days?" Enid asked. "You said it has been difficult with all the stress."

"For a while, I had no visions at all and had to cancel some client appointments. But then I talked to Karla, and she helped me put it all in perspective." Cassandra looked away briefly, as if deep in thought. "You know, you wouldn't think something like that could happen here, in Columbia, I mean."

"Sadly, evil knows no boundaries," Enid said. "But I'm glad Karla was able to help you. Can I just verify a few things for the article?" Enid asked.

"Sure."

"You said you've had this gift since you were a young girl, is that right?"

Cassandra nodded.

"And you said your grandmother, the first seer in your family passed her gift of seeing the future to your mother, who couldn't handle the burden of seeing someone's future and killed herself at thirty-three. Is that right?"

Cassandra blinked away the tears and nodded.

Enid sensed that for a moment, Cassandra was that young teenage girl again, reliving those painful memories. "My mother was a great storyteller and talented cook. To everyone else, she was just like any other mother. But I knew she was tormented by what she saw. Before she died, I hated her at times for passing the gift to me—as though it was something she could have prevented."

"You were young and confused. That's understandable," Enid said.

For the next half hour, they discussed Mara's death and Cassandra's vision of the murder so Enid was sure to get the details right. She also wanted to handle Cassandra's story as sensitively as possible.

Before Cassandra left, Enid reached out and took her hands. "I think you're going to be very happy back in Appalachia. And I think Drake may be a part of your future. Whatever happens, please be happy."

Cassandra blushed slightly. "Thank you. And what about your future?"

"I think you were right about my experiencing a death, although thankfully it was symbolic, as you said." She told Cassandra about her and Josh's meeting in Madden.

"That's wonderful. Let's stay in touch. I want to know how your life turns out, and I'll fill you in on mine."

Enid watched Cassandra leave and felt a sense of loss, like a close friend was moving away. But then she reminded herself, she had only known Cassandra briefly. For a few moments, Enid reflected on all the people who had left footprints on her path over the years.

CHAPTER 71

When Silas finished reading Enid's article, he slapped his palms on the desk. "Brilliant," he said. "This exclusive is going to bring in all kinds of new readers. Of course, I wish you were staying, but then you're going to own your own small-town newspaper. How awesome is that?"

"Actually, it's pretty scary."

"May I tell you something?"

Enid nodded. "What's that?"

"You are beautiful, brilliant, and destined."

"Destined?" Enid asked.

"I'm so very grateful our paths have crossed, even briefly. And I can't thank you enough for this article. We will miss you here, but you're destined to pursue bigger dreams." He laughed. "Like single-handedly trying to save local news."

"But I'm not—"

"I'm not making fun of you. I admire and respect you. You're taking on a big mission, and I wish you all the best." He slapped his palms on the desk again. "When you get settled in Madden, I'd like to run an article on your personal journey, your quest for the truth. Whataya say?" Before Enid could answer, he continued. "What made you change your mind about running the paper?"

"I'm not sure there was any one thing, more like a combination of things." She didn't mention Cassandra's vision of the symbolic death Enid would experience. "But I recently read a book about Elizabeth Timothy that gave me new insights."

"Ah, yes, the first female publisher in America. In the 1730's I believe."

"That's right. She worked in partnership with Benjamin Franklin."

"What was it about her that inspired you?" Silas was busy scribbling notes.

"Are you interviewing me already?" Enid said, smiling.

"Something like that. Go on."

"I can't imagine the odds she must have faced during that time period. Women were relegated to the kitchen then, so if Elizabeth Timothy could overcome the obstacles she faced and run a newspaper, then I can draw from her courage and run the *Madden Gazette*."

Silas scribbled more notes hurriedly. "I'll get more details from you later. This will make a great article. Oh, and give Jack my best. I sure hope he can beat the Big C."

. . .

When Enid got home, she felt both exhilarated and exhausted. The events of the past few weeks had taken a toll on her. With no more outstanding articles to turn in, and feeling a bit adrift, she went to the kitchen to make a cup of tea.

Looking out the window as she filled the tea kettle with water, she saw Sophie and Kibo in the yard next door. Enid set the kettle aside and went outside. "Hi, Sophie. Got a minute?" Enid called out.

"Hi, Sure," Sophie said.

Enid walked next door, going through the wooden gate that led to Sophie's backyard. "I won't keep you. In fact, I need to start packing."

"Packing? You moving too?"

Enid told her about their move to Madden and their new jobs.

"That's so exciting!" Sophie said, waving her arms in the air and scaring Kibo, who ran away in surprise.

"So when are you moving to Atlanta?" Enid asked.

"I'm all packed up and the movers come tomorrow. I was going to run over later this afternoon and say goodbye to you and Josh."

"I wish you all the best," Enid said.

"You too. Did they ever catch the killer, the one with the tattoo I sketched?" Sophie asked.

"Not yet. But they will." Enid wanted to believe they would. "I can't thank you enough for your help. That sketch was a big piece of finding out what happened."

"I'm glad I could help. In fact, working with you and Cassandra made me realize I need to get back into police work. Maybe I will be replaced by artificial intelligence soon, but I'll enjoy it while I can. Then I can always learn to do AI prompts as a living."

"That'll work, a good plan," Enid said, laughing.

They talked for a few more minutes and then Enid leaned down to rub Kibo's head, as he had wandered back over to sit at Sophie's feet.

CHAPTER 72

There's no place like Madden on a quiet Sunday morning. On this crisp, late fall day, all seemed right with the world. Sitting on their front porch, Josh sipping coffee and Enid with her beloved cup of Earl Grey, she watched Jack walk up the sidewalk to join them.

"You're looking well this morning," Enid said to him.

Jack walked up on the porch and leaned down to kiss Enid's cheek. "How' my favorite newspaper owner?"

Before Enid could answer, Josh laughed and said, "Don't give her a big head. She's hard enough to live with now."

"Stop it," Enid said. "This is a pleasant surprise," she said to Jack who had settled into one of the porch rockers.

"I wanted to come by personally and tell you how much I enjoyed the first edition of the *Madden Gazette*. You've brought a much needed, fresh perspective to the paper. Not that I'm surprised. And your note from the editor was so heartfelt. I was moved by your sincerity."

Jack then turned to Josh. "And how's the esteemed Madden Police Chief? Got all the crime cleaned up yet?"

"Well, Miss Emma claims someone stole a few pieces of her silverware that were outside on the porch table. I told her it was probably crows. They love to steal shiny things."

"Was she happy with that explanation?" Enid asked.

Josh laughed. "No, but when I went by there to talk to her, sure enough a bunch of crows were picking through her yard."

"What did she want you to do?" Jack asked. "Shoot the crows?"

"No, but she did suggest the city should hire someone to shoo the crows away. She also claimed the crows might have also stolen her checkbook, but then her daughter came in and said she had taken it with her for safekeeping."

"You must feel so needed," Enid said, smiling.

"Oh, I definitely do. And the mayor wants to meet with me tomorrow morning to establish some 'priorities,' as she called them. So, I really feel needed." Josh's cell phone pinged and he looked at the screen. "Got to run. Crime never stops."

After Josh left, Enid laid her head back against the wooden rocker and briefly closed her eyes. When she opened them, she turned to look directly into Jack's eyes. "I can't thank you enough for trusting me with running the newspaper. I hope I can live up to your expectations."

Jack leaned forward and put his hand on her arm. "My dear Enid. You have already made me so proud. You'll do fine. In fact, you will surpass anything I could have done. This is what you were destined to do."

There was that word again, *destined*. Silas had said the same thing to her. Enid didn't believe in predestination, but she did believe in following her instincts. As her mother had told her, the heart knows what the mind can only ponder.

"Josh seems to be happy too," Jack said. "He slipped right back into the role like he had never left."

"Yes, he does seem happy. Oh, I almost forgot, would you like to come back for lunch today? I'm cooking, but don't let that scare you away. It'll be something simple, probably vegetable soup and cornbread."

"Sounds delicious, but Rachel is coming over today. I think she wants to check on me." He smiled slightly. "She thinks I'm dying."

"She sent me a really nice text this morning, congratulating me on the first Sunday edition of the paper. If she has time today, ask her to stop by and say hello." She sighed. "You know, it's so wonderful to have friends close by. I've really missed that. And as far as you dying, don't you even think about it."

"Well, I'm doing my part, and the experimental cancer treatments at Duke University Medical Center seem to be working." He shrugged. "But life is what it is. We'll deal with it. Right?"

Enid didn't trust herself to answer unemotionally, so she just nodded.

As Jack stood to leave, he put a copy of the newspaper in Enid's lap, open to the editor's note. "You need to frame that. It says it all."

Madden Gazette – First Sunday Edition
From the Editor's Desk

Dear Readers,

As the new owner and senior editor of what was the *Tri-County Gazette*, I am thrilled to introduce a fresh chapter in our shared story. Starting with today's edition, the newspaper has returned to its original name, the *Madden Gazette*, which will provide coverage for Madden and Bowman County. This change reflects not only the evolving identity and growth of our beloved town but also the transformative journey we are all part of.

For those who do not know me, I didn't grow up in Madden, but it is my home. As many of you know, I moved here several years ago and worked with the former owner, Jack Johnson, who continues to be a contributor to the paper as well as my mentor and dear friend. Returning to Madden now, I see our town with a renewed perspective, witnessing its growth and the emergence of new stories waiting to be told. Sometimes our journey leads us back to where we started, but with new eyes and a wiser heart.

I encourage you to stop by the newspaper office, say hello, and share your stories with us. Part of what compelled me to return here was the commitment to write stories about you, the citizens of Madden and our county neighbors, and about what matters to you. I want to learn more about you. And while this newspaper honors tradition, we also know that Madden will grow and thrive only if we all commit to honoring the past while embracing the future.

At the heart of the *Madden Gazette* is our unwavering mission: Truth First. This guiding principle has been the cornerstone of our reporting, ensuring that we deliver honest, accurate, and meaningful news to our readers. In an age where information is abundant but trust is scarce, we pledge to uphold the highest standards of journalism, giving you the truth you deserve.

Beginning this week, the *Madden Gazette* will publish twice weekly, on Sundays and Thursdays, with the goal of expanding further as our town continues to flourish. Expect deeper investigative features, engaging community spotlights, and interactive sections designed for you—our readers—to voice your thoughts and stories.

Let's embark on this journey together, fostering a newspaper that truly embodies the spirit of Madden, one that supports and celebrates our emerging stories.

With anticipation and warmth,

Enid Blackwell

∞

AUTHOR NOTES

This book, like each of the volumes in the Enid Blackwell Mystery Series, was inspired by an actual event. In 1990, while living in Charlotte, North Carolina, I was deeply affected by the murder of Kim Thomas, a young mother, in her home. The proximity of this horrendous crime to my own residence made it all the more shocking and unforgettable. The memory of that tragic event has stayed with me all these years. When I decided to write about a fortune teller foreseeing a murder, the Thomas case seemed a fitting inspiration.

Initially, the Charlotte police arrested Kim's husband but later cleared him. To this day, no one has been officially charged, despite annual claims of new DNA or other evidence. I won't delve further into the details, but if you're interested, an online search will provide more information about Kim Thomas' murder.

Cicada 3301 was an actual group of highly intelligent puzzle solvers active online between 20212 and 2014. Additionally, the double brood cicada emergence taking place this fall in South Carolina is real—an event that has not occurred in 221 years. I found both pieces of information fascinating and incorporated them into the story. However, Intellecta and Umbra are just figments of my imagination.

As for the fortune teller's vision, I do not try to convince you, the reader, to accept its possibility as real. Instead, I offer you the option to explain it away logically if it doesn't align with your beliefs—or to accept there are mysteries in our world we simply cannot explain.

If you are a fan of the Enid Blackwell Mystery Series, you know that Enid has endured a great deal. I hope you find the ending of this book satisfying, as it may be the last in the series. I've learned never to say "never," having originally planned to write just one book, which then became four, and ultimately a series of seven. There are always more stories to tell, so who knows what the future holds!

I have several other projects I want to pursue, and I hope you'll continue to support my work. Please follow my newsletter or social media for updates on new releases. Words cannot express my gratitude for the loyalty and appreciation you, my readers, have shown me. Writing a book is hard work, but it's also a labor of love—love of words, storytelling, and readers like you.

Thank you for being part of my journey.

Raegan

ACKNOWLEDGMENTS

Of all the pages I write, the acknowledgments page of each book is always my favorite. Without the support of others, none of this would be possible.

First and foremost, I want to thank my wonderful spouse, William Earl Craig. He calls himself my "roadie," as he's responsible for maintaining our book inventory for in-person events, packing the truck for festivals, and helping me set up and break down each event. But he's much more than that. He's my rock, my foundation, and my chief cheerleader. He supports me in countless ways that allow me to do what I do, year after year.

I also want to thank Irene Stern, my friend, developmental editor, and supporter. She has contributed to my success in many ways, including taking care of my feline writing companions when we're away.

My gratitude also goes to Deputy Chief Harry Polis Jr. of the Richland County Sheriff's Department. He has provided invaluable technical law enforcement advice throughout this series. Any errors are mine alone, despite my best efforts to maintain accuracy.

I'd like to add that nothing in this book is meant to be disrespectful to the Richland County Sheriff's Department. This work of fiction is the first book of the series set in an actual city, Columbia, whereas my settings are usually fictitious to avoid offending local law enforcement. Our sheriff's department does an outstanding job, and we are grateful for their professionalism and community protection.

And a big "thank you" goes to my friend and fellow author, Patricia McNeely, who wrote a book about Elizabeth Timothy. In 1739, Timothy became America's first female newspaper publisher and editor. Pat's book about her inspired the ending of this book.

Another key resource for this book was Dr. Kathleen Connolly, a licensed clinical mental health counselor with a unique hobby of reading tarot cards. Her input in the early stages of this book was invaluable.

Creating unique characters is one of the things I enjoy most about writing. I'd like to acknowledge a wonderful man named Alex who often waited on us at a fast-food restaurant, because he was my inspiration for Drake Harrow—Big D. Thank you, Alex.

There are many writer friends and others who have supported me along the way. I won't list them all for fear of leaving someone out, but you know who you are. Thank you, dear friends and fellow writers, for your friendship and invaluable support over the years.

ABOUT THE AUTHOR

Choosing a name is a privilege not often afforded to us, except, perhaps, when one is a fiction writer. In this domain, I am known as Raegan Teller, a name I've chosen with care and purpose.

With Welsh heritage from my father's side, I opted for an Irish name, Raegan, meaning "spiritual strength," to honor my Celtic roots while avoiding the pronunciation challenges Welsh names often present. The surname Teller, synonymous with "storyteller" in English, reflects my passion for weaving narratives that captivate and intrigue.

Behind the pen name, I inhabit the real-life world as Wanda Craig, with a diverse career background that spans from business writing and copy editing to roles in marketing, executive coaching, corporate training, and even insurance claims adjusting. My journey also includes a unique stint selling burial vaults during my school years, an experience that oddly resonated with my fascination for mystery writing.

My affinity for mystery and suspense novels runs deep, influenced by every author whose work I've had the pleasure of reading. My literary tastes are eclectic, finding my current favorite is the author of the last compelling book I've devoured. However, the authors I gravitate toward are those whose narratives frequently explore family dynamics and the emotional depth of their characters, with the elements of murder and crime serving to enhance their personal journeys and the turmoil faced.

As Raegan Teller, I strive to be counted among such storytellers—those who can delve into the complexities of human emotions and relationships while unfolding a mystery that keeps you turning the page. I hope you find that my stories resonate with you, offering both intrigue and a glimpse into the intricacies of the human heart.

PLEASE…
A humble request from the author

Thank you for taking time from your busy schedule to read this (or any other) book. The world needs more readers like you.

I hope you enjoyed *Murder Vision*. If so, please do me a big favor and leave a review on Amazon and/or Goodreads. Reviews encourage other readers to explore authors with whom they may not be familiar.

Thank you in advance for taking the time to do a review!

www.Amazon.com

www.Goodreads.com

…

If you'd like to contact me directly, please visit my website: www.RaeganTeller.com/contact. I'd love to hear from you.

Made in the USA
Columbia, SC
18 March 2025